TARTAN TWO-STEP

A HIGHLAND HOLIDAY NOVEL

New York Times Bestselling Author

GRACE BURROWES

Published by Grace Burrowes Publishing, 21 Summit Avenue, Hagerstown, MD
21740.

Cover design by Wax Creative, Inc.

ISBN: 1941419488
ISBN-13: 978-1941419489

AUTHOR'S NOTE

Well, I wrote myself into a conundrum. Seems the Scots spell whisky without an e, while Americans spell it with an e. Magnus, our hero, thus makes whisky, while Bridget, our heroine, makes whiskey. What should an author (much less her poor copy editor and proofreaders) do? I went with the Scottish spelling, for several reasons. It's the first one to hit the page (our story opens in Scotland), the spirits at the center of Magnus's dilemma were made in Scotland, and Bridget and Magnus said they weren't particular about the spelling, as long as I got the happily ever after right.

So, whisky, it is—with a happily ever after too, of course!
Dedicated to those who go forth into the unknown in a spirit of courage, hope, and determination

CHAPTER ONE

Magnus Cromarty swirled the glass of whisky beneath his nose and breathed in the scent of betrayal.

"Tell me what you think," he said, as casually as he'd offer his cousin a new blend of coffee.

Elias Brodie went unsuspecting to his doom. He didn't bother to nose his wee dram, he took a sip and winced. "This is not up to your usual standard, Magnus."

"No need to be diplomatic."

Now, Elias took a whiff of the whisky. "A hint of wet dog, muddy boots, rotten eggs, or something..."

"The technical term is foxy. The damned stuff is foxy, like cheap burgundy or fraternity moonshine. This was supposed to be my signature batch of whisky, Elias, the year that all the judges at all the international competitions sat up and took notice of Cromarty Distilleries, Limited."

Elias set down his glass. "They'll take notice of that and promptly call the poison control hotline. Can you fix it?"

Whisky-making was as much art as science, which was part of what Magnus loved about being a professional distiller.

"I don't know. Do you trust me to serve you an antidote?"

"There is no antidote. The finish is as bad as the nose."

Magnus crossed the study and fetched two clean glasses, a pitcher of water, and a bottle of whisky.

"Give this a try."

Elias was used to these sessions and knew better than to resist direction. He obliged Magnus, though this time he took a sniff of his drink before trying a taste.

"That is lovely. That is..." He held the glass beneath his nose.

"That is what my best batch should be," Magus said. "That is damned fine whisky."

Elias peered at the label. "It's *American*? Is nothing sacred? I've never heard of Logan Bar whisky."

Magnus poured himself a scant portion, inhaled, and took a taste of six-year-old Logan Bar single malt. In the dark of a blustery Scottish evening, sunshine bloomed on his tongue. The nose had notes of butterscotch and apples, a touch of citrus, and a hint of banana taffy.

Exquisite, ladylike, and elegant on the palate too.

"The Logans are sitting on a damned gold mine," Magnus said, "and they don't realize it."

"It's their gold mine," Elias countered. "Americans take their property law quite seriously."

"I take my whisky more seriously still. You have to admit this is outstanding for a young single malt."

"I'm sure we have better here in Scotland," Elias said, taking another sip, then another.

Magnus put his glass aside, lest the contents distract him from the discussion. Elias was the senior director on the board of Cromarty Distilleries, Ltd., and his business acumen had preserved Magnus from more than one wrong turn. Elias was family too—a second cousin—so Magnus could be honest with him.

"That's the problem with the rest of my board, Elias. All they think about is Scotland. Whose eighteen-year-old batch isn't finishing worth a damn for the third year in a row. What's Dewar's got up their sleeve, and can we get them to include our overstock in their next blend?"

Elias propped his feet on a hassock, and because he had the Cromarty height, they were large feet. His right sock had a hole near the big toe, which was damned silly. Women had adored Elias since he'd first pinned a kilt around his chubby toddler knees. Surely some girlfriend or fiancée might have bought the man a decent pair of socks?

Magnus made a mental note to stuff a few pairs of his favorite organic wool hiking socks into Elias's overnight bag.

"Your board of directors has an average age of eighty-seven," Elias said, pouring himself another dram. "This American whisky is charming. I don't picture you acquiring anything charming."

This discussion was taking place in Magnus's study, a temple to Scottish Baronial interior design. The furniture was heavy, comfortable, and upholstered in plaid. The carpet was more plaid, and the curtains yet still more plaid. Some multiply-great-grandmother had chosen to inflict on her menfolk the Cromarty hunting tartan, a jarring weave of green, black, yellow, and red.

And the lot of it was even older than Magnus's board members.

"This whisky is more than charming, Elias, it's exactly what I need to get Cromarty's into the US market. Logan's has the brand recognition that can get my whisky out of the country clubs and into the honky-tonks and hookup bars."

Elias held his glass up to the light. "Hookup whisky? You aspire to peddle *hookup* whisky? Most of your board members won't know what a hookup is. Won't you command a better price at the finer establishments?"

Magnus's grasp of the term hookup was a dim memory at best, but his dream of putting Cromarty Distilleries on solid footing was all too real.

Though, if Magnus couldn't convince Elias to consider an American partner, he'd never convince his board.

"Americans are willing to pay a decent sum for their drink of choice, regardless of venue. I'm not in the same league as the snobs. I haven't a twenty-eight-year-old crop that will sweep all the awards and enthrall the Malt Whisky Society. I make a good, vastly underrated whisky. Americans love to find a bargain, and with the right entrée, Cromarty's can be that overlooked gem that a savvy cowboy knows to order for his date."

Though not if Magnus's flagship bottling had all the appeal of vintage rat poison.

"Honky-tonks and savvy cowboys," Elias said. "Not a market the average Scottish distillery would pitch to, I'll grant you that. I like this whisky more the longer I drink it."

And *that* was why Magnus had noticed the Logan Bar distillery. The whisky spoke for itself, in tones all the more seductive for being intelligent and charming.

"You like that whisky now," Magnus said. "You'll be in love before we finish the bottle."

"I'll be asleep in your guest room within the hour. Where did you say this distillery is?"

"Montana."

"Never been there. I hear it's full of cowgirls." Elias drained the last of his drink. "Will you run away to join the rodeo on us, Magnus?"

Elias had played the international polo circuit, hung out with the racing set—cars and horses, both—and had at one time been engaged to some earl's daughter. He had the sort of natural athletic talent that should have earned him the undying enmity of his fellow man, and was a genuinely decent person.

"You sound wistful when you mention running away, Elias."

"And you are married to that damn pot still," Elias retorted, pushing to his feet. "I will approve the expenditure of funds to send you to negotiate with the Americans. You'll need the full board to approve a final offer, and that will be an uphill battle. I don't care for the idea of acquiring an American business in the current international environment, but this is the only way you'll leave the distillery for more than a bank holiday."

"You're approving a trip to Montana so I can watch a rodeo?"

"No, Magnus. I'm approving this trip so you can get acquainted with a few cowgirls."

As long as those cowgirls didn't mind paying for a fine Scottish single malt, Magnus would be their new best friend. If one of them could repair the damage done to his signature vintage, he'd go down on bended knee and kiss her fancy cowgirl boots.

* * *

"Montana State has more than fifteen thousand students," Bridget MacDeaver said, "and out of all those young minds eager for knowledge, why do the ones who are also eager for a beating have to show up here on Friday night, as predictably as saddle sores and taxes?"

Bridget's brother Shamus turned and hooked his elbows on the bar so that he faced the room. "A fight means Juanita can change up the Bar None's décor. You ladies like hanging new curtains."

Bridget didn't bother kicking him, because Shamus was just being a brother. In the mirror behind the bar, she watched as Harley Gummo went nose to nose with yet another college boy.

"One of these days, Harley's going to hurt somebody who has a great big trust fund, and then our Harley will be getting all his mail delivered to Deer Lodge."

Montana State Prison, in the southwest quarter of the state, called Deer Lodge home.

"What's it to you if Harley does a little more time?" Shamus asked, taking a sip of his beer.

"He'll ask me to represent him, and I can't, though he's a good guy at heart."

Also a huge guy, and a drunk guy, and a guy with a temper when provoked. College Boy was provocation on the hoof, right down to his Ride A Cowboy T-shirt and the spankin'-new Tony Lama Black Stallions on his feet.

"Pilgrims," Shamus muttered as College Boy's two friends stood up, and the other patrons drifted to the far corners of the Bar None's dance floor.

"Do something, Shamus. Harley's had too much."

Bridget's brothers—step-brothers, technically—were healthy specimens, all over six feet, though Harley came closer to six-foot-six.

"He has too much too often," Shamus said. "This is not our fight. Let's head out the back."

Behind the bar, Preacher Martin was polishing a clean glass with a white towel. Bridget knew a loaded sawed-off shotgun sat out of sight within reach of his left hand. Preacher looked like the circuit parsons of the Old West— full beard, weathered features, slate gray eyes—and he'd been settling fights by virtue of buckshot sermons since Bridget had sat her first pony.

"We can't let Harley just get in trouble," she said, "or let that idiot jeopardize what few brain cells he hasn't already pickled."

"Bridget, do I have to toss you over my shoulder?"

"Try it, Shamus, and Harley will come after the part of you still standing when I've finished putting you in your place."

Bridget hadn't the family height, so she made sure to punch above her weight in muscle and mouth. Three older step-brothers had taught her to never back down and never make empty threats.

The musicians—a pair of fiddlers—packed up their instruments and nodded to Preacher. A few patrons took their drinks outside.

Bridget was off her stool and wrestling free of the hand Shamus had clamped around her elbow when Harley snarled, "Step off, little man," at the college boy.

A stranger strolled up to Harley's left. "Might I ask a question?"

"Who the hell is that fool?" Shamus murmured.

"Never seen him before," Preacher said, towel squeaking against the glass. "Bet we won't see him again either."

The stranger was on the tall side, rangy, and dressed in blue jeans and a Black Watch flannel shirt. His belt buckle was some sort of Celtic knot, and his hair was dark and longish. Bridget put his age about thirty and his common sense at nearly invisible.

He was good-looking though, even if he talked funny.

"A shame to see such a fine nose needlessly broken." Bridget took noses seriously, hers being one of her most valuable assets.

Shamus shot her a women-are-nuts look.

Harley swung around to glower at the stranger. "What did you say?"

"It's the accent," the guy said, patting Harley's arm. "I know. Makes me hard to understand. I wanted to ask what it means when you tell somebody to step off. I haven't heard that colloquialism before, and being far from home, I don't want to offend anybody if I should be told to step off. Does it mean to turn and count my steps like an old-fashioned duel, or move away, or has it to do with taking back rash words?"

The stranger clearly expected Harley to answer.

"He's either damned brave or a fool rushing in," Shamus said.

"He's just standing there," Bridget replied, because a brother in error should never go uncorrected. "He sounds Scottish."

"He sounds like he has a death wish."

"You don't know what step off means?" Harley sneered.

"Haven't a clue," the stranger said. "I'm a fancier of whisky, and I'm sipping my way through my first American holiday. Don't suppose I could buy either of you a drink, if that's the done thing? I wouldn't want to offend. My name is Magnus, and this is my first trip to Montana."

He stuck out a hand, and Harley was just drunk enough to reflexively stick out his own.

"That was brilliant," Bridget said. In the next instant, College Boy was shaking hands too and introducing himself, then shaking with a puzzled Harley.

"Never seen anything like that," Preacher commented. "Harley Gummo ambushed by his mama's manners."

There had also been a mention of whisky, which recommended the Scotsman to Bridget more highly than his willingness to intervene between a pair of fools. *Somebody* should have intervened. For a stranger to do so was risky.

Bridget should have intervened.

Harley and College Boy let their new friend escort them to the drink station a yard to Bridget's left at the bar. She overheard earnest explanations of the rivalry between the Seahawks and the 49ers, which then degenerated into an explanation of American football.

Man talk. Safe, simple man talk. *Thank God.*

"I do believe I see Martina Matlock all by her lonesome over by the stage," Shamus said. "If you'll excuse me, Bridget."

He wasn't asking. Martina was all curves and smiles, and Shamus was ever a man willing to smile back on a Friday night. He embodied a work hard/play harder approach to life, and of all of Bridget's brothers, he was the one most likely to miss breakfast at the ranch house on Saturday morning.

"Find your own way home, Shamus," Bridget said.

Harley and his recently acquired buddies had found a table, and College Boy's companions took the two remaining free seats. The musicians unpacked their instruments, and Preacher left off washing glasses to help Juanita with the line forming at the drink station.

Magnus—was that a first name or a last name?—ordered a round of Logan Bar twelve-year-old single malt for the table, the first such order Bridget had heard anybody place all night.

As Preacher got down the bottle, Bridget approached the stranger. "May I ask why you drink Logan Bar?"

"Because it's the best American single malt I've found thus far. Would you care to join us?"

His answer could not have pleased Bridget more. "You're on your own with that bunch of prodigies, but if you want to dance later, come find me."

"The lady doesn't dance with just anybody," Preacher said, setting tasting glass shots on a tray and passing over a menu. "Get some food into Harley, and this round will be on the house."

Magnus took the tray. "My thanks, and my compliments on a fine whisky inventory."

His voice sounded like a well-aged whisky, smooth, sophisticated, and complex but forthright too. A touch smoky, a hint of weathered wood and winter breezes.

He leaned a few inches in Bridget's direction as the fiddlers arranged chairs on the stage. "I'll take you up on that dance, miss, just as soon as I instruct my friends regarding the fine points of an excellent single malt."

The finest single malt in the country. "You do that."

Bridget didn't wink and didn't smile, and neither did Magnus. He appreciated her whisky and was about to teach others to do likewise. If he made a habit out of advertising her single malt, Mr. Magnus could be her new best friend.

Or the Logan Bar distillery's new best friend, which amounted to the same thing.

* * *

Magnus could explain whisky all day and half the night. He had a routine that included the history of distilling—if the monks did it, we know it's good for us—and a demonstration of the traditional whisky glass's ability to hold a correct sipping portion when toppled on its side.

When Harley and the three college students were sagely sipping their drams, Magnus rose.

"If you'll excuse me, gentlemen, I've a dance to catch. The sandwiches should be here shortly, and I'd be obliged if you'd consider this my treat. I would never have puzzled out that part about the four downs and ten yards."

American football was as tedious as cricket, though considerably more profitable.

Harley considered his drink. "You asking Bridget to dance?"

It was more the case that Bridget had asked Magnus. "I thought I would. Why?"

"Go easy," Harley muttered. "And mind your manners."

"Of course."

The lady had asked Magnus about his choice of whisky, and was thus another potential convert. She was back on her barstool near the drink station, and as Magnus approached, he was mildly surprised to realize that Bridget was... pretty.

Her name suited her, for she had freckles sprinkled across her cheeks, dark auburn hair, and green eyes that held neither flirtation nor guile. She was between average and petite in stature and appeared to be drinking ice water with a slice of lemon.

"If the offer of a dance is still open, I'd like to take you up on it." How much easier to start a conversation when the woman had done the initial asking.

"I'm Bridget," she said, offering her hand. "And we either dance now, or the floor will soon be too crowded."

Magnus took her hand. "Let's seize the day, shall we? Or the night?"

In Scotland, he would never have stood up with a strange woman. He'd been dragged to endless *ceilidh* dances as a child and spent most of them nipping from the adult's drinks. As an adolescent, he'd seen the potential rewards for actually learning the dance steps and subjecting females to his company on the dance floor. What the females had got out of the business, he could not have said.

The fiddlers tuned up, the lights dimmed, and as luck would have it, Magnus was about to spend the next five minutes slow dancing with a pretty stranger.

"You're sure?" Bridget asked, taking another sip of her lemon water.

"I'm sure."

"Over there," she said, sliding off her stool and marching through the tables.

Magnus followed and got looks from the other men, particularly one man sitting with a leggy blonde in the corner. The other women didn't look at him so much as they inspected him.

The Scots had invented the you're-not-from-around-here glower. Magnus smiled back at all of them. Bridget had asked him to dance, after all.

The introduction was in triple meter, the violins in close harmony. Magnus arranged himself and his partner in waltz position, though Bridget kept him at a firm distance.

"I'm not very good at this," she said. "I know most of the line dances, but not this couples' crap."

Americans could be blunt. Magnus liked that about them. "We'll stick to a box step, then," he said, guiding her through an awkward square. "Or we can sit this one out."

"I offered, and sooner begun is sooner done."

"Why did you offer?"

She was looking down, clearly trying to anticipate their movements rather than let Magnus lead. "Ask me when I haven't grown two extra feet and lost my sense of direction."

"We're dancing in a square. We'll stay right here, getting acquainted with left, forward, right, and back, until—"

She tromped on his foot. "Sorry."

"No worries." He pulled her closer when another couple went careening past. "I'll talk you through it. Left, forward, right, back. Left, forward, right, back."

Verbally directing Bridget meant thinking in mirror opposites, but that spared Magnus from focusing too closely on being near a woman for the first time in months. Years, possibly. He was not married to his pot still, but he'd outgrown casual encounters long ago.

By degrees, Bridget relaxed, and soon, Magnus's directions were no longer needed. Bridget stopped watching her feet, and for two whole minutes, Magnus simply enjoyed partnering a lady on the dance floor.

"Thank you," he said as the violins died away to a smattering of applause.

"Thank *you*," Bridget replied, grinning out of all proportion to the moment. "I haven't slow danced since twelfth grade, when Jimmy Jack Cavanaugh knocked me on my keister in front of the whole class. I'm back on the horse now."

"You mean to pay me a compliment."

By waltzing with him, Bridget had obviously cleared some social hurdle. If her smile was any indication, she'd be waltzing again soon.

"Jimmy Jack went ass over tin cups in front of the whole class too, and then headfirst into the Homecoming queen's bustle. Ruined her dress, and Joellen Plymouth still sets a lot of store by her wardrobe. So where are you from, My-Name-Is-Magnus?"

Magnus was tired—he'd driven four hundred miles before finding his hotel—and the room was loud. Deciphering Bridget's meaning took him a moment.

"Scotland," he said. "West of Aberdeen."

She resumed her perch on the barstool and patted the empty seat beside her. "And you like whisky."

"I enjoy good whisky in moderation. I'm on holiday, so I drove up from Denver and toured a few distilleries."

Interesting businesses, and far more varied than the single malt industry in Scotland. Americans didn't stick to barley. They also made grain into bourbon, rye, corn whisky, blended concoctions, experimental products... The whole market was more complicated than its Scottish counterpart and no less competitive.

"Everybody who didn't catch the microbrewery wave has opened up a distillery," Bridget said. "Are you drinking?"

He was staying in the hotel two doors up from the Bar None Tavern and Taphouse. Instead of merely sipping from an interesting flight, he could savor a dram on a chilly night.

"Perhaps you have a recommendation?"

She looked him up and down, far more carefully than she had before they'd taken to the dance floor. "Preacher, pour us some of the Edradour."

Edradour was usually referred to as the smallest *legal* distillery in Scotland and still made its whisky on the farm where operations had started in 1825. They valued excellent quality over quantity, but Magnus hadn't tasted their product recently.

"What are we drinking?" he asked as the bartender poured two pale gold drams into tasting glasses.

"Fifteen-year-old single malt finished in Madeira casks," she said, the way some women might have discussed Belgian dark chocolates.

"You know something about whisky-making."

"Enough to know that whisky is aged in oak barrels and those barrels give it most of its flavor. Hush now and let me pay my respects."

Bridget was interesting when she focused on whisky. She took a few slow breaths, closed her eyes, and brought the glass under her nose. A whisky's first impression was called the nose for that reason—the impact was primarily olfactory, which meant the same drink could come across differently to different people.

"Farmland," she said. "I love that, with a hint of horses and freshly turned fields." Her smile was dreamy, as if she could see the farmland, hear the horses munching grass in their pastures, and feel the sun's reflected warmth rising from the cropland ready for planting. "A barn full of fresh hay, and then there's peat, of course, but gentle peat. The hint of last night's fire."

She spoke in tasting notes, in the precise sensory descriptions favored by whisky connoisseurs.

"And the palate?"

She took a sip and held the glass away. "The peat remains unobtrusive, and the wine comes through after a polite tap on the door. Green tea, cooking apples—Winesap, not those boring Red Delicious—and whole wheat toast, scythed grass, a touch of black pepper. God, to drink this on a picnic blanket with afternoon sun beaming down."

Magnus did as Bridget had done, nosing the whisky before sampling it, and Bridget's description was astonishingly accurate.

"What would you say about the finish?" he asked.

She took another taste, her eyes closed again. "Still bucolic, but with a hint of the pungent quality of livestock immediately upwind. I like a contradictory whisky, and this one has both elegance and earthiness." She opened her eyes and gazed at Magnus directly. "Scrumptious."

Elegance and earthiness. Exactly.

He'd taken another sip of his whisky before he realized that her last comment—*scrumptious*—might not have been exclusively aimed at the whisky.

Bridget wasn't a cowgirl, as Magnus's cousin had probably meant the term. Her hair was French braided into a tidy bun, her green blouse looked to be silk and showed not a hint of cleavage. Her jeans were comfortable rather than fashionable. She wore some kind of ballet-slippery things on her feet and no makeup that Magnus could detect.

The only scent he picked up from her in the increasingly crowded confines of the Bar None was a subtle hint of lavender.

"Was that another compliment, then, Bridget?"

She ran her finger around the rim of her glass. "I'm not sure. Let me finish my whisky, and we'll find out."

CHAPTER TWO

Bridget rarely drank whisky. She sampled, evaluated, analyzed, and loved it, but didn't consume it. Tonight was special, in a queasy, upset, uh-oh-feeling way.

She'd argued with her brothers. Not a squabble, a spat, a dustup, or difference of opinion, this had been an argument. Patrick had slammed doors, Luke had trotted out his best epithets, and Shamus had threatened to spend the summer skiing in New Zealand.

Bridget had raised her voice. She never raised her voice.

She also never slow danced, but that had gone better than her attempt to bellow sense into her brothers.

"You are very serious about your whisky," Magnus said.

The Edradour was seriously wonderful, a comfort and an inspiration. "I'm serious about most things. What about you?"

"Serious to a fault," he said, holding his glass up to the light and swirling the contents. This Edradour was light-bodied, meaning the whisky didn't cling to the sides of the glass.

"Not too serious to take a vacation." What would that be like? A vacation? To leave not just the Logan Bar, but Montana, or even the United States? Go someplace where walking down the street didn't mean greeting somebody who'd gone to third grade with you?

"I'll tend to a bit of business before I go back to Scotland. Is something troubling you, Bridget?"

Just the rest of her life. "Had a difference of opinion with my brothers. We'll get past it." They'd get past it just as soon as Bridget capitulated to her brothers' wishes.

Which was not going to happen.

"Would it help to talk about it?"

"Nope." Talking might lead to more yelling or possibly crying. The brothers had ambushed her at the damned dinner table this time. Ganged up on her and started in with the consider-the-bigger-picture and we're-thinking-of-your-best-interests bullcrap.

"Would it help to complain about it?"

"My brothers are stubborn, and there are three of them and only one of me. They think I should go back to lawyering, but I'm not meant for that."

"I studied law. I never intended to go into private practice, but a legal education has been useful. When I do need to rely on outside counsel, I'm not at their mercy."

"A legal education is only useful if people listen to you," Bridget said, closing her eyes and inhaling the scent of fifteen years of nature's alchemy. "They don't listen to me."

And that hurt bitterly. The men whom she called family, the ones who'd probably die to protect her, couldn't be bothered to give her a fair hearing. Shamus might try, if his older brothers weren't pacing and pawing in the same room, but Shamus might also bolt for southern climes.

He was at that moment sitting nearly in Martina Matlock's lap. No chance he'd be willing to have a reasonable discussion out of Luke's and Patrick's hearing, and the Bar None was no place to air family differences.

Enough brooding. "Tell me about yourself, Magnus. What are you doing in America, and how do you come to know your whisky?"

If Bridget hadn't been watching him, she would have missed his smile—a fleeting, self-deprecating lift of one side of his mouth and a momentary glint in his eyes.

Blue eyes, not that eye color mattered for doodly-dang-squat.

"I am an only child," he said, an interesting place to start his self-disclosure. "I manage a business that my family began generations ago, which isn't unusual in Scotland. I was overdue for a change of scene, and I'd never seen the American West before."

All very prosaic, and yet, he wasn't a prosaic guy. He'd walked up to Harley Gummo and diffused a fight that could have turned ugly.

"And?" Bridget prompted.

"And what I've found here is well worth the journey," he said, turning those Highland-blue eyes on Bridget. "Unexpected and intriguing."

Well, now. Bridget fumbled around for a snappy comeback—*I'm all yours, Braveheart*, struck her as a little undignified, also not quite true.

Magnus turned on his stool as if to survey the dance floor where scooting, swinging, flirting couples were shuffling back to their tables for drinks between sets.

"I think this is where you toss your drink at me," he said, "except I'd ask you not to waste such a fine single malt. Witty banter was never my strong suit, and I'm out of practice."

"I'm not much of one for bantering myself so spare yourself the effort.

Where did you have your first sip of good whisky?"

"On my mother's lap, I suppose. Possibly my father's."

"And your favorite whisky is?"

The American whisky industry employed a number of Scots, and Bridget loved to hear them talk. The accent was charming, but even more attractive was their passion for the water of life. The most dour and retiring Scot would wax eloquent in the face of a well-finished eighteen-year-old single malt, and bad whisky reduced them to unintelligible tirades.

Bridget loved those tirades, because without comprehending a single word, she could agree with the whole sentiment.

Magnus talked about whisky as if it were a member of his family—difficult, dear, and deserving of every loyalty. Scotland had more than two hundred distilleries, and he rattled off names and products like a horse breeder spoke of lineage and track records.

Listening to him talk, the betrayal Bridget felt from her brothers faded, aided by the Edradour, but also by the magic of hearing a true believer talk about his passion.

Which also happened to be Bridget's passion.

Somewhere between an argument about Islay versus Campbeltown peatyness, the thought strayed through Bridget's head: What would Magnus the Scot be like in bed?

Bold with notes of soft wool, slow hands, and comfortable silence?

Frisky, surprisingly playful, with an inventive streak and stamina toward the finish?

"I've bored you," Magnus said. "My apologies, but many Scotsmen are passionate about whisky. What of you? How did you become enamored of the water of life?"

The fiddles had re-tuned, and Preacher had turned the lights down again.

"I like challenges," Bridget said. "Are you up for another turn on the floor?"

Shamus was leading Martina from their table, and her walk said she had plans for her partner after the last waltz.

"I would be honored." Magnus stood and held out his hand.

Bridget let him escort her to the same corner they'd started out in last time. "If I fall on my butt, I'm taking you down with me."

He arranged them in waltz position. "Promise?" His expression was solemn.

Magnus spoke plain English, but cultural differences might mean...

"You're teasing me," Bridget said as the introduction started.

"I would never make sport of a lady."

"You just did. I should warn you that thanks to my brothers, I would make sport of a gentleman at the least provocation."

The introduction was unaccountably long, which meant Bridget was standing more or less in Magnus's arms and he in hers. That should have felt awkward, or flirtatious.

Mostly, it felt nice.

"I think you're bluffing," Magnus said as they moved into a relaxed version of their box step. "I think you would be very considerate of a gentleman's sensibilities."

Innuendo lingered in that observation, and Bridget didn't bother batting it aside. Talking to Magnus had warmed parts of her the whisky couldn't reach, and helped her gather the composure the day's earlier arguments had scattered.

Her brothers were damned idiots. Shamus and Martina twirled by, and Martina gave her a little wave and a thumbs-up.

Bridget closed her eyes and tucked closer to Magnus, who accommodated the shift in position as easily as if they'd been dancing together for years. He felt good—warm, solid, and masculine with none of the wandering hands or bumping hips Bridget would have endured from other guys she'd stood up with in recent memory.

When the music ended, she excused herself to use the ladies' room and found Martina reapplying eyeliner.

"I don't know where you found him," Martina said, "but if I wasn't with Shamus tonight, I'd be arm-wrestling you for that guy."

Bridget tucked a few stray wisps of hair back into her French braid. "He's just passing through."

Martina snapped her eyeliner closed with a twist. "They're the best kind. If you're going to be stupid and talk yourself out of a little harmless fun, I'll tell your brother you stole his Indian head nickels when we were in fifth grade."

"You stole them, and we were in fourth grade."

In the mirror, Martina gave her a look. "Go for it, Bridget. Shamus said he owes you an apology, and that means somebody's temper got out of hand. A little horizontal two-step always improves my mood. You have any protection?"

"You are a bad influence, Martina Matlock."

"Shamus likes that about me," she said, digging in her purse and passing over a three-pack of condoms. "Be adventurous, not stupid." She gave Bridget a hug and sashayed out of the ladies' room on a cloud of Tom Ford fragrance.

Bridget mentally cataloged scents—citrus, mint, thyme, some close relative of jasmine—and considered the condoms. They were nowhere near their expiration date.

"Be adventurous, not stupid," she told her reflection, and that was good advice. Where Magnus was concerned, she could be tempted to be both.

"But he's only passing through, so adventurous will do just fine."

* * *

"The first thing you will do," Luke Logan said, turning the chair around and straddling it so he faced his brother across the kitchen table, "is apologize to Bridget."

Patrick stared straight past him, but then, what had Luke expected? "I already put my quarters into the potty-mouth jar."

Luke had put ten bucks in. "You could put your whole soul into the potty-mouth jar, and that's not the same as apologizing for raising your voice to the only person remaining in this household who qualifies as a civilizing influence."

Wrong thing to say. But for nearly a year, everything had been the wrong thing to say to Patrick Logan. Every look was the wrong look, every silence was the wrong silence.

"Bridget gave as good as she got." Patrick sounded eight years old and guilty as hell.

Luke had had more conversations with his brothers than the Montana night sky held stars, most of them trivial or related to running the ranch. This conversation could not be allowed to become trivial.

"Bridget will always give at least as good as she's gotten. That's no excuse for how you acted."

"You weren't exactly the United Nations peacekeeping envoy."

"So I will apologize. I'll do it in front of you, in front of Lena, in front of my damned horse. You were out of line, Patrick."

Patrick sat back. "We all were. Shamus would rather be catching the last of the spring skiing, not buried in our bookkeeping. He always gets restless as winter ends."

True enough, which had nothing to do with anything.

"He gets restless because we paid corporate taxes this spring, same as every year." They'd paid as much as they could. Shamus had until September to figure out how to make that amount be enough to appease the bottomless IRS pit.

The kitchen door swung open, and Lena stood there in her nightie and bare feet, clutching a book. Her braids were lumpy, meaning she'd done them herself.

"I finished my homework and brushed my teeth and watered Mama's violets, Daddy. Will you read me a story?"

She held one of those books about rabbits and possums and old Mr. McGregor. They were stories for a child younger than eight, in Luke's opinion.

Patrick scrubbed a hand over his face. "Sure, Pumpkin. I'll be up in a minute."

"You always say that." Lena's tone was hesitant rather than accusing. Everything about the girl had become hesitant, while her father's approach to life had become aggressively heedless.

"See the clock?" Luke asked. "I will keep track of the time, and when it has been five minutes, I will remind your daddy that he's given you his word, and up the stairs he will go." On the end of Luke's boot, if necessary.

"Thanks, Uncle Luke." Lena scampered across the kitchen and gave him a good squeeze around the neck, bashing him in the ear with her book, then scampered out the door without even looking at her father.

"Get back into counseling," Luke said. "Find salvation, find another woman, take holy orders, or bay at the full moon, but you can't go on the way you have been."

Patrick tossed the ketchup bottle in the air and caught it. "Yes, boss."

"You'd better be up those steps in four-and-a-half minutes, or you'll have another apology to make."

Patrick rose and took a longneck out of the fridge. "What's one more when I have so many? Leave me alone, Luke."

And leaving Patrick alone also wasn't the right thing to do, but Luke apparently had a bedtime story to read—another story. At least for the damned rabbit, there would be a happy ending.

* * *

"You were holding Miss Bridget a mite close," the bartender said.

"She was holding me just as closely," Magnus replied, and that had felt better than it ought to have. By the end of the second dance, Bridget had been pliant and relaxed in his arms, following his lead instinctively, though he'd been doing little more than swaying to the beat and trying not to get too obvious an erection.

Which had also felt better than it should have.

The bartender braced both hands on the bar and leaned close. "Friendly warning. You mess with that little gal, and Harley will be the least of your troubles. She has three brothers who will swing first and ask questions when they're done stompin' on your Scottish ass."

Magnus would place Bridget closer to thirty than twenty-five and put her intelligence—emotional as well as academic—at well above average.

"You disrespect the lady if you think I could impose on her and survive the encounter. She has a mind and will of her own, and those she calls friends ought to respect her judgment."

Gray eyes grew as cold as a Hebridean winter sky. Too late, Magnus recalled that America was saturated with guns by Scottish standards.

Then a grin split the bartender's face, and he extended a hand. "I'm Thaddeus Martin. Everybody calls me Preacher, 'cept Juanita. She calls me whatever she damned well pleases. Any friend of Bridget's is a friend of ours."

Magnus shook, because making friends with bartenders was part of his job. At an establishment serving liquor, bookkeepers were also surprisingly influential when it came to what inventory was ordered and in what quantities, but bartenders actually dispensed the product and monitored those consuming it.

Bridget emerged from the hallway leading to the facilities. She had a neat way of moving, neither timid nor bold. She was comfortable here, alert but not on guard, and she had no need to call attention to herself.

Somewhere in the middle of that last dance, Magnus's body had begun to notice *her*, and thus Magnus had begun to notice his body. He worked out, he played golf. He'd been dragged on his share of hill-walking dates and preferred not to die of an avoidable coronary, so he watched what he ate.

Magnus had come of age regarding sexual attraction as a normal preoccupation for the male in his reproductive prime. Managing that preoccupation fell somewhere between a delight and an ongoing chore. Since turning thirty, the preoccupation had faded, and Magnus had told himself that was normal too.

Maybe spending a pleasurable few hours with a friendly stranger when on holiday was also normal.

"Shall we enjoy another dram?" Magnus had to bend close to Bridget to be heard over the crowd now stomping and whooping on the dance floor.

"Your choice of single malt, and then let's move to the lounge."

That was a yes. Magnus chose a lovely eighteen-year-old Speyside that never failed to impress. He paid the bar tab and the total for the group at Harley's table, then followed Bridget from the bar. She led him down a plank-floored corridor lined with vintage rodeo posters, and the noise of the dance floor faded behind them.

"Tell me about living in Montana," Magnus said as they took a small table in a quiet corner. "I've never seen terrain like this before."

"I suspect life in Montana is like life in your Highlands. Self-sufficiency is prized, but we try to look after one another. Tons of scenery, and the weather does whatever the heck it pleases. This is a great whisky."

"This whisky is an old friend. You don't speak of your home state with any great affection." And that was sad.

"Maybe I need to travel elsewhere to see what a bargain I have here. The standing joke is we have ten months of winter and two months of road construction—or relatives."

Bridget leaned her head against the cushioned upholstery, exposing a graceful line of shoulder, throat, and jaw.

"You are tired." Magnus was too, having driven beyond his scheduled itinerary. He'd run out of distilleries to visit and hadn't been interested in starting on the breweries. Driving on the wrong side of the road and sitting on the wrong side of the car meant the whole undertaking was more nerve-racking than a holiday ought to be.

"I'm weary to the bone," Bridget replied, "but it's always that way by the end of winter. The calving and lambing are brutally demanding, and just when you think spring has finally beaten winter into submission, one more blizzard—the third one more blizzard of the month—comes roaring down on an Alberta Clipper." She took another sip of her drink. "I argued with my brothers at the supper table."

The location apparently exacerbated the offense. "I'm sorry. They upset you."

"They live to upset me, and I return the favor."

Magnus asked the question his father had taught him to pose when harm had been done among family members. "Can you make it right?"

"No, I cannot. They want too much, and I'm saying no because I mean no."

That was a relief, actually. If Magnus offered his company for the night, Bridget would turn him down flat unless she was genuinely interested. No should mean no.

"Maybe time will help. I nearly came to blows with my great-uncle recently. Fergus is eighty if he's a day and speaks the Doric dialect with an aggressively unintelligible accent. He venerates the past and accuses me of venerating profit."

Elias had been the only other person present during that altercation. He'd made what peace he could between Magnus and a curmudgeon determined to turn a distillery into a monument to maudlin sentiment.

Bridget brushed a glance over Magnus. "Are you ashamed of what you said?"

A useful question. "No, but I might have said it more respectfully."

She patted his hand. "Don't do that. If you'd been more polite, he would have steamrolled right over you. Some people don't listen unless you shout, and I've begun to suspect that's my fault too."

Magnus caught her hand and kept their fingers linked. "You shout out of habit, do you?"

"I let them ignore me until ignoring me becomes a habit. I've trained them, the way a horse trains us to react when it paws in the crossties."

The moment called for flirtation, a kiss to her knuckles, a witty quip, a toast, but Magnus was too annoyed with her brothers to bother with any of that.

"Untrain them, Bridget. Or perhaps this disagreement was the first step in that direction?"

She smiled that big, beaming, happy smile. "You catch on fast, Magnus. Makes me wonder where else you might be a quick study."

"Are you flirting with me?"

Her smile wavered. "If you have to ask, then it's not very effective flirting, is it? Tell me some more about this whisky."

"For the first time in years, I'm not interested in talking about whisky." Magnus wanted to know how she kissed and what her hair looked like when not all tucked up in that fancy braid. He wanted to learn the contours of her bare shoulders and how she best liked to cuddle.

"What are you interested in, Magnus?"

He was interested in *her* and being intimate with her, but why was this conversation so difficult? Magnus recalled the moves—they were hardly complicated—but Bridget was complicated. She wasn't on the prowl, wasn't trolling for a ride, wasn't *forgettable enough* for a man who'd be back in Scotland a few weeks hence.

"I'm interested in inviting you to my room," Magnus said. "My hotel is two doors up."

Oh, that was smooth. Bridget looked at him as if he'd spoken in Uncle Fergus's Doric dialect, which was barely related to English on Fergus's most sober day.

"Accompanying strange men to their hotel rooms is not my usual style."

Nor was inviting strange women to bed Magnus's style. He'd done his share of rebounding in stupid directions, taking what was on offer, but Bridget wasn't on offer in that sense, nor was she a stupid direction.

Magnus wasn't quite sure what Bridget was, but he liked what he knew of her, and attraction seemed to grow from that liking rather than the reverse.

But the lady apparently wasn't feeling the chemistry. *Bollocks.* "Then we will enjoy the rest of our drinks, and you will recommend the local sights to me. I'm not due at my next destination until the day after tomorrow, which puts me at loose ends."

He was ahead of schedule, which for a vacationing man was probably a form of failure.

Bridget slid closer on the bench they shared, so she and Magnus were hip to hip. "I could use a distraction right about now, Magnus. I mean no disrespect, but you're passing through and I'm plotting DEFCON 1 for my brothers. You would be nothing but a distraction, and then so long, cowboy. Happy trails and all that."

That had been Magnus's public service announcement until five years ago, though he preferred sailing analogies to talk of cowboys.

Magnus looped an arm around her shoulders. "I'll be your distraction, Bridget, and you can be mine. Shall we order something to eat?"

"Now that is a fine idea," she said, settling against him. "I was too angry at dinner to do justice to the cooking, and I intend to be up tonight well past my bedtime."

Magnus passed her the menu and signaled the server.

* * *

College for Bridget had been a blur of book learning stashed between doing her part for the ranch and figuring out from Grandpap MacDeaver how to run the distillery business—not simply how to make whisky, which education had begun before Bridget could read. Whisky-making was regulated by local, state, national, and even international bodies, though Logan Bar had yet to test the crowded and shark-infested whisky-export waters.

Grandpap had favored staying in control to staying up with the times. Bridget had promised to honor that legacy. He'd gone so far as the let Mama change the name of the business upon her marriage—from MacDeaver's to Logan Bar—but that had been his only concession to the passage of time.

Running the business, as opposed to minding the still, took a level of know-how Bridget hadn't gravitated to instinctively. Her strength was her nose, not a head for numbers. Law school had allowed her a semblance of a social life. She'd had the occasional hookup, friends with benefits, casual relationships, and a few near misses.

"I'm not a prude," she told her reflection in the mirror of Magnus's hotel room. "I'm not Martina either."

Martina spent about eight seconds on each bronc, as it were, and made no apologies for enjoying variety—not that she should.

Bridget hadn't been in the saddle since… she couldn't recall since when.

She emerged from the bathroom to find Magnus sprawled in a wing chair. He was an attractive man, even when he was just checking messages, though Montana was full of handsome specimens.

"Everyone okay back home?" Bridget asked, taking the second wing chair.

"Everyone's fast asleep," Magnus said. "Or just about to wake up. Have you let somebody know where you are?"

That was hookup safety rule number one, wasn't it? "Have you?"

"My cousin Elias. I hope I woke him up too, given all the times he's sent me cheery little texts from Monaco or Budapest or Singapore."

Magnus surprised her. Guys didn't observe the hookup safety protocol, but Magnus had. Even Harley's friends didn't try to talk him down from stupid decisions, but Magnus had. Guys didn't linger over a shared dessert of huckleberry cheesecake when the rest of the evening had been agreed to, but Magnus had.

He'd studied business law, with a side of land use—a big deal in Scotland, apparently—and had an undergrad in environmental science.

"You ever been married, Magnus?"

He put the phone down. "I am not married, Bridget, and neither are you. I also don't have children or a dog, though I am permitted to share my quarters with a pair of geriatric cats. Having second thoughts?"

"Having I-don't-recall-the-tune, can-you-hum-a-few-bars thoughts." The whisky glow had worn off, which also didn't help a gal get her buckaroo on.

Magnus rose from the chair, scooped her up, and resettled with her in his lap.

Bridget was too surprised to fuss him for it.

"Hum a few bars, she says to a man who's notoriously tone deaf. I liked it when you sat next me, right next to me. I like how indignant you became when my fork ventured too close to your half of a forty-pound piece of cheesecake. I like that arguing with family doesn't sit well with you, but I wish you could put that aside for a moment and kiss me."

She scooted around so she straddled his lap. "I can manage that last."

She'd brushed her teeth twice, and Magnus had found a moment to brush his as well. Another surprise, maybe the best one so far.

Thank God, he wasn't a pushy kisser. He let Bridget make the overtures, and she wasn't in a hurry. Heaven knew when she'd find another dance partner, so she intended to savor the one she'd lassoed.

Magnus apparently intended to savor her too.

He slid his hands around her waist, then up her back, tracing bones, exploring muscles, and easing away tension. He threaded his fingers into her hair and cradled the back of her head as she took a taste of his mouth.

They slow danced through their first kiss, and Bridget let go of worries she'd been clutching too close for too long. Things at home had hit the fan, but in this space, with this man, everything was easy and sweet.

In another few minutes, Bridget was lying across Magnus's lap, unbuttoning his shirt, and toeing off her flats. Her phone buzzed, but it took her a few moments to distinguish the sensation in her back pocket from all the pleasure gathering inside her.

"Phone," she muttered against Magnus's mouth.

He eased away, and Bridget scooted around to glower at her screen.

Martina. *Everything OK?*

Bridget texted back the hotel and room number. *Going just fine. For a damned change.*

She got a smiley face in return, turned off the ringer, and set the phone beside Magnus's on the end table.

"You, sir, are wearing too many clothes."

He rose with Bridget in his arms. "I can fix that. Would you like to use the shower?"

"I'm good." Her hair was still damp in its braid, in fact, which would make it all ridiculous tomorrow—another reason to be unhappy with her brothers.

Magnus set her down on a hundred-acre bed. "I'll join you in five minutes. If you want to borrow one of my shirts, you're welcome to rummage through my suitcase."

The offer was tempting. Bridget instead filled a glass of water at the kitchenette sink, set her pack of condoms on the night table, and shucked out of her clothes. The shower ran briefly, and doubts resurged.

She was about to... there were a zillion words for what she was about to do. Shag, screw, do the nasty, slam the jam, win the pants-off dance-off, do the horizontal greased-weasel tango.

Cowboys were a poetic lot.

Mostly she was about to take a small, prosaic, unplanned risk. Beneath a frisson of trepidation and a lingering buzz of arousal was some pride. She climbed onto the bed and got under the covers. *I am not married to that damned distillery, Lucas Logan, so there.*

Magnus strolled out of the bathroom wearing only a towel around his hips. "That is a pensive expression, madam."

He had just the right amount of chest hair—not a bear-skin rug, not a Ken-doll caricature of a masculine chest. He was well muscled and well proportioned, and as he threw the deadbolt and chain at the door, Bridget wished he'd lose the towel.

But then, she was the one with the sheets tucked up under her arms.

"Lights on or off?" Magnus asked.

Considerate of him. "Up to you."

He killed the lights in the room, which left a single shaft spilling out of the bathroom. He stood in that beam of light and unwrapped the towel from his waist. Without the towel, well-built became a work of art. His body flowed from muscular legs to smooth flanks, to trim waist, tight butt, long back, and shoulders exactly the right breadth.

He'd hold up well, which was the evolutionary objective of strong conformation.

"Condoms are on the night table," Bridget said, lest there by any misunderstanding on that entirely nonnegotiable point.

"I have some as well," he said, prowling across the room. "We'll use yours, if you'd rather."

Whatever else was true about Magnus, he understood a woman's need to be cautious and feel safe.

"Maybe we'll use both, but we'll start with mine."

Magnus sat on the bed at her hip. "Anything I should know? Last-minute warnings? No-tickle zones?"

He was getting it right, moment by moment, move by move. What a pathetic relief that was.

"I'm a traditionalist, if that's what you're asking. I haven't known you long enough to be bored with the tried and true."

"You're a realist," he said, leaning over to kiss her cheek. "I like that in a lover."

A lover. How comfortably he used the term.

Bridget scooted down to her back, and Magnus followed, nuzzling her neck and chest, then climbing over her. For a moment, he lay on her, only the covers between them. He let her have some of his weight, but didn't mash her into the mattress.

"What about you?" Bridget asked, ruffling his damp hair. "Any no-tickle zones?"

"Just be yourself," he said. "Yell if you want to yell, steal the covers, tell me never to call you   darling, laugh at me, but please be yourself."

"Call me Bridget," she said, patting his butt. "And I'll call you Magnus."

CHAPTER THREE

His name was actually Horatio Rupert Magnus Cromarty, but what man—what creature of any species—wanted to be called Horatio or Rupert when his clothes were hanging on the back of the bathroom door?

Before Bridget left, he'd tell her his full name, because that was gentlemanly, not because a passing fancy should become anything more.

For the moment, Magnus concentrated on the pleasure of having Bridget stretched out beneath him on a bed. He'd purposely not gotten under the covers, even though he'd put his time in the shower to good use.

Whether he was reacting to the end of a drought, the fresh mountain air, or the woman herself, his fuse was short. He'd forgotten how that felt, forgotten that lovely, deceptive, I-could-go-all-night sense of erotic rejoicing.

Bridget ruffled his hair in slow, easy strokes.

"If I were a cat, you'd have me purring."

"Get under the covers, Magnus."

"Yes, ma'am."

She might have been a traditionalist in the sense of being at ease with a man sprawled over her in the most unimaginative of intimate positions, but she was an inventive traditionalist. She tugged gently on Magnus's hair, all over his scalp, and that was oddly relaxing.

She ran her nose over his neck, chest, and brows, cheeks, lips, and chin, as if he were an intriguing glass of single malt and entitled to tasting-room protocols.

Bridget wasn't shy about the purpose of the meeting either, wrapping her legs around his flanks and hauling him close.

Magnus reciprocated by exploring the caresses she liked best on her breasts, which was lovely, because he adored a woman who enjoyed having her breasts touched. The urge to join with her hummed through him, along with an odd sense of rightness.

Life should not always be about specific, measurable, attainable, realistic, and timely goals, nor about quarterly earnings or mission statements. Sometimes, life should be about pleasure, connection, and being human.

Bridget brushed her thumbs over his nipples. "Magnus?"

"Aye, love?"

"Now would be nice."

He sat back, wishing he'd left the lights on. Bridget's hair was still in its tidy braid, though a few wispy curls had escaped.

She wrapped her fingers around his cock, and Magnus let her play until *now* became a necessity.

"You have the sweetest touch," he said, reaching for a condom. He could get used to that touch.

"You're not shy. I like that. If we're not in bed to touch each other and be touched, then we're not really in bed together, are we?"

To his sorrow, he knew exactly what she meant. Celeste had taught him what it meant to make love with a woman who wasn't truly in the bed *with him*. He'd been a sexual accessory, a social accessory, a financial accessory.

And a willing one.

The condom was traditional—no fancy textures, flavors, or enhancements. "We have whisky-flavored frenchies in Scotland. I haven't been able to bring myself to use one."

He braced himself on his arms, then tucked closer. Bridget got a grip on him and showed him where she wanted him.

"Whisky-flavored?"

"And plaid. Can't forget national dress for the tadger."

Bridget was silently laughing as Magnus eased himself inside her, and the sensation was lovely. Intimate, affectionate, happy—and outstandingly erotic.

And then he paused, ambushed by tenderness. What a gift—to laugh in bed with a lover.

"Hello, Magnus," Bridget said, kissing him as she met him with a lazy roll of her hips. "Welcome to the Wild West."

Even her kiss held a smile. "Hello, Bridget. A pleasure to be here."

If a man paid attention, he realized that some women were more difficult to read in bed than others. Some ladies didn't move, or moved out of sync, or to a rhythm Magnus couldn't catch. Others made it hard to distinguish between growing arousal and frustration. Still others went about the whole business with a confusingly impatient air.

Bridget was perfect. Her sighs and reactions were entirely intelligible, and if she wanted Magnus's hand on her breast, she simply put his hand there and gave his fingers a squeeze. Her timing matched his. Her tempo fit his as well.

It wasn't supposed to be like this on a first encounter, or even on a honeymoon.

"Strong legs," he muttered as she locked her heels at the small of his back.

"Time in the saddle," she panted. "Do that up and over—God, yes, like that."

He hitched himself higher, and she did something with the angle of her hips that sent him nearly to the brink.

Three seconds later, Bridget was keening softly against his neck and hammering herself against him. Magnus hammered back, and pleasure tangled up with a sense of relief, of coming home and finding all was well, despite a long, wearying absence.

He propped himself on his elbows, lest they both suffocate from a surfeit of satisfaction.

Bridget turned her head so her cheek was against his forearm. "Dayum, Magnus."

That translated easily and wonderfully. She stretched, then nuzzled the crook of his elbow, which tickled. She wiggled next, and Magnus endured while she treated herself to a digestif orgasm—or two, possibly three.

"I needed that," she said, stroking his shoulders. "Lordy, Lordy, did I need that."

He kissed her nose. "So did I."

For a moment, he wallowed in the pleasure of being close to the woman who'd wrung him out thoroughly, but the housekeeping wouldn't wait for long. He sat back, the small of his back protesting.

"Water?" he asked.

"Please."

Bridget propped herself on her elbows while Magnus held the glass to her lips so she could drink.

She flopped back to the pillows. "I need a nap, Magnus, but don't run off. I have plans for you."

He drank from the same spot on the glass she had, because he was an idiot, then he climbed from the bed and peeled off the condom.

"Back in a moment."

The bathroom light was harsh, and the mirror reflected a man whose hair was sticking out in eleven different directions. Magnus's heart, however, was happy. He'd gotten lucky, not in the sense people usually flung the term around. The sexual pleasure had been lovely—better than anticipated, certainly—but his sense of well-being went beyond that.

Bridget suited him, and he suited her in more than the erotic particulars. He and she might have only a single night to delight in each other's company, but it would be a wonderful night.

He was overdue for some wonderful and suspected Bridget was too.

That it could be only a single night of shared wonderful was sad. He pushed the sadness away, scrubbed his fingers over his hair, and made a few plans of his own.

* * *

Magnus slid into the bed behind Bridget and wrapped himself around her. "You're supposed to be napping."

He cuddled up close, nothing diffident or standoffish about his afterglow manners. He draped one arm loosely around Bridget's waist and tucked the other beneath her neck. His body radiated heat along her back and butt, and yet, he didn't crowd her.

How was it possible she'd miss a guy she'd known less than a day?

"Tell me about Scotland." For whatever time they had, Bridget wanted to spend it pretending they had more.

"Scotland the brave." Magnus drew the covers up a few inches higher around Bridget's shoulders, which had been getting chilly, now that she considered it. "Scotland is a complex little country. It would fit inside Montana four, almost five, times, but its experience—particularly in the Highlands and islands—is complicated. We're some of the most formidable soldiers in the world, but our national identity is more conquered than conqueror."

Magnus's fingers drew lazy circles on Bridget's nape and shoulders as he spoke. She could listen to him talk all night. The accent was part of it, but so was the sense that she was connected to him by the words he wove.

"That business about necessity being the mother of invention rings true for us," he went on, "and we take great pride in our innovators and entrepreneurs, and yet, it's as you say: We try to look after one another. Looking after people who don't want to be told what to do—*ever again*—is a challenge."

"What's good about Scotland?"

"The whisky," he said, kissing her shoulder. "The humor, the scenery, the courage, and the resilience. The resilience of the Scots who immigrated here is half the reason Americans aren't still a colony cowering along the Eastern Seaboard of North America, but there's ruthlessness and greed too. We've a lot of Viking blood, especially in the west."

He rambled on about obliteration of Gaelic culture, Clearances—they had something to do with sheep—and the idiot Tories, until Bridget could no longer keep her eyes open. She drifted off for a nap and woke to the realization that her lover was aroused.

Magnus moved in lazy strokes, rubbing himself against her intimately.

"Not without me you don't." Bridget extricated herself from his embrace and straddled him. "How about like this?"

He covered her breasts with his palms. "Like this is lovely."

When the man was right, he was right. Bridget didn't usually care for girl-on-top, because it left her less privacy—which didn't make a lot of sense, considering the context. With Magnus, she wanted to enjoy the view and to enjoy *herself*.

He made that so easy. He was positively gifted when it came to pleasuring a lady's breasts, whether he was using his hands or his mouth. He could be playful, challenging, relentless…

Bridget loved the relentless part. She got him dressed for the party and crouched over him.

"Inside me now, Magnus. Please."

He settled his hands on her hips and drove home in one slow glide. "Exactly where I want to be."

They smiled at each other in the shadows, and then Bridget got the festivities started all over again. She meant to savor him, to treat herself to a few teaser orgasms, because with Magnus she could.

Her plans went awry—the Scots had a saying about that. She caught fire, and Magnus—the fiend—poured everything she'd ever craved in a lover onto the flames. His hands were everywhere, on her breasts, tangled in her hair, stroking her back. He was *with her* as she surrendered to desire and *with her* as she drifted down from a wild, beautiful ride.

"So that was Scottish ingenuity," she panted, subsiding onto his chest.

"More like Highland hospitality."

He made her smile, made her wish that in the morning she didn't have to leave. That was sweet and surprising. Nothing and nobody had ever tempted her away from the Logan Bar ranch.

Except… that wasn't quite accurate. The ranch was beautiful, but it was a Montana ranch, the most jealous of mistresses. If the livestock wasn't demanding attention, the land was, and if the land and livestock were running smoothly, the finances and equipment never did.

Bridget wasn't that attached to the ranch. She hadn't been born there and didn't particularly want to die there. What held her in Montana was her distillery.

Magnus kneaded the muscles of her backside gently, a comforting intimacy as passion faded and the next day's realities threatened to harsh the glow. He slipped from her body, and yet, Bridget didn't want to move.

"Will you stay with me tonight?" he asked.

She lifted her head to peer at him, but there wasn't enough light to read his expression. "You mean as in stay until morning?"

"And for breakfast. I see no need for you to sneak off like some cattle reaver who's been up to no good."

Staying until morning was a bad idea, a tempting bad idea. "More Highland hospitality?"

"Greed," he said, brushing her hair back from her brow. "Pure, selfish greed, lass, and that's not my tadger talking, though I'm a well-pleasured man at the moment."

And that was probably an example of Scottish courage.

"As it happens," Bridget said, sitting up, "I'm feeling greedy myself. I warn you, I'm as possessive about my butter and maple syrup as I am about my cheesecake."

She'd like to be possessive about Magnus, but the last thing she needed now was a complication. Magnus had complication written all over him, and he wasn't offering anything more than a shared breakfast anyhow.

Lovely of him to offer that though. To Bridget, it meant more than he'd know.

"If you'll keep the bed warm for me, I'll nip into the loo," he said, patting her butt.

She almost said, *I could get used to this Highland hospitality.* Instead, she pitched off of him, drew up the covers, and took the warm spot when he strolled over to the bathroom.

When Magnus came back to bed this time, Bridget spooned him. "What do you dream of, Magnus?"

He was quiet for so long she suspected he'd fallen asleep.

"I thought I knew," he said, drawing her arm more snugly around his middle and lacing his fingers with hers. "A business that supports my elders. Commercial success to wave in my cousin's face. A respected place among my peers and maybe a bit of revenge on those who assured me I'd fail in two years flat. Those are all understandable goals, but they don't sound very lofty, do they?"

"They sound human." Bridget could understand those goals all too well. *I am not married to my distillery, Luke Logan.* She wasn't married to anybody or anything else either.

Which was just fine. Mostly.

She tucked close and let sleep claim her, until Magnus woke her at dawn. They made love a third time, slowly, drawing out the pleasure and putting off the parting. Breakfast was a friendly affair over a room-service tray of flapjacks, coffee, and bacon.

After separate showers—ladies first—Magnus walked Bridget to her truck and gave her a final kiss to her cheek.

She climbed into her Tundra, gave him one wave good-bye, and turned her mind to the challenge awaiting her at home.

Her brothers had invited some fancy Brit to the ranch with a view toward selling the bastard her distillery. She had until Sunday night to convince them that their betrayal would fail. Come fire, flood, famine, or fraternal disloyalty, nobody was going to take that business away from her.

Nobody.

* * *

"Elias, you bastard. I hope your tadger falls into the River Tay the next time you're trying to impress one of the ladies with your angling."

Two in the goddamned a-of-m Montana time, meant Elias was probably enjoying his second cup of some exotic Italian caffeine while a lovely spring morning got underway in Scotland.

"Fishing analogies," Elias replied around a loud sip. "I'd forgotten your fishing analogies. Does this imply you've been casting a line or two?"

Magnus lay back against the same pillows he'd shared with Bridget the previous night. "The spring fishing in Montana would make your piddly Deeside antics look like Uncle Fergus swatting at the midgies. A different hatching begins each week, the variety is unbelievable, and the guides appreciate a good whisky."

He'd spent his Saturday with one of those guides, a young man who'd known every bank, bug, and tall tale related to the valley's angling industry.

"Are we overworking your analogy, or did you truly go fishing?" Elias's question was casual, but then, Elias was at his nosiest when he was trying to appear casual. He'd learned that tactic from the aunties, who could pry a young man's worst fears from him over a cup of tea and a nibble of tablet.

"Do you know what a streamer is, Elias?"

"Of course I... What's a streamer?"

Magnus launched into an explanation of a curious type of tied fly—much longer than the usual variety—and how it could be manipulated to lure trout.

"So you got your pathetic arse into a river," Elias said. "I thought you were supposed to be in Denver today."

Elias was the best of cousins, despite his excellent memory for detail. "I'm ahead of schedule. I'll drive up to a couple ski resorts tomor—this morning and then arrive at the Logan ranch this evening."

Another loud, luscious sip of coffee. "You're going skiing?"

Scotland had a few ski resorts, though they were backyard bunny slopes compared to the American version.

"I'm going on reconnaissance, Elias. The nearest resort includes more four-star accommodations than most cities in Scotland, covers more than five thousand acres, and includes a conference center, multiple spas, summer resort facilities, and—"

"You're off to sell goddamned whisky," Elias growled. "I send you on the first holiday you've taken—not in years, Magnus. The first vacation you've *ever* taken, and you can't be content to go raiding at some boutique distillery as a means of writing off the expenses, you must turn the whole exercise into business."

"Selling whisky is what I do, Elias." Though Magnus recalled Bridget's question: *What do you dream of?* He'd been dreaming of her when Elias had interrupted his sleep. "Did you call to scold me for pursuing my livelihood in a location where that might be quite profitable? They are catching onto the concept of food miles here, whether they know it or not. Local distillers have cachet."

"Whisky isnae food, you dolt."

"And you aren't Uncle Fergus. Is he speaking to you yet?"

"Aye. Cursing at me. Says you're off on a fool's errand. Americans have been making their own whisky for hundreds of years, according to Fergus. Even they can figure out a three-ingredient recipe in that much time."

Despite the hour, despite the lingering dreams of Bridget, the part of Magnus's mind that was always open for business had awakened.

"How do I get him off the board of directors, Elias? The old boy's grown forgetful and difficult."

"And the forgetfulness is probably half the reason for his bad disposition." Elias sounded as if he might have been talking around a mouthful of warm, buttery scone. "You don't want him off the board, Magnus. If he retires or otherwise becomes incapacitated, Cousin Aileen could take his place."

Now there was a nightmare to strike fear into an honest distiller's heart. "She's... two years his junior?"

"And a more rabid opponent of the grape and the grain, you never did meet."

There were plenty of teetotaling Scots, but most of them grasped that two hundred distilleries added a great deal to the national economy, in employment and tourist appeal.

"Better the devil I know," Magnus said, running his hand over the pillow he'd apparently been clutching in his dreams. "Are you through depriving me of my beauty sleep?"

"God knows you need it. Can I at least conclude your last text was about a frolic instead of a spying mission?"

"What was my last text?" Magnus could recite what he'd texted verbatim. He'd considered each word and whether to even send it.

"The one about 'have arrived at such-and-such hotel and am enjoying the local sights.' At midnight, you were enjoying local sights?"

"Montana by moonlight would take your breath away, Elias. Keep your Amalfi Coast and your Moroccan camel treks. This place is special."

Magnus hadn't meant to say that, but Elias was thousands of miles away. The admission wasn't as damning as if they'd been sharing a bottle in Great-Grandda's Plaid Purgatory.

"If you can notice that much, there's hope for you. Stick to the well-groomed slopes, please. If anything happens to you, I become the acting CEO of your pot still, and I've no wish to take on that thankless task."

"Love you too."

Elias ended the call on a snort.

A friendly, cousinly snort.

Magnus set his phone on the night table and rummaged among his emotions for homesickness.

He missed his distillery. Missed the yeasty, fruity, wonderful scent of whisky aborning. He missed the cheerful sense of industry his employees brought to a trade that hadn't changed much since their great-granddas and great-grandmams had first sampled a wee dram.

He did not miss being hounded by the accountant for quarterly spreadsheets, did not miss the constant haggling and negotiating over warehouse space, and most of all—he might not admit this even to himself in the broad light of day—he did not miss that sense of utter frustration when a batch wasn't finishing well and the entire crew suspected it.

Whisky made the stock market look like a sure bet. The finest ingredients, most lovingly blended, entrusted to the best-quality casks, could yield a purely pedestrian product. The best distilleries, the lucky ones, had a distiller who could rescue that product with a few years of finishing in the right barrels.

Even a few months in the right barrels—sauterne, port, Madeira, bourbon, sherry—could bring out hidden depth and quality in a year that might have otherwise been disappointing.

Cromarty Distilleries, Ltd., lacked what was known in the business as a cask whisperer, and unbeknownst to the board, Magnus desperately needed one.

* * *

Shamus had delivered the gut punch: They couldn't afford to refund even a two-week booking on the ranch's guesthouse. The fancy Brit had paid in advance and booked the whole house for himself, and that money had already been spent on barley seed.

"We could put the refund on a credit card," Luke said. "Give the guy back his money, let everybody in the valley know we're starting off the year turning away paying customers."

"No credit cards," Shamus snapped. "Haven't you people learned anything?"

Bridget passed Lena a slice of pizza—plain, extra cheese, because in this one particular, Lena still expressed a preference. The Sunday afternoon pizza run had become something of a ritual for them in recent months, a gesture in the direction of female bonding. More and more, Bridget and Lena were coming home to a weekly bickering session around the kitchen table.

"Or," Luke went on, as if Shamus hadn't spoken, "we could tell the nice man we've changed our minds. We don't want his money, we won't honor his reservation, and oh, by the way, the weather's supposed to turn crap-awful on Tuesday."

"The weather turned nasty the day you invited this guy to steal my distillery," Bridget snapped. "I'll put his refund on my credit cards, or on the distillery, and you idiots can pay me back over time." With interest, of course.

"You will do no such thing," Shamus said. "I can ask the bank…"

"You can't ask the bank." Patrick spoke up for the first time. He looked like hell, suggesting he'd spent Saturday night cozied up to a bottle, another weekly ritual. "Not again. Why not let the guy have his two weeks, show him around the ranch until he has saddle sores on his saddle sores. He can catch some spring powder on the slopes, and Bridget can give him a tour of the distillery. We can't force you to sell to him, Bridget, but anything less than the usual Logan Bar hospitality would be just plain stupid when he's paid for the whole guesthouse at top rates."

That was the longest speech Patrick had given in weeks.

"We could take him on a trail ride," Lena said.

Patrick cast a haunted look toward the window, where a mild spring day was lying to everybody about what waited for them on Tuesday.

"That's a fine idea," Bridget said before Patrick could pee all over his daughter's suggestion. "Never met a greenhorn who didn't want to play cowboy a time or two. He won't be setting one prissy foot in my distillery though."

"Technically," Shamus said, helping himself to his fourth slice of pepperoni and black olives, "it's not exclusively your distillery."

"You had to go there," Luke muttered.

"He's just being honest," Bridget said, though she refrained—barely—from pointing out that these three were not her brothers by blood. "It's not exclusively my distillery, not my ranch, but it's my hard work that made the distillery about the only profitable aspect of the whole Logan Bar operation. My hard work that put a free lawyer at the disposal of the family businesses. And the distillery—of which I am part owner—*sits on my land*."

Patrick shoved away from the kitchen table and went to the window, turning his back to the room. Lena followed, half a slice of pizza in her hand.

"We don't need to have this discussion now," Luke said.

"Bull-doots we don't," Bridget retorted. "His Royal Majesty will be pulling in to the guesthouse parking lot before sundown, and you expect me to roll out the red carpet for the man who'll kill my dreams."

And for what? So the ranch could limp along for another generation? Ever since Bridget's mother had died, the ranch had drifted. Mama had been the bookkeeper, innovator, guardian of traditions, and voice of common sense for a business as diverse as it was difficult. She'd been a kind, tolerant, and even-keeled step-mother to three grieving adolescent boys, and she'd thrived on the challenges of ranch life.

Ranches could be highly profitable, between tourist draws such as fishing and cross-country skiing, livestock, crops, timber, horses, and wool, but ranches went under every year as well.

Development had hit Montana years ago, turning good land into dude ranches, trust-fund mansions, upscale hunting lodges, and ski chalets. Foreign oil imports had dropped radically, but so had fossil fuel consumption domestically. Any ranch that depended on mineral leases to make ends meet was on borrowed time. Beef consumption was dropping, but Montana weather made crop farming a dicey proposition.

Change had come to the ranching way of life, and the Logan Bar had yet to adjust.

Or the Logan brothers had yet to adjust.

"I don't see as we have much choice," Patrick said. "We took the man's money, we can't pay it back easily, and if we ever do need to sell the distillery, sending the first potential buyer down the drive without a how-de-do won't help our prospects. Why can't you at least listen to what he has to say, Bridget? You might learn something about the European market or the latest technology."

"I keep up with the tech through the industry publications. Because I have not one dime to expand with, I don't give a hearty heck-yeah what the European market is doing."

Lena took her father's hand, and abruptly, Bridget wished she'd kept her mouth shut.

A distillery was a business. A legacy too, and a livelihood for Bridget, but *Lena had lost her mother*. What would happen to the girl if the ranch went under? Her daddy was halfway to lost already, and her mama was pushing up daisies.

"I will make an effort to be hospitable to the raider you buttheads have invited into our midst," Bridget said, "but I make no guarantees. If he gets too uppity, if he doesn't show my operation proper respect, then you prodigies can just explain to him that you offered him a distillery that's not for sale. As far as I'm concerned, he's here to kick tires and take a write-off vacation, nothing more."

A sigh of fraternal relief went around the room. They'd been worried, and that was good. For their high-handedness, for their lack of trust in Bridget and respect for her, they should be worried.

"Lena, you going to help me slice the apple pie?" Bridget asked. If Judith had been alive, they would have at least had a salad to go with this cardiac disaster of a menu.

Lena was taking a bite of pizza. She dropped her father's hand and pointed out the window as tires crunched over gravel.

"The enemy has arrived," Bridget said, shoving away from the table. "And you can expect the longest two weeks of your lives to commence the minute his majesty puts his suitcase down in that guesthouse. You will keep him away from me and from my business to the greatest extent possible, and you will let me choose when to show him the distillery."

"Yes, ma'am." Three for three. They were perfect gentlemen when they'd gotten away with being idiots. Bridget could never hate her brothers, but they surely did turn up tiresome more than was convenient.

A knock sounded on the front door. A good solid rap of the knocker. Lena scampered from the room, waving the crust of her pizza. Neither her father nor her uncles made any move to call her back, which meant Bridget would have to admit the enemy to the castle herself.

The family was falling apart, and thus the ranch stood little chance of surviving. All the more reason for Bridget to protect the distillery. She tromped across the great room with a sense of doom and barely beat Lena to the front door.

The great room was intended to welcome and impress, with a huge river rock fireplace along the far wall, exposed beams, woven rugs over hardwood floors, knotty pine paneling in all directions, and diabolically comfy furniture. The place needed dusting, though, needed fresh flowers and the little touches Mama had instinctively added.

Bridget dredged up a false smile. This guy wasn't her enemy, but he wasn't the ranch's savior either. She had two weeks to explain that to him.

She swung the door open and stepped back. "Welcome to the Logan—"

Magnus stood on the front porch, his cheeks ruddy, his dark hair tousled by the Montana wind. The sheer pleasure of seeing him lasted about a nanosecond before reality slammed through Bridget.

His interest in whisky, his Scottish accent, his claim to be on vacation.

On holiday, to use his term. It all made a rotten kind of sense.

"You low-down, slithering, disgusting, creeping excuse for a vile, humping, conscienceless reptile," Bridget growled. "Get off this property and don't come back."

She slammed the door, only to see Lena staring at her. The girl's chin began to quiver, and she bolted straight up the stairs as Luke, Patrick, and Shamus all emerged from the kitchen.

CHAPTER FOUR

Did reptiles hump?

That inane question swirled through Magnus's brain as he wrestled with the notion that the woman he'd glimpsed for half a second in the open doorway had borne a delightful resemblance to Bridget.

A girl had stood by her side. A mixed-race little sprite with what looked like spaghetti sauce on her cheek and a crust of bread in her hand.

Then boom—literally—the enormous door had slammed shut.

It opened again. "Excuse my sister for her unique sense of humor," a tall blond man said. "You must be Mr. Cromarty. Welcome."

Bridget—*had* that been Bridget?—was nowhere to be seen, but two other tall blond men were in evidence, trying to smile.

"I am Magnus Cromarty. Have I found the Logan Bar ranch?" The turnoff to the drive was well marked, with a timber sign anchored in native stone, but that had been several miles ago.

"You have," the official greeter said. "I'm Luke Logan, and these are my brothers, Shamus and Patrick. I'll show you around your new home away from home, and if you have any luggage—"

"I'll show him around."

Bridget stood on a flight of steps leading from a truly impressive room. The American West was embodied in this room as a rugged, lovely, comfortable haven. The woman on the steps was furious, though, and nothing would protect Magnus from her wrath.

Which made no sense.

"Thank you," Magnus said. "I wouldn't want to put anybody to any bother."

Bridget descended the rest of the steps and clomped to the front door. "You won't be any bother at all, I can guarantee you that, mister. Luke, fetch his gear. Patrick, see to your daughter. Shamus, you can start cleaning up supper before the cats get after the pepperonis."

These must be the infamous brothers, though they scurried off at her command like chastened puppies.

"Bridget?" Magnus didn't dare touch her, though he wanted to. She had clearly added him to the list of men with whom she was furious, and he had no intention of remaining on that list.

"That would be me," she said, rounding on him. "What sick sense of humor inspires a man to charm his way right into the enemy's skivvies, Magnus? I don't expect much from the male of the species, but that's a new low in my experience."

"How did I become your enemy?"

"We'll discuss that later, when my brothers aren't lurking in the bushes, thinking up more inspired ways to ruin my life." She snatched a patchwork quilted jacket from a peg on the wall and flounced out the door.

A gentleman didn't argue with a lady, not when her expression promised to geld him at the first opportunity. Magnus followed Bridget across the driveway to a handsome stone and timber house with a roofed porch. Luke Logan followed with Magnus's suitcase and carry-on.

"Thank you," Magnus said.

"Your groceries got here a couple hours ago," Luke said. "If you need anything, we're just a—"

"Beat it, Luke," Bridget said. "Braveheart and I are due for a parley."

Luke's gaze skittered from his sister to Magnus. "You two know each other?"

"No," Bridget said, just as Magnus answered, "We're acquainted."

"That's... that's good, I hope," Luke said, taking himself down the steps. "Bridget, we'll save you a slice of pie."

That was a warning of some sort, obvious even to Magnus, who had no siblings.

"Inside," Bridget said, producing a key from the pocket of her jeans. "Get inside and prepare to explain why in the hell I should give you the time of day much less a tour of my distillery."

Her distillery? "Because," Magnus said, "if ever you should come to Scotland, I'd be happy to give you a tour of my facilities."

"I've seen your *facilities*, Magnus. I never want to tour them again."

* * *

Bridget's sense of betrayal was wonderfully righteous, and yet, a stupid corner of her heart hoped that Magnus hadn't spent the night with her in anticipation of stealing her distillery. Then too, her rage felt a little too good, a little too handy.

She had many, many reasons to be angry, and they weren't *all* Magnus's fault, even if he was in Montana to take her business from her.

He leaned against the guesthouse kitchen counter, looking windblown and wary in his jeans and a flannel shirt. He also looked tired.

"Are you hydrating?" Bridget asked.

"Bridget, I'm not a sot."

Did anybody sound as offended as an indignant Scot?

"The elevation here is nearly a mile above sea level," Bridget said, opening the fridge. "If you're used to living at lower altitudes, then you need time to adjust. You're also probably not accustomed to how dry it can be here."

She filled a glass half way with organic raspberry juice—he could afford organic raspberry juice, of course—and topped it off with seltzer water.

"Drink that."

He crossed his arms. "Not unless you join me, Bridget. You told your brother that you and I are due to parley. That means discussion, not you giving orders while the rest of the world scurries to do your bidding."

She took a sip of his drink, realized what she'd done—damn, it was good—then shoved it at him.

"Nobody scurries to do my bidding, Magnus. That's a problem I aim to fix. The Logan brothers suffer a deficit of scurry-ness, but they're educable, given enough patience and a cattle prod."

"Right now, one of them is cleaning up the kitchen; the other is seeing to the child. Luke is making sure there's a piece of pie waiting for you when you hop on your broomstick and rejoin them at the dinner table."

"You think so?"

"I think they scurry better than you notice. This drink is exquisite."

Real men didn't describe fruit drinks as exquisite, but Bridget had every reason to know that Magnus was a real man.

She fixed herself a glass and put the juice and fizzy water back in the fridge. Magnus had ordered a crisper full of fresh veggies, several different kinds of cheese, artisan bread, butter, eggs, and…

And Bridget was snooping, so she closed the door to the refrigerator and put on her trial-lawyer face.

"You want to talk," she said, "I'll listen." She'd hated the courtroom, but had found that out only after devoting three years of her life and all of her savings to law school.

Magnus held a chair for her at the small round table by the window. Bridget pulled the curtains closed, lest any nosy brothers get to spying, and took a seat. Magnus sat across from her, and for a moment, she battled with the pleasure of simply beholding him.

She'd parted from him yesterday morning, telling herself she'd stored up a fine little memory, but she'd also stored up a fine little heartache to go with it. She *liked* Magnus—or liked the Magnus she'd met at the Bar None—and had steeled herself against never seeing him again.

Now, she wanted to know if there was a way to keep liking him without losing her distillery or her pride.

He slid her drink across the table to her. She ignored it, though even the sight of his hands brought back memories.

"Did you, or did you not," Bridget said, in her best cross-examination-from-hell voice, "know that you were taking the manager of the Logan Bar distillery up to your hotel room Friday night?"

"I did not."

That was the right answer, delivered with more of that growled indignation. "Can you prove it?"

He looked around the room at cheerful red-checked curtains, hardwood floors, handmade cabinets, and gleaming white appliances. The dish towels matched the curtains, and a tree of red ceramic mugs sat near the coffeemaker.

Mama would have had some daffodils in a mason jar on the table and a few homemade muffins wrapped in cellophane on the counter.

"I told you my name, Bridget," Magnus said. "How many Magnuses have you met? Do you expect me to believe you didn't know even the first name of a guest who'd booked this place for two weeks?"

"Shamus handles the bookings."

"If that's the same quilted jacket you wore Friday night, then my business card is in the inside pocket."

Bridget fished out a cream stock card with gold embossed lettering. "You didn't give me this card, and I never use the inside pocket."

He took a sip of his raspberry juice. He would have made a good trial attorney, with a poker face like that.

"You never asked me for it. I tucked it in there while you were in the shower yesterday morning. You never gave me your last name, never offered a phone number or email address."

"Did that bother you?"

He gave her a look that brought to mind the feel of him easing inside her, the sheer pleasure of his touch on her back and shoulders, a dozen small acts of consideration.

I have been smoldered. For the first time, hopefully not the last, I have been well and truly smoldered.

"I gave you my card, Bridget. Make of that what you will."

She studied that card: H.R.M. Cromarty, Distiller, with one of those complicated British addresses that happened when a house, village, and neighborhood all had names. If all the arrangements had been made by internet, Shamus would never have heard Magnus's Scottish accent, and Scotland was, technically, British.

"Now that I see it in writing," she said, "the name is familiar. H.R.M. Cromarty—M for Magnus, I suppose. I know your twelve-year-old, and I think you put out an eighteen-year-old single malt, but I can't recall it."

Magnus finished his drink and took the glass to the sink. "You don't know the eighteen-year-old because I don't export it. The twelve-year-old has been to some competitions."

That a man could be sexy washing out a juice glass surely qualified as a grave injustice.

"I don't export anything," Bridget said. "Don't have the volume, don't have anybody to handle the red tape. So you and I just ran into some bad luck on Friday night? Two people destined to be on opposite sides of a range war ended up in the same bed?"

He stayed at the sink and turned to face her. "In the same bed, making passionate love. All three times. If you can put that behind us so we can discuss mutually advantageous business opportunities, I can. In fact, I already have."

* * *

"Bridget stays out all night for the first time in years," Luke muttered, "then she comes sashaying home without a word of explanation for a wickedly happy smile. We start the spring rental season with the only ray of financial hope this ranch has had since the last time I beat sense into you, and she tears a strip off Cromarty before I can do my welcome-to-the-Ponderosa speech."

Shamus wrung out a washrag at the kitchen sink. "Bridget texted Martina on Friday night. I knew where she was, right down to the room number."

"You aiming to strangle that rag?"

Shamus wanted to strangle something. "I should have texted Bridget. She should have texted me or you. Put the damned ketchup away. It gets all cruddy if you leave it in the lazy Susan."

The ketchup was already cruddy, but Shamus needed to grouse and Luke was the safest target. Went with being the oldest brother and the biggest, and sometimes the asshole-est.

"You were busy," Luke said, unscrewing the cap to the ketchup. He washed off the lid and wiped off the ketchup bottle.

"I was busy with Martina. If she could bother to send a text, I could have. I'd seen Bridget dancing with Cromarty and wished her good hunting." Without a thought for her safety, which might be a compliment to her self-sufficiency, but it was no compliment to Shamus's fraternal loyalties.

Luke put the ketchup in the fridge. "They danced together? As in, boot-scoot-rooty-toot-toot or something else?"

"Slow danced, and that was weird as hell. I've seen Patrick prowling around any number of dance floors, and that's just getting his weekend on, but Bridget isn't Patrick."

"Bridget isn't happy," Luke said, using a fork to take a bite of apple pie right from the one-third remaining in the pie plate. "Damn, this is good."

Shamus snapped him with the rag. "Don't eat from the pie plate."

"You already washed my dish."

That retort was twenty years old. "Say we sell this guy our distillery. Then what?"

"Then we have money," Luke mumbled around a bite of pie. "You said so."

"We have money, but what does Bridget have?" Martina had asked that question, in the patient, long-suffering tones of a veteran first-grade teacher trying to coax one right answer out of the kid who'd been held back.

"If we sell the distillery," Luke replied, "Bridget has a place to live, three brothers and a niece with a roof over their heads, a law degree she refuses to use, also some money in the bank. Whoever buys the distillery will have to either rent the property from her or buy a few acres. She could run this ranch one-handed, but she'd rather compete with distilleries ten times her size."

"She loves that distillery." Possibly more than she loved the step-brothers who'd been foisted on her when she was eight years old, a horse-mad girl who'd yet to grow into her front teeth.

Luke took another bite of pie. "Comes a time when you put away your toys, Shamus. You do the work that needs doing. Nobody needs to drink whisky."

"Nobody needs to eat beef," Shamus countered. "Pretty soon, nobody's going to need oil and gas, at least not at the prices they're paying now. Nobody needs to go fishing or skiing or hiking or horseback riding, but thank God, they spend money doing it anyway. That distillery has been in her family for a hundred and fifty years."

"We're her family now."

Family didn't work like that, but Luke was in his mule-in-the-manger mode, so there was no point trying to reason with him. He could be the peacemaker and voice of reason, but he could also be the older brother who came close to bullying anybody who disagreed with him.

Because he believed he knew best, of course, not because he was a mean-ass son of a bitch with a wide streak of close-mindedness and a few too many personal frustrations stuck in his craw.

"We should move some hay to the mares' pasture tomorrow," Shamus said. "If the snow is as bad as predicted, they'll need it."

"And if the snow doesn't show up, or melts by Tuesday afternoon, we'll have wasted four of our last stash of round bales."

"Foaling season is coming. No time to be putting the ladies on short rations, Luke."

The horses were a sore point. Every ranch needed reliable mounts to go with its reliable vehicles, reliable equipment, and—for the larger spreads—reliable aircraft. The horses were a legacy from Judith. She'd scheduled and paid for breedings last year, and the results could start showing up any day.

Or night. Mares delighted in dropping foals at three in the morning.

"You can take a couple bales out," Luke said. "One of us will have to babysit Cromarty if Bridget's going to stay on her high horse."

"You take one more bite of that pie, and Ima hafta whup up on you, Lucas."

"You want the last piece?"

"The last piece is for Bridget."

Luke set his fork down, and guilt flashed in his smile. "Little bitty thing like her doesn't need a whole lotta pie."

That taunt was also twenty years old. "She needs her piece. Did anybody stack firewood for the guesthouse?"

"Phooey. Don't we have ranch hands around here somewhere?"

"It's Sunday. You stack the firewood, and I'll check on Patrick and Lena."

Put like that, Luke was heading for the kitchen door. "Two bales for the mares, Shamus, and then you can take his lordship skiing."

Shamus loved the thought of triple black diamond spring powder, but babysitting a greenhorn wasn't his idea of fun. They invariably underestimated the toll eight thousand feet of elevation took on them and got sidetracked flirting with the lifties.

"Bridget can take him skiing if he's that keen to go. I have first-quarter bookkeeping to catch up on."

"You can do that when we're snowed in on Tuesday. Gotta love Montana." The kitchen door swung shut, leaving Shamus with the rest of the mess to clean up.

Nobody had to love Montana. The place was beautiful, demanding, and full of contrasts. There was tons of money if you knew where to look, but it was hard to make a living. A frontier mentality jostled right up next to Hollywood living, and the weather had to be experienced to be believed.

Cleaning up after one more Sunday supper that had disintegrated into bickering and unhappiness, Shamus admitted that he wanted out. He wanted off the damned ranch, and out of Montana, and away from the people he loved most in the whole world.

If they sold Bridget's distillery, she'd have one less reason to stick around the Logan Bar ranch. So maybe selling out to Magnus Cromarty would be doing her a favor. Shamus had seen her slow dancing with Cromarty—twice.

His lordship might have scheduled this trip in hopes of acquiring a distillery, but he was already on the way to lassoing Bridget's heart.

And that was a good thing—Shamus hoped.

* * *

Magnus would never forget the feel of Bridget in his arms, the soft rhythm of her breathing as she drowsed beside him in bed, her voice bellowing off-key over the sound of the shower: *It's nice to git yore ass outta bed in the moooooorning.*

But nicer to stay in bed.

There would be no putting that night behind him, but he needed time to think, to move chess pieces, to adjust to fate's latest practical joke on a tired Scottish lad far from home.

Bridget clearly needed breathing room too, and what Bridget needed mattered to him.

"I thought the distiller at Logan Bar was Mary MacDeaver," Magnus said. "You're Bridget Logan."

Bridget tipped her chair back on two legs. "Don't they have Catholic girls where you come from? I'm Mary Bridget MacDeaver. My mother married Dan Logan when I was eight years old. Her property and his shared boundary, and they'd both lost a spouse."

She apparently didn't account these as happy recollections.

"Can you do business with me, Mary Bridget MacDeaver? I'm here to explore the possibility that my distillery and yours could develop some mutually beneficial schemes, up to and including one of us buying the other out."

Even under the influence of the most beguiling twenty-eight-year-old single malt, Magnus would never consider selling his business. Uncle Fergus often grumbled about the benefits of teaming up with a larger outfit, but the aunties would haunt Magnus through eternity for even thinking of such treason.

"I have no interest in acquiring any asset of yours, Magnus, and I'm not interested in your schemes."

He ignored the double meaning. He couldn't ignore how different Bridget looked in this spotless rented kitchen from how she'd looked yesterday morning. Then, she'd been relaxed, rested, and equal to a plate of American pancakes complete with bacon, maple syrup, and butter.

Now she was tense, drawn in on herself, and ready for battle.

"The word *scheme* has a less sinister meaning in the United Kingdom," Magus said. "You'd probably use the word *plan*."

"Not interested in your plans either."

Such magnificent stubbornness. "Your people were Scottish."

"Great-Great-Grandpa came over in the 1860s in search of gold. His daddy had been in the whisky business back home. When Jack MacDeaver got tired of looking for gold, he decided he'd distill it instead."

That much lore was on the Logan Bar distillery website. "So do what Jack MacDeaver would have done, Bridget: Keep an eye out for opportunity at all times, even when you're mad as hell, half starved, and winter is closing in. Never let sentiment get in the way of imagination."

She rose and refolded the towel hanging over the oven handle. "Is that some sort of Scottish battle cry?"

More of a business motto. "One of my cousins consults to nonprofits. Elias is a canny fellow, and he says much business comes down to common sense. I'm here for the next two weeks. Use those two weeks to assess what I can do for your distillery, if anything."

"My distillery is in honking good shape, thank you very much. I'll be civil to you, Magnus, and let bygones be bygones, but I don't care how much cash you wave at the pack of jackals I call brothers. I'm not selling."

"Then don't sell. This dance goes on all the time in Scotland. The big outfits that sell blended whiskies are forever pitting one small house against another, forgetting to move inventory out of a warehouse that's been promised to a competitor, and otherwise conducting what you'd call a range war, all very amicably."

She shoved back to sit on the counter. "I get the sense at the whisky competitions that for most of your kind, distilling is a vanity business. A frolic and detour to entertain visiting busloads of Swiss businessmen. The distillery and the land it sits on are all I have left, Magnus. I'm deadly serious about preserving my heritage."

He treasured that about her, though she was wrong about the Scottish whisky industry. "Then we understand each other. We aren't competitors, much less enemies, Bridget. We don't even sell in the same markets. I'm here for two weeks, our previous dealings don't impact our business relationship, and we can be cordial without creating any confusion about motives or agendas."

Bridget's thoughtful expression said she was buying his load of tripe. She didn't want to hate him, though she might before Magnus had packed his bags and returned to Scotland. He might hate himself, come to that.

"If you can forget we met on Friday night," Bridget said, hopping off the counter, "I can."

Not exactly what he'd proposed, and her characterization was a bit lowering. "We have a bargain."

Magnus met her in the middle of the kitchen, hand extended. She shook firmly, then passed him a set of keys.

"If you need help figuring out the woodstove, ask over at the house. Don't smoke up the whole place because you're too proud to get directions. We're due for a load of snow on Tuesday, and Montana weather can be deadly. Always— and I do mean always—have warm clothes, food, and water in your vehicle. Always be sure somebody knows where you're headed and when you should be back."

Exactly like traveling in the Highlands.

"Yes, ma'am. I will scurry to comply with your every order."

She smiled, a sad echo of the grin she'd flashed on Friday night. "Keep your scurry handy, and we'll get through the next two weeks. You're not getting your Scottish paws on my distillery, though, Magnus. That's a vow."

It wasn't her distillery, in a business sense, or not exclusively hers. Her brothers had been clear about that. Magnus wasn't too concerned about the details of ownership. He'd like to buy her business if he could find terms she'd accept, but what he needed more than the title to the Logan Bar distillery was her.

He needed her, rather desperately.

* * *

Patrick was an artist, or had been prior to his wife's death. Lena had apparently inherited his proclivities, because when she was upset, she drew. Her tongue peeked out of the left side of her mouth—her mom had done the same thing when concentrating—and her expression was furious.

"What are you drawing there, Lena Lilly Logan?" he asked.

"Horses."

She always, always drew horses, of all the goddamned subjects to choose, but she'd been as fixated on the equine even before her mother had died.

Patrick peered over Lena's shoulder at a plunging, rearing trio of steeds. Her childish composition bore an eerie echo of the sculpture of Laocoön and his sons being attacked by Athena's serpents. Old Laocoön had tried to warn his people about the Greeks' tricks: Equō nē crēdite, Teucrī...

Don't trust the horse, Trojans...

Patrick sat on the bed next to Lena's desk, knowing she'd draw until she was ready to talk. He'd been the same way, and Judith had had the patience to outlast his muse. Now the bottle called to him as strongly as a blank sheet of drawing paper ever had.

And his sister ran a distillery. Athena—the goddess of wisdom—was still in the business of sending serpents to plague the unwary.

"You drawing any particular horses?"

Lena sat back, scowling at her creation. She had her mother's eyebrows and nose. If a nose could be fierce, Judith's nose had been fierce.

"That one in the middle is Blitzen."

Blitzen was Luke's preferred mount. A big, ornery gelding who could go all day without faltering. "What about the other two?"

"Barley and Albert."

Bridget's and Shamus's horses, respectively, though neither in real life had a mean bone in their bodies. That was the trouble with horses. They didn't have to be mean, stupid, badly trained, or ill to kill you.

"They look pretty upset," Patrick said.

He was upset. He wanted to cuddle Lena in his lap as he'd done when she was small, wanted to assure her that come the weekend, they'd kidnap her mama and go for ice cream, and that would make everything all better.

Death had kidnapped her mother, and not even Patrick's soul would ransom Judith back.

"They can't find Da Vinci," Lena said, erasing an extravagant length of mane, then shading it in again. "He ran away."

Da Vinci was Patrick's horse, who'd been returned to the working string, the last Patrick knew.

"Was Da Vinci a bad boy?" Patrick asked around a perpetual lump in his throat.

"He colicked," Lena said. "He wants to get down in the grass and roll, but that will only make it worse."

Colic could kill a horse, and it was an awful way to go. Lena was absolutely right that rolling around could turn a bellyache into a twisted bowel, in which case death was often a mercy.

"You might try using colored pencils next time."

Lena gave him a look so like her mother that Patrick rose from the bed. "I have to do my homework now, Daddy."

"You get your smarts from your mama. I'll leave you to it."

He brushed a kiss to the top of her head, patted her shoulder, and escaped. After the dustup at the kitchen table, and Bridget pitching a fit at their guest, Patrick could use a nip to take the edge off.

He shouldn't. The sun hadn't set, it was Sunday, and his daughter was upset. But he would, because the alternative...

"Where are you going?" Shamus asked, meeting Patrick in the hallway.

"Straight to hell, not that it's any of your danged business."

Shamus took him by the arm, which was plain down stupid in Patrick's present mood. "We are not having this argument outside Lena's bedroom door. Is she okay?"

What little girl could be okay when her mama was dead? "She's doing her homework."

"She does her homework on Friday nights, Patrick."

"Maybe she didn't finish it."

They'd reached the top of the steps, and a weird urge crossed Patrick's mind to toss himself over the railing. The French had a phrase for those kinds of thoughts, something about flirting with the abyss.

"She always does her schoolwork," Shamus said. "She asks me for help with the math, goes to Luke with history questions, and saves everything else for Bridget."

"But no questions for dear old dad, which is good, because I don't have any answers."

"What do you have, Patrick?"

Patrick sat on the steps, because that was safer than standing at the top of the staircase. If he tossed himself over the railing, the pain of landing might wake him up from the nightmare his life had become—but he could just as easily pitch Shamus over.

"I have a powerful thirst that will not leave me alone," Patrick said, "and a baby brother who takes after it."

Shamus sat beside him, something they'd done as kids when eavesdropping on the adults had been one of life's imperative missions.

"Maybe you should travel," Shamus said. "You love all that cultural shit."

"If you need to get outta Dodge, Shamus, then go. I do not need to travel." Of the entire family, Patrick was the only one who'd traveled. A year in Paris studying art, another year racketing around Europe, then the Caribbean, where he'd met Judith.

And by Judith's side, he would stay. Of that he was certain.

"She died," Shamus said. "You didn't. Lena didn't. I'm not saying to forget Judith, or disrespect her memory, but she'd be miserable seeing what you've become."

Shamus was trying to help. That's what Shamus did. Luke was the leader, Shamus was the loyal follower, while Patrick was the…

Problem.

"I've become a widower, Shamus. It's a miserable condition." Even saying the word—widower—conjured rage, helplessness, and sorrow.

"You're still a father, a brother, part owner of a beautiful spread, and an artist. You throw all that away, and you're not the man Judith thought you were."

Now there was a helpful truth. Patrick pushed to his feet using Shamus's meaty shoulder as leverage.

"I'll check on Lena in a little bit," Patrick said. "What was Bridget's hissy fit at the front door about?" Give Shamus another problem to focus on, and he might leave off preaching for two goddamned minutes.

"Bridget met up with Magnus Cromarty on Friday night. I gather he either neglected to tell her he would be staying here, or she neglected to tell him her family owned the Logan Bar guesthouse. Luke is stacking firewood for Cromarty."

Eavesdropping, then. Spying. Bridget had arrived to the ranch a fully formed little female at the age of eight, but Luke, Shamus, and Patrick had never really figured out how to be her brothers. Judith had pointed that out.

"Will Cromarty buy the distillery?"

"I hope so. Luke does too."

"Which might cost us Bridget. Heck of a note."

"We've already lost you and Judith, and Lena's fading. What's one more casualty for the sake of the great Logan Bar ranch?" Shamus was off down the stairs like a flushed rabbit, suggesting he hadn't meant to be so honest.

Honesty was overrated, particularly between family members. Patrick let that thought propel him into the study, where the antique glass-front liquor cabinet sat in one corner. He never drank his sister's brew, because Bridget made the good stuff, too good for getting drunk.

He twisted the cabinet handle, intending to pour a shot of Kentucky bourbon, but the handle didn't give.

Several moments of rattling and jiggling went by before Patrick realized that somebody had locked the dadgummed liquor cabinet. He felt along the top of the cabinet for the key, but no luck.

"Bastards."

The solution was simple. He took the wrought-iron poker from the fireplace, tapped the glass, and broke through one pane. Easy enough to reach through and get what he needed, and to hell with people who thought they could tell a grown man what to do.

He took the bottle with him to the door, but stopped when a vestige of artistic instinct prodded him to identify what was different about the room.

In the early evening light, he scanned furnishings that hadn't been moved for decades. Nobody messed with the study, except to dust and clean. This had become Shamus's preserve, full of records, ledgers, and family diaries. Henry Logan II, founder of the Logan Bar, had built the fireplace with his own hands, and the gun cabinet...

The gun cabinet was different. Not Henry's sturdy old made-over grandfather clock, but a modern oak facsimile of an antique.

No glass front, and Patrick would have bet his bottle of bourbon, half empty though it was, that the spiffy new gun cabinet was locked.

Probably a good thing. There was a child in the house, after all, and glass broke all too easily.

* * *

CHAPTER FIVE

This distillery and the land it sits on are all I have left, Magnus.

Bridget hadn't meant to be that honest, because she couldn't afford to trust H.R.M. Cromarty any farther than she could swing a whisky bottle.

And yet, here she was, driving him up the canyon road not a day later, Patrick pale and quiet in the backseat of the ranch's least ancient Durango. The sky was still a deceptive hurt-your-eyes blue, but the weather lady had raised tomorrow's expected snowfall by four inches.

"Don't suppose you remembered to hydrate?" Bridget asked.

"I had my usual three cups of tea."

Magnus was a stranger to her today. He was in jeans, flannel shirt, and boots, the same as he had been the first time she'd seen him. He probably wore the same Celtic knot belt buckle, but he'd also donned sunglasses—a necessity above the snow line in spring—and his demeanor was subtly cooler.

He was a paying guest at the ranch, not a former lover. Certainly not a future lover either, which was what Bridget had asked for.

"Three cups of tea isn't hydrating, Magnus. We'll be at seven thousand feet for much of the day, and if you hit the slopes, that number goes up. 'Even Bridget felt the toll a day in the mountains took.

"I'm not hitting the slopes. Not this trip."

Implying there would be other trips?

"Then what the hell are we doing up here, mister?" Patrick asked. He hadn't spoken for miles, though he'd at least shaved before joining this expedition.

"I'm a purveyor of fine whiskies. I'm investigating a lucrative foreign market."

"Why did you drag me along?" Patrick preferred Kentucky bourbon, for breakfast, lunch, and dinner, lately.

"Because I asked your brother Shamus, and he said for what I have in mind, you would be the better resource. He's known to the staff and management at this resort and has been employed here as a ski instructor, ski patrol, snowboard instructor, and lift operator. Too many people know him on sight."

The mountain village came into view, though *village* was a stretch. An alpine lake—necessary at any facility that made snow—curved along one side of the road, and low-rise chalet condos flanked its shore. Behind the condos, four- and five-star hotels rose, and every amenity—every god's-blessed amenity known to man, woman, couple, kid, or family dog—was available for a price.

"I hate this place," Patrick muttered.

"It's not exactly pristine wilderness, is it?" Magnus replied. "The resort must bring a good deal of money into the local economy, though."

"It's wilderness." Bridget pulled into a tidily plowed parking lot. "Not the kind of wilderness nature intended. Shamus used to spend half his year up here." Now Shamus spent half his time locked in the study trying to make a nickel do the work of a dime.

"So why are we here?" Patrick climbed out, and in the brilliant alpine sunshine, he looked like roadkill.

"Ask Magnus." The air was different at this altitude, colder of course and drier than hell, but also fresh as heaven. Lena claimed that even the air in Montana's mountains felt big.

"We're scouting the territory," Magnus said, tucking a purple plaid scarf around his neck. "Every restaurant, bar, casino, and coffee shop on the premises."

"The heck you say." From Patrick.

"All day won't be long enough to get that done," Bridget said.

"Then we make as much progress as we can, and we'll split up. Bridget, you're to collect menus. Get the room-service menus if you can't get anything else, but ask for a copy of everything that has to do with what's being consumed here. Wine lists, dessert trays, bar food, anything."

That made an odd sort of sense. Just as a cowboy's nature was arguably discernible from the state of his rig, tack, and ride, so a resort should leave some sort of fingerprints on what it served to whom, at what prices, and where.

"I'll be in the casino," Patrick said.

"Where the drinks are free?" Magnus asked, striding off in the direction of the nearest high-rise. "No, you will not. We have much to accomplish. Come along, laddie. Do cell phones work up here?"

Most people wouldn't have known to ask. "They do," Bridget said.

"Then we'll meet in three hours at the location of your choice and compare notes. Patrick, you will see that I *hydrate*, or Bridget will be in a temper with us both."

Bridget was already halfway to a temper—so much more adult than a hissy fit—torn between wanting to protect Patrick from a stranger's judgment— Patrick would not resist the booze offered from every direction—and envying

Patrick time spent in Magnus's company. Magnus on a mission was much like Magnus as a lover.

Utterly focused, confident, competent, and magnificent to behold.

"I have work to do," she muttered.

For a moment, though, she watched Magnus and Patrick stride along amid the towering snowbanks. Magnus was talking, and Patrick was listening.

When was the last time Patrick had listened to anybody about anything?

They disappeared amid a throng of people heading for the lifts—skiers, snowboarders, maybe some lifties—all decked out in brilliantly colorful, high-tech winter play clothes.

That bunch was here to play. Bridget was here to work. Some things never changed.

* * *

"Just the lady I've been longing to see," Nathan Sturbridge murmured. "Funny we should meet up here."

Martina came to the Cowboy's Cupcake almost every day for lunch, as did many people who enjoyed good food. The fare was fresh and well presented, and not too godawfully expensive. The Cupcake rode the line between being a local eatery and a tourist spot.

For Nate, the Cupcake was one more place to pick up women, which would probably scandalize the pair of ladies who owned the place.

"Hello, Nate." Martina studied the chalkboard menu hanging behind the counter.

The woman was purely beautiful. Flawless skin, true-blue eyes, features that even an airbrush couldn't have improved upon. Her figure looked to deliver on the promise of her face, though Nate had never gotten close enough to see if the curves were real. For some women, the more gifts God gave them, the more they fretted about the one or two endowments that had been left off their list.

"What are you having," Nate asked, "and can I talk you into sharing a table with me?"

She didn't so much as turn her head. "What do you want?"

"No need to be unfriendly. I have four rabid clients waiting to jump my handsome ass over at the courthouse, and if I take lunch back to the law office, my paralegal will expect me to answer eight phone calls before I even sit down. You'll protect me from tourists deciding to share my table when all I want is a peaceful meal."

"Go away, Nate."

Martina had standards, which trait Nate had to admire. What exactly those standards might be, when she'd two-step and boot-scoot with a different guy every weekend, Nate did not know, but standards were a good thing.

"C'mon, Martina, you know I worry about Bridget. The woman has a lot on her plate." Most of which Nate had put there, and thus Bridget still needed constant surveillance.

A pair of girls walked in wearing jeans, down vests, and fuzzy boots, the shop bell tinkling as the door closed behind them. Nate put them at junior-senior year, maybe taking an extra spring break.

"Wind's picking up," Martina said. "Temperature will be dropping before sunset."

"Thank you for the weather report. How is Bridget doing?"

"You should ask her."

"We didn't part on the best of terms, Martina, and I don't entirely blame Bridget. She had the potential to be a damned fine lawyer." Though she'd lacked confidence. Too bad about that.

"While you have more confidence than brains." Martina placed her order, some exotic bean-and-bacon-topped-with-fancy-flowers salad and a cheese scone.

"Don't be twitchy, Martina. I'm worried about somebody who was once my business associate. Bridget was sitting alone at the bar on Friday for longer than was decent, and then she went off with some stranger."

Harley Gummo had passed that much along, though Nate had the sense there was more that Harley wasn't saying. If Bridget was turning into a drunk like her brother, she might start throwing around wild accusations about her former partner.

A woman on the path to ruin would say just about anything, not that anybody would believe the poor little darlin'.

Nate ordered a roast beef sandwich. This was Montana, for God's sake. Eating beef and driving a pickup came under the heading of civic duty.

Martina paid at the register. "Bridget didn't give me the details, Nate, and they are nobody's business but hers."

"I don't like to think of a member of the bar comporting herself in a less than sensible manner," Nate said, sparing a smile for the young lady behind the counter. "Bridget isn't quite as all-fired in charge and on top of things as you might think."

Martina had been a cop in Helena. Five years of that had probably been enough for her, and truth be told, she was too damned pretty for the job anyway. She still had a good dead-eye stare, though.

"You tell one more lie about a friend of mine, Nate Sturbridge, and I will put out the word that you have trouble getting it up."

The two girls in line behind him had gone silent.

"I guess that means you're not joining me for lunch."

Martina shot a look over Nate's shoulder at the girls and collected her food. "Nobody with any sense should join you for lunch."

Then she sauntered out into the gathering wind and dropping temperatures. Nate watched her ass on general principles, then winked at the woman ringing up purchases, and tipped his hat to the high school girls.

* * *

"You are perfectly capable of driving yourself up here on your own," Patrick Logan observed. "Why drag Bridget along?"

"Because I'm tired of driving on the wrong side of the road," Magnus replied, scooting back to avoid being whacked in the face with a snowboard.

"That is bullpoop."

"No, it is not." Though it might qualify as a metaphor. "On the interstates, there are far fewer decisions to make. You pick a lane and stay in it for a hundred miles. On the surface streets is where it gets confusing, and backroads are probably the most difficult of all. Then too, there's the altitude, which tires a fellow out."

"You are a bad liar."

"Thank you. If you were looking to pick up women after a day of skiing, where would you start?"

Patrick was wearing dark sunglasses, but even so, his disgust with the question was obvious. Nonetheless, he looked around at four or five possibilities. That so much commercial enticement should be situated atop beautiful mountains fell somewhere between genius and sacrilege.

"That one," Patrick said, pointing across a small square dotted with evergreens, benches, and grimy piles of snow.

"Why?"

"No families spilling out the front door, no amusement-park vibe to the décor, the gamblers won't be there, and it's not shouting a five-star price tag." He took off his sunglasses and shaded a hand over his eyes. "It won't be too dark inside during the day, given the orientation and fenestration, and the path from there to the hotels will be well lit at night. That matters to the ladies."

At some point, a lady had mattered to Patrick Logan. "What's fenestration?"

"Arrangement and design of the windows. Are we going to stand here all day working on your boyish tan or get on with this?"

Without the sunglasses, Patrick Logan looked like a wilderness survivor. His complexion was sallow, his face gaunt, his eyes weary.

"Get on with this," Magnus said, "though for a holiday, a Scot will almost always look for a place to lie in the sun. We're like seals. Give us a warm sunny rock, and we're in heaven. All you have to do is go in there and ask for a shot of Logan Bar twelve-year-old single malt."

Patrick stopped walking. "I don't drink Bridget's whisky. I don't drink single malt whisky, period."

"And you won't be drinking any here. They don't stock it, so when the bartender offers you something else, you look aggrieved, sigh mightily, and tell him you'll try elsewhere."

"While you do what?"

"Ask for a copy of the menu and wine list, as if I want to take them up to my room to placate a demanding partner."

Two brunettes went laughing through the doorway several yards away. Their noses were red, their hair windblown, and they wore the loose, synthetic attire of athletes after a workout. One of them glanced at Patrick and Magnus, her gaze merely curious.

"She's happy, Patrick. We're going into a happy place. Try not to look like you kick kittens for entertainment."

"You promise me they don't stock Logan Bar?"

"They do not stock Logan Bar. Bridget assured me of this, and your sister is not given to mendacity."

Then too, Magnus had been the one asking at the bars here yesterday. At every likely establishment he'd passed since leaving the airport in Denver, he'd asked for Logan Bar single malt.

Patrick shoved his sunglasses back onto his nose. "I see what you're doing, and for Bridget's sake, I'll accommodate you."

"Oh, right," Magnus said, holding the door. "For Bridget's sake. For whose sake will you sell me her distillery?"

"We haven't sold it to you yet, your lordship. Go flirt with a waitress and let me do my thing."

As it happened, Magnus had a lovely wee chat with a waiter, who might have been flirting with him, though Americans were friendly, and Magnus was rusty when it came to reading signals from his own team. Magnus left with a menu, wine list, bar list, and a recommendation to stay away from one particular bar in Bozeman, because the patrons were prone to violent disputes.

Patrick was waiting for him when he left, sitting in a wooden rocker several yards to the left of the front door.

"Now what?"

Magnus took the rocker beside him. The seat was both hard and cold, which was probably intentional. People sitting in rocking chairs weren't spending money.

"Now we lather, rinse, repeat, until every bartender on this mountain has heard two requests in two days for Logan Bar single malt."

"And then?"

"And then they'll hear four more, because I'll make that happen too. By the end of the week, when Bridget calls the person ordering liquor for the resort, ready to give them a discount because the delivery is local, they'll be willing to take a shipment. After that, the whisky will sell itself."

"Sneaky but not quite crooked. I like it."

"Credit old Tom Dewar. He went to London to peddle his wares, but before he called on a tavern owner, he'd pay a couple of blokes to ask for Dewar's the day or two before Tom hit the door."

"Dewar's, as in Dewar's White Label?"

"As in the imported Scotch whisky Americans drink more than any other. It's blended, which means many distilleries have seen a piece of that success."

"You aren't doing this for Bridget."

Magnus rose as a trio of young ladies accompanied by one young man went into the bar. "As it happens, I am doing this for Bridget. While you lot were happily consigning the woman to law school, nobody was teaching her to market some of the best damned whisky I've ever tasted. She's sitting on a gold mine and thinks it's a business barely hanging on."

Patrick pushed to his feet more slowly. He might have been a year or two older than Magnus, but he moved as if recovering from a long illness.

"A gold mine you want to buy."

"One she does not want to sell, and I'll not purchase this business against her wishes, Patrick. What you three don't seem to understand is that *she* is what makes that distillery so valuable. Where to next?"

Patrick pointed across the square to the saloon. "They'll serve liquor, but also kids' meals. Might as well get that over with. So who showed you how to market?"

"Nobody. I watched and learned and made mistakes. I married an excellent marketer, though, so I at least had a first-rate example."

That shut Patrick up, and the rest of the exercise passed without incident. He seemed to gain some color as they trooped about the village, while Magnus felt increasingly as if he were lugging cinder blocks with him everywhere.

"Bridget wants us to meet her in the hotel cantina," Magnus said, swiping the message on his phone. "That would be…"

"Over there," Patrick said, jerking his chin to the left.

"You have an excellent sense of direction."

"I can't help it. If you pay attention to your surroundings, you get oriented. We're parked over there, and we started out on the far side of that hotel."

Magnus would have bet money Patrick was right on all counts. "Is this an American wilderness skill?"

"It's an artist's skill. If Bridget asks, I made you drink two bottles of water."

"I won't lie to your sister." Bridget wouldn't give him a third chance to earn her trust.

"Then I will. You really ought to be upping your fluid intake. This is serious altitude, and we'll be here for hours."

And Magnus's head was starting to pound. "Then I'll have a liquid lunch."

Patrick laughed, a bitter sound. Magnus abruptly realized the man had a drinking problem. Puzzle pieces snapped together—Patrick's reluctance to ask for a drink, his ability to size up a watering hole, his appearance.

"Patrick, you have turned down endless opportunities to drink today. That should tell you something."

He walked along in silence beside Magnus for thirty yards, as happy families, overly boisterous young people, and a few red-nosed, hard-core skiers moved around them.

"This morning's expedition tells me I've used up my resolve for now, and if liquor is served at this cantina, I'll be wetting my whistle."

Bridget waved to them from down the plank sidewalk.

"Don't be an idiot. You have the power to say no, and you've just exercised that power over and over again. At least think about how you managed that feat."

"Thinking is part of the problem," Patrick said. "All I do is think."

Brood, then, seethe and regret. "I had a couple years like that, then I decided to get even."

"You can't get even with death."

Patrick was a widower with a small daughter. Shamus had shared that intelligence. "You get even with death by living the hell out of your life."

"Don't cuss in front of my daughter, or I'll whup up on you."

"Point noted." And in that point, Magnus detected some hope for Patrick Logan.

Bridget looked happy, and she had a stack of menus sticking out of her shoulder bag. "Mission accomplished," she said. "It was easier than I thought. Never met such a friendly bunch of people as the wait staff on this mountain. What were you two up to?"

"Much of the same," Magnus said, patting his rucksack. "Though we did a bit of reconnaissance too. Patrick has been nagging me to drink water."

Bridget beamed at her brother. "Thanks, Patrick. I could use some myself. The sandwiches in the cantina are built for mountain appetites, and I'm hungry."

Patrick came along peacefully, which was fortunate. To keep Bridget smiling, Magnus would have dragged her brother by the hair anywhere she pleased. They sat at a quiet table and surveyed fare that would have done an Edinburgh pub proud but for the absence of fish and chips and sticky toffee pudding. No alcohol, though.

Bridget had probably chosen this place for that reason.

"I'll have a Reuben, no dressing, don't forget the pickle," Bridget told the waiter.

"Same," Magnus said. "Patrick?"

Patrick eyed the door, and Magnus nearly stepped on his foot. The bottle was singing its siren song to a man who'd scared himself with his own fortitude.

"Burger, medium, fries, hold the onions. If you'd bring some vinegar, my friend here would appreciate it."

The waitress scribbled down the order, fetched them three tall glasses of ice water, and left with a cheery "I'll be right back."

"Thoughtful of you, Patrick. I haven't learned to appreciate ketchup yet."

"Drink your water." Patrick nudged the glass closer to Magnus. "So, Bridget, did our guest happen to mention that he's married?"

* * *

In the time it took Bridget to bring her water glass to her mouth, she re-experienced the sense of betrayal that had swamped her when Magnus had shown up at the Logan Bar ranch house. She was furious with Magnus, but also—in the same instant—furious with herself.

Would she never learn to guard her trust?

Then a snippet of remembered conversation popped into her head, and she gripped the cold, wet glass more tightly.

"Magnus isn't married. He told me that himself."

"Then he was married. Good-lookin', well-heeled guy with a distillery all to himself parted from a wife somewhere along the way. Bet that's a story worth telling."

Magnus flipped a forest green linen napkin across his lap. "Patrick asked for a dram of Logan Bar at every establishment within walking distance. Because he failed to earn your scorn today with irresponsible drinking, he'll earn it by being overly protective. Will somebody please explain to me why, when it's barely above freezing outside, there is ice in this water?"

"Because that's how we do it," Bridget said. "If you don't want ice, all you have to do is ask. Why did you put Patrick up to asking for drinks before noon?"

Magnus's theory—that Patrick was purposely making himself an object of disgust—bore consideration. *Later*, when Bridget had some food in her belly and a few more answers.

"I asked Patrick to inquire about Logan Bar single malt, just as I did previously, so that when you cold-call the wine and spirits manager at the end of the week, he or she will be more inclined to buy from you."

Now that was a prime strategy, and more than a bit inventive. "I've tried calling her. She doesn't get back to me."

The waitress returned and set chips and salsa on the table.

"Hello, Olivette," Magnus said, sticking out his hand. "I'm Magnus Cromarty, and I've a wee proposition to put to you."

His smile was damnably sincere, and if he'd read the woman's name tag, Bridget hadn't seen him do it. The waitress, a pale blonde on the leggy side, wiped her hand on her half apron and shook willingly enough.

"Nice to meet you, Mr. Cromarty."

"Magnus," he said, peeling a fifty-dollar bill from his wallet. "And I've a favor to ask. At some point before Friday morning, can you and a friend go into two or three of the fine establishments in this village and ask for Logan Bar single malt whisky?"

He passed her the money, which disappeared faster than snowflakes falling on a rushing stream. He also served up a heaping portion of Highland charm, hitting just the right note between brash and humble.

"Do I have to drink the whisky?"

"The bartender won't be able to fill your order because they don't stock Logan Bar here yet, so no, you won't get to taste it."

Strange men passing out fifties probably weren't all that unusual at the resort, but the young woman still hesitated.

"Is it any good?" she asked.

Magnus gave her a soulful look that nearly earned him a kick under the table. "My dear young lady, you are asking about one of the finest single malt potations this Scotsman has ever tasted. It's made not twenty-five miles from here, and the very essence of Montana's wild grandeur graces it from nose to finish. This is sipping whisky, if you take my meaning. An excellent value for the price, distilled by a Montana-born and -bred lady."

He made *sipping whisky* sound like a drink only the most sophisticated of adults should be allowed to sample.

"Logan Bar single malt?"

"Aye, lass. Ask for it everywhere."

She gave Magnus the sort of smile that suggested he'd be living in her dreams long after the fifty had been spent.

"Order up!" sang out from the kitchen.

Olivette scampered off, a loyal minion acquired in two minutes flat for fifty bucks, and without so much as a wink or a promise.

"You can do that only because you're Scottish," Patrick said. "She would not have been so accommodating if I'd asked."

"I can do that because I am sincere," Magnus replied, peeling another fifty from his wallet. "I am asking her to undertake a simple task for cash proffered, because I believe in the product she'll request. You could do the same easily."

Patrick regarded the money as if it could rattle its tail. "What is that for?"

"One of the better hotels is right next door. The bellhops are lounging at their station, and you could recruit one or two of them for a similar errand. Look for one with red hair who's obviously good at what he does."

"Why?" Bridget asked.

"Because red hair is more likely to indicate Celtic ancestry," Magnus said, tucking his wallet away, "and competence suggests somebody who didn't start here last week. An employee who's been here all season will make more of an impression on the bartender than a roving stranger would."

"Give me ten minutes," Patrick said, shoving away from the table. "Either one of you touches my fries, you die a slow, painful, vinegar-soaked death."

Bridget was about to tell Patrick she'd be happy to talk to the bellhops, but Magnus put his hand over hers.

"Let him give it a go," he said as Patrick stalked off. "Distilleries are supposed to be family businesses, and he needs breathing room."

"He'll turn it into drinking room." Or he might not. Patrick was too proud to drink himself insensate in public—or he had been thus far. "But I know what you're doing, Magnus Cromarty."

"Showing you how to market a very good product?"

He was doing that too, for which Bridget would thank him, maybe. "You are making sure you don't have an audience while you explain to me about your former wife."

Magnus dipped a corn chip into the salsa and bought himself a little time munching it into oblivion.

"Why do you want to know about ancient history, Bridget? We're to be business acquaintances, nothing more."

"Nice try. I'm guessing she had something to do with your whisky-making, and now you're here, trying to have something to do with my whisky-making. It's a long walk down the mountain and mighty chilly this time of year."

An empty threat, but a woman with three older brothers learned to bluff well.

"I'll tell you about my marriage if you'll tell me why you don't practice law."

The food arrived, and sheer hunger distracted Bridget for the time it took to put away half of a hot, cheesy, too-good-to-be-healthy Reuben. Then Patrick came slouching back, looking pleased with himself, and Bridget resigned herself to getting an answer later.

But get an answer, she would.

CHAPTER SIX

By the time Magnus climbed back into the Durango, he'd parted with several hundred dollars in cash and been given the phone numbers of two waitresses and a snowplow operator. Scottish accents were apparently a rarity at the resort.

He'd also developed a screeching banshee of a headache, and when Bridget pulled into the Logan Bar driveway, he wanted nothing more than to lie flat in a darkened room.

"Our Highlander isn't looking too good," Patrick said, slamming the car door much more loudly than necessary.

"Just a wee headache." Magnus also had an empty belly and an all-over achy feeling.

Bridget gave him a scowling inspection. "You didn't hydrate. Darn it, Magnus. You were so busy being God's gift to lonely waitresses you didn't drink enough. Do you have any aspirin?"

"Say yes," Patrick suggested. "She'll fuss you within an inch of your sorry life otherwise."

"I avoid falsehoods at all cost." Besides, being fussed by Bridget was a lovely prospect.

"You get in there and down at least two glasses of water," Bridget said, jabbing a finger at the guesthouse. "I'll bring you some over-the-counter painkillers, and you will take them."

"Tried to warn you," Patrick muttered, boots crunching on the gravel as he headed for the main house. "Thanks for a fine day in the fresh air. Been nice knowing you, sorta."

Bridget watched him go, her expression troubled.

"You have two more just like him," Magnus said. "One wonders why you aren't the one with the drinking problem."

"Don't you dare insult my brothers, Magnus Cromarty. Patrick has been through a lot, and as much as you love and know your whisky, he's better at art and design than you will ever be at anything. Go stick your nose in a horse trough, and don't stop drinking until I bring you some aspirin."

The temperature had dropped to the point that any horse trough would be frozen over.

"Yes, ma'am."

Magnus did drink two glasses of water—no ice, for God's sake—and while he didn't feel better, he'd been thirstier than he'd realized. Also more tired. When Bridget came through the front door on a gust of chilly air, he was lying flat out on the couch, boots off, mentally lecturing himself to get up and check his emails.

"Altitude sickness does this," Bridget said, unscrewing the cap of a small white bottle. "Knocks you on your ass. Smart people stay there for a good long while. Take these."

"Not on an empty stomach," Magnus said, sitting up. "May I make you dinner?"

She sat back on her heels, her gaze anything but friendly. "Why?"

Magnus was tired, he was discouraged, and he felt like crap. He was fresh out of public-relations smiles and blather.

"Whoever he was, Bridget, you need to toss him into the ditch. I'm offering to make dinner because I'm hungry, and my mother put a few manners on me. You spent the entire day humoring my agenda. Some reciprocity is called for."

Bridget rose. "Weather's coming. You can feel it in your bones, the need to slink off somewhere cozy and safe until nature has had her tantrum. What's on the menu?"

What did the weather have to do with anything? "Fine dining, by bachelor standards. Salad, quiche, and brownies."

Bridget was in the kitchen, banging drawers and cupboards. "From the Cupcake's bakery?"

"I believe so."

"Don't tell my brothers. They'll come stampeding over here in search of leftovers before you've opened the box. Be still my heart, for I do declare this is arugula and avocado salad with pecan dressing."

She went on murmuring sweet raptures to various boxes from the fridge while Magnus sipped water, folded napkins, and set out plates.

"Do you say grace?" Bridget asked, taking a seat at the kitchen table. "I do. We thank Thee for this food, and for Valrhona chocolate, which transcends the whole notion of food and approaches a level of sustenance so sublime I call dibs on the first brownie, amen, do you understand me, Magnus Cromarty?"

He was beginning to. "Amen. I am duly warned. Of the establishments we visited today, which ones do you think are best suited to Logan Bar single malt?"

The food was good, but not so good as to distract from the conversation.

Bridget apparently hadn't considered the venues in her own backyard as a source of revenue, beyond making a few casual inquiries.

Magnus would change that.

"You can sell the local resorts on your whisky," he said, "not only on the basis of its quality and Montana heritage, but also on the basis of food miles. The less transport a product needs, the smaller its carbon footprint, the more responsible its consumption, and the cheaper its delivery price."

Bridget considered her last bite of spinach quiche. "Is that Scottish thinking, that food-miles business?"

"It's certainly European. We've been paying upwards of eight dollars per gallon of gas for years, and that's on purpose, to discourage excessive consumption of nonrenewable energy sources."

"While you drill the heck out of the North Sea."

"One admits the contradiction. We also have smaller distances in many cases and superior public transportation. Are you interested in European markets?"

Magnus was interested in Bridget's willingness to correct him, in the relish with which she went after good food, and in the keen mind that had walked away from a career in law to focus on whisky-making instead.

"Had to take some comparative government courses as an undergrad, and the European Union and Britain came under discussion. You planning to eat that crust?"

Magnus passed her his plate. If he'd been sharing this meal with Celeste, she'd have chosen the wine, then spent half the meal analyzing it while Magnus admired her expertise.

"What were you thinking of just now?" Bridget asked.

"The past. Why do you ask?"

"Because it made you sad. When I watched you charming all those young people up at the resort, you looked as if you were nothing but a good time with a fat trust fund and a cool accent."

"No trust fund, but the accent's genuine." He'd leave the "good time" assessment to the lady.

Bridget set down her fork. "So tell me about the past."

"Let's tidy up, shall we?" Magnus rose and took his dishes to the sink. Darkness had fallen, and his headache had receded thanks to Bridget's little white pills, or maybe to the water she'd pushed on him all during the meal.

"Tidy up all you want," Bridget said, bringing her plate over. "But whoever she was, she left claw marks in private locations. I need some time to contemplate impending bliss before I tackle my brownie. Tea or coffee?"

Impending bliss had to do with what was in the last white box sitting on the table, not with what lay behind the zipper of Magnus's jeans. He liked this about Bridget, liked her focus and her self-possession.

He'd also really, really liked making love with her. "Tea, please, decaf for me.

Should we start a fire?"

"Yes. If the wind picks up, you'll be glad you did. Nothing keeps up with an Alberta Clipper like a well-stocked woodstove. You finish the dishes, and I'll get after the stove."

She set about crumpling up newspapers, arranging kindling, and muttering to the woodstove much as she had to the dinner offerings. Magnus had a vision of Bridget as an old woman, talking to her pot still, sniffing the wort, checking thermostats, and holding a one-sided conversation with a batch of whisky she might not live long enough to consume.

She would convince herself such a life was a happy one. Thousands of miles away, Magnus might be trying to convince himself of the very same thing.

Perhaps altitude sickness affected the mind.

The dishes took no time, and Bridget used the discarded food boxes to fuel the nascent fire. Magnus put together a tea tray and brought it to the coffee table.

Desire intruded among thoughts growing melancholy. Not even a desire for sex, per se, but a desire for intimacy. He recognized the yearning because he'd felt it often during his marriage.

"You domesticate well," Bridget said, sitting cross-legged on the rug before the glass front of the woodstove. "Is that because you were married?"

Magnus sat on the couch, the better to keep his perspective during what was bound to be a thorough cross-examination.

"Or did I marry because my wife realized I'd be a good sort in the kitchen? Probably a bit of both. The idea of coming home at the end of the day to somebody who wants to talk to me, who will listen to me, had a lot of appeal. I'm an only child, and my father was gone before I turned twenty-five. My mother remarried a Hungarian, and I see her a couple of times a year."

Bridget nodded, as if he'd just confirmed her suspicions. "About this wife, Magnus. Was she part of the business?"

Magnus poured himself a cup of tea, a fragrant Darjeeling, but being decaf, the taste wouldn't deliver what the nose promised.

"Celeste was to be my partner in all things. She grew up in a whisky-making family near Inverness, knows everybody, has charm oozing from her fingertips. When she decided to share all of her know-how and ability with me, I was nearly drunk with my good fortune. Shall I fix you some tea?"

"I'm good. Drop the other boot. She screwed you over."

"Nobody has put it that bluntly, but yes. She screwed me over. Began colluding behind my back with a rival outfit."

"Is colluding polite talk for jumping the fence?"

"Eventually. Celeste is an interesting woman. She can be your best friend, the confidante you never realized you longed for. Witty, trustworthy, loyal… but it's not real. She hungers always for more, and I count myself fortunate she became bored with me as quickly as she did."

"A predator," Bridget said, propping her chin on her knees. "She snacked on you, then left you for the buzzards."

Bridget's metaphors were pure prairie, but oddly accurate when applied to a whisky princess. "She told me it was just business. I've come to hate that phrase."

"Marriage was just business?"

"Or the divorce was. I kept the distillery, and thanks to family members on my board of directors, I hadn't quite given Celeste the keys to my kingdom. I owe one cousin in particular a great deal." Uncle Fergus still blamed Magnus for *driving that bonnie lassie away.*

But then, Uncle Fergus was half daft.

Bridget studied the fire. "I don't have any cousins."

Magnus shifted to join her on the rug, though the floor was drafty. "They come in handy, when they aren't trying to run your life." And Magnus really should check his emails.

"So you were rode hard and put away wet, and now you're out to make your ex regret galloping into the sunset."

Magnus was out to save his distillery. "I admit to an element of wanting to prove myself, but it's fading. I suspect Celeste's second husband is about to be treated the same way I was."

Bridget took an absent sip from Magnus's teacup. "A competent criminal doesn't let patterns develop. They don't leave any kind of fingerprints on their crimes."

"You were a good lawyer, I suspect. Why aren't you practicing law?"

How could the woodstove be burning away so brightly and the room be getting colder?

Bridget rose and headed to the couch. "I didn't care for it, but that's not something you realize until you've spent three years preparing for the bar examination, and you're sitting across from a juvenile shoplifter who was just trying to make sure his baby sister had a can of formula. You can't solve the big problems with lawyers, judges, and social workers."

"You can't solve them with whisky either."

"So why have you made whisky your life's work? The floor's cold, Magnus. Get up here and answer a few more questions for me."

Did he or did he not want one of those questions to be an invitation to share her bed? Magnus was surprised to realize he was leaning toward not.

He'd promised himself he wouldn't lie to Bridget, but he wasn't being honest about the reasons for his trip either. Another shared night would only complicate matters. Nonetheless, he got off the floor and took the place right beside her.

* * *

Watching Magnus at the resort had been a revelation, and not a little unnerving. He went after opportunity like a free climber scaling a rock face. Determined, relentless, unstoppable. Even when he was going sideways—teasing, flirting, making small talk—he was closing in on his objective.

Which, apparently, was increasing sales for the Logan Bar distillery.

He subsided onto the sofa with the careful movements of somebody who'd done too much and rested too little. Bridget pulled the log cabin star quilt from the back of the sofa and spread it over their legs.

"You'll hear the wind howling tonight," she said. "Don't let it bother you."

She'd used a double fat bat on this quilt and backed it with flannel. A warmer blanket would be hard to imagine. Shades of red, brown, and cream predominated, and the backing was chocolate.

"We have wind in Scotland. What more did you want to ask me?"

How could such a bright man have been so thoroughly taken in that he'd marry his enemy? If Magnus could explain that to her, maybe she could figure out why she'd gone into business with hers.

"Tell me about Cromarty Distilleries, Magnus."

Predictably, he started with the founding of the business in the early decades of the nineteenth century and didn't fall silent until he'd described the single malt already laid down that would be tapped to celebrate the business's bicentennial year.

"Now there's another marketing idea I would never have come up with," Bridget said. "Celebrating anniversaries for the distillery."

"Not all anniversaries are happy," Magnus said. "My cousin Elias's parents were killed in a plane accident, and when that time of year comes around, still—more than twenty years later—we don't quite know what to do for him."

For Magnus Cromarty, not knowing what to do would be awful. Bridget didn't fare much better with the same conundrum.

The woodstove was roaring merrily, and Magnus was a comforting warmth along her side. She could turn the moment from friendly to fond to frolicking, and not much would have changed come morning.

Bridget didn't reach for Magnus's hand under the blanket, didn't curl down and rest her head on his thigh, though the temptation was a hard ache in her heart.

Why had Magnus spent the entire day and much of his trip up from Denver increasing sales for a distillery he had no intention of buying?

She pondered that question until the man beside her had fallen asleep. She rose, tucked the blanket around him, closed the dampers on the woodstove, and took herself out into a frigid, windy night.

* * *

Magnus woke to an unrecognizable world. Everything beyond the window was white. No shapes were discernible, no light source organized the morning sky. Gravity alone provided orientation, though some considerate soul had set the coffeepot alarm.

He extricated himself from the warm embrace of an old-fashioned patchwork quilt, knuckled sleep from his eyes, and tried to recall where Bridget's aspirin was.

For that matter, where was Bridget?

A tour of the kitchen revealed that the hot pot had been primed with a stout, black breakfast tea. Magnus added cream and sugar and considered having a brownie for breakfast.

One didn't, though in the Western Isles of Scotland, some families still indulged in a wee dram of whisky as part of their morning routine.

Somebody thumped on the door. Magnus opened it, and the air that hit him was cold enough to wake Uncle Fergus halfway through a board of directors' meeting.

"Morning," Luke Logan said. "Bridget sent me over to make sure you don't die of stupidity."

"A worthy errand." Magnus closed the door as Luke stepped inside. "One probably has to be awake to die of stupidity though."

"Stay inside, or you'll disprove that theory in less than an hour. Falling asleep is part of freezing to death. We've strung the ropes between buildings, but nothing short of Sasquatch asking to use your bathroom should send you outside until this weather blows over."

This was merely *weather*? "You hang ropes between the buildings?"

"Getting lost in a whiteout is easier than ordering your third drink on a Saturday night. People have died six feet from their own front door. You know how to work the woodstove?"

A gust of wind rose to a moan—an actual moan. "Not in any detail."

"A fool." Luke stripped off heavy sheepskin gloves. "But an honest fool. All you need to know is two things. A fire needs air and fuel. These are your dampers." He spun cast-iron fittings and explained about adding enough wood, but not too much, and letting the fire breathe, but not too deeply.

"You have about a week's supply of wood on the porch, if you're careful. Five-gallon jugs of water are under the sink and in the hall closet. Flashlight and batteries are on the table by the door, and when the power goes out, the generators are on a five-minute delay. If the power's not up in five minutes, the generators will come on automatically, so don't go screwing with the fuse box or panicking."

All of this information had been posted on tidy notecards in prominent locations about the premises. "Yes, Mother. Next you'll be telling me where the deck of cards is."

Luke's bootsteps thumped across the living room to the kitchen. "That is a box from the Cupcake's bakery."

"That is my box, you heathen. What sort of host steals from his guest?"

"One who can pitch you into the snow one-handed." Luke peered inside the box as the scent of dark chocolate fragranced the air. "Baby Jeebus, deliver me, it's an undefended batch of brownies found wandering in the wild."

Magnus took a peek. All present and accounted for. "You will bring one of those brownies to Bridget with my compliments."

Luke sniffed. "Are you nuts? There's two brownies in there. One for me and one for you. I'll let you have first pick because I'm a generous guy."

"Either of those brownies—which I bought and paid for—would put a family of four into a diabetic coma. I don't care for sweets first thing in the day." Though pancakes with Bridget had been lovely.

Waking up wrapped around Bridget had been lovelier still, and making love with her…

"A fool and his brownies are soon parted." Luke closed the box. "You checked your email today? The internet sometimes goes down when the weather's acting up."

"I make it a habit never to look at a screen until I've had at least one decent cup of tea."

Luke pulled on his gloves. "Do they serve indecent cups of tea where you come from?"

"Take your plunder and go. Bridget gets first pick of the brownies."

"Plying her with chocolate won't do you any good," Luke said. "When she makes up her mind, not even brownies from the Cupcake will change it. We might vote to sell you the distillery if you make the right offer, but Bridget will hate you and us for cutting the deal."

"So why make the offer? You've only the one sister, and she has only that distillery."

"She has us, goshdangit, and the Logan Bar. Mind you stay inside with your decent tea. Shamus said he emailed you a few files."

He stomped out into the elements, while Magnus sipped a lukewarm cup of tea and put together an omelet—green peppers and salsa, with a side of familiar resentment. On this working holiday, Magnus felt half sick with a headache, worried as always for his business, and not entirely sure whether or how to go forward where the Logan Bar distillery was concerned.

He fired up his laptop and opened his email queue to the usual browser load of business—Elias had contributed heavily to the stack—and a single email from Shamus Logan. Delightful.

The power blinked on another gust of wind.

Magnus fished his cell phone cord and adapter out of his rucksack, plugged in the phone, and saw no less than three texts from Elias.

Call me.

Call me now.

Call me right this fecking damned minute.

Elias was prone to jerking Magnus's chain, but not to panicking. Neither was Magnus. He scrolled through his emails, starting with the one from Shamus.

No message at all, just an attachment labeled "Logan Bar Distillery General Ledger."

Magnus's phone rang—Elias again. "Magnus here."

"Finally. Why in the hell didn't you answer my calls?"

"Because it's barely morning and cell reception is dodgy when there's a foot of fresh snow and more on the way."

Magnus would not lie to Bridget, but neither would he let Elias harass him.

"It's as well you waited a few hours. We were in a proper frazzle, but there's less reason to worry now."

Less reason? "Elias, why are you calling?"

"Fergus had a heart attack. The doctors say it's a warning, and a few changes to diet, a wee ramble every day, some pills, and this won't be what sends him to heaven."

A feeling colder than the Montana blizzard washed through Magnus. "What does Fergus say?"

"Mostly profanities, and that drinking city water is what killed his great-uncle Alasdhair, so somebody had better produce a flask of Cromarty fifteen-year-old or the NHS will get an elder-abuse complaint."

"I want to grow up to be just like him." Even if he was a thorn in the side of the distillery at every opportunity.

"As do we all, but you have a board meeting next week, and Fergus ought not to attend. Without him and without you, there won't be a quorum."

Fuckity-boo. "I can fly home."

"Make the reservations at least. Old people can take a turn for the worse."

"You are such a voice of comfort, Elias. If there's anything Fergus needs…"

"I let him have a nip from my flask. Seemed to settle him. Enjoy your snowstorm." The call ended, and Magnus stared off at the endless white beyond the window.

How in the hell—how in the freezing hell—did anybody enjoy a snowstorm?

* * *

"I'm bored." Lena had made this announcement several times as the morning had worn on. Her father was out in the shop, tinkering with some ailing piece of machinery. Shamus was buried in ledgers, Luke was in the foaling barn with a crew of ranch hands, bedding stalls and putting the stable to rights before foaling season.

Leaving Bridget to babysit when she ought to have been reviewing her first quarter's general ledger.

"You have library books, Lena."

"I've read them all."

"You can sketch."

"I sketched after breakfast."

"Haven't done a princess movie marathon for a while."

"Princesses are stupid."

Lena was an only child, and Bridget knew exactly how that felt at the Logan Bar. Nobody to fit in *with*, plenty of people to be ignored by. Mama had smoothed the way for Bridget up to a point, while Lena was having to blaze her own trail.

Bridget set aside the spreadsheet that Shamus had so kindly printed out for her. "When I'm bored, it helps me to brighten somebody else's day."

"The uncles are busy, Daddy's in the shop, and Estelle chased me out of the kitchen."

Estelle, the housekeeper, was long on domestic skills and short on patience.

"I guess we'll have to be inventive. Come with me to the sewing room, Lena Lilly."

The sewing room had been Mama's sanctuary, the one part of the ranch house where nobody, not even Estelle, intruded.

Lena's braids needed tidying, but it was a snow day. If a girl couldn't relax at home on a snow day, then it was time to leave town.

"I don't like to sew," Lena said. "I like your quilts, though."

"One of the things I enjoy about quilting is that my brothers don't do it. I'd be happy to teach you, if you were ever interested, but I'm also happy that it's something I have for myself."

"Like your distillery?"

"Exactly like my distillery. The quilting is from my mama, the distillery is from my grandpap."

Lena stopped outside the sewing room door. "Mama gave me the horses."

Another Logan family mess. "And Luke said you could pick out a kitten from Diana's litter."

In deference to the weather, the queen of the stable cats had been given temporary quarters in the mudroom. Her kittens were at that almost-weaned, endlessly cute phase, where they pronked across any open surface, hissed and snarled at each other, then curled up to purr contentedly against their mama's furry belly.

Only three kittens, thank God. Diana alone had been allowed to retain her reproductive functions, and where she'd found a paramour was a mystery. Once or twice a year, she produced a litter. Because old age, coyotes, and other varmints made off with the occasional barn cat, the feline population stayed under control.

"Choose a color of yarn," Bridget said, gesturing to her supplies. She often tied off small quilts rather than stitching them. The resulting look was more homey, and the project was more quickly completed.

"Bright red," Lena said, passing Bridget a skein. "What's it for?"

"Boredom busting. For you, and for somebody else who's probably unhappy to be trapped inside today."

What was Magnus doing with his snow day? He'd sent over his entire stash of brownies, which somehow felt symbolic. Bridget had left him fast asleep on the couch despite all temptation to the contrary, in part because Magnus—true to his damned word—hadn't cast a single lure since setting foot on the Logan Bar ranch.

Bridget cut off a four-foot length of yarn. "Come with me, and we'll see what mischief we can stir up."

"Can I go out to the foaling barn when we're done? The snow stopped by the time I was done drawing."

Lena would get in the way of men who'd try to watch their language and fail. "Give the sun a little time to warm things up outside."

The mudroom was cold, but a baseboard heater kept it above freezing. Diana's box sat up a few inches off the floor, a sturdy wooden affair Patrick had made in his shop.

Two of the kittens were curled into perfect marmalade fur balls among the fabric scraps Bridget used to line the box. The third—a little tortie—had propped its front paws on the edge of the box and surveyed the mudroom with a bright-eyed attitude of conquest. Diana remained curled up in the scarf and mitten box across the mudroom, regal in her maternal calm.

"Tornada is awake," Lena said. "She's always awake."

"Then she can start the festivities." Bridget tossed one end of the yarn across the mudroom and trailed it slowly before the kitten. Lena took over after the first ineffectual pounce, and Bridget was edging toward the door to the back hallway when the other door—the one that opened on the garage—opened without warning.

Patrick stomped into the mudroom, followed by Magnus. They brought with them the scents of cold, wet wool, and engine grease.

"Close the door, Daddy!" Lena yelled. "You'll let the kittens out."

Tornada made a dash for the door, which might have resulted in the kitten getting lost permanently in the garage. Magnus got the door closed before the kitten could escape, but Patrick stumbled, and a heart-rending yowl rose from Tornada.

"What is that goddamned idiot cat doing in here?" Patrick's speech wasn't slurred, but the profanity was unusual.

The kitten's distress changed to sheer feline screaming when Lena picked her up. "You stepped on Tornada. You stepped on her, and now she's hurt."

"What in the heck is going on in here?" Shamus asked from the hallway door.

"Close the door," Bridget snapped. "One of the kittens got underfoot."

"She didn't get underfoot," Lena cried over the kitten's mewling. "Daddy stepped on her, and now she has to go to the vet."

Oh God. Not the vet. Vet bills could be astronomical, and in the case of a half-stomped kitten, what was the point?

"Can we move this discussion elsewhere?" Magnus asked.

Discussion wasn't going to happen. There'd be yelling and tears, and a hard decision, and a devastated little girl.

"Bring Tornada to the kitchen, Lena," Bridget said.

They filed out of the mudroom, leaving an anxious Diana calling for her equally upset daughter. Patrick had yet to shave, and while he didn't quite reek of spirits, he'd missed sleep yet again.

"Luke didn't tell you to stay put until the snow stops?" Bridget asked Magnus.

And why, why oh why oh why, did Magnus have to see the Logan family once again grappling unsuccessfully with life?

"The snow stopped more than an hour ago, and Patrick seemed to be having trouble navigating between buildings. The kitten's leg looks to be in a bad way."

Patrick steadied himself with a hand on the wall as they moved toward the kitchen in a procession led by Lena bearing the distraught Tornada.

"Luke will deal with the kitten," Bridget said, "or Shamus will."

"I'll do it," Patrick said. "I'm the one who messed up."

He sounded contrite, not that contrition would console Lena when the kitten was put down.

Luke came in the front door just as the group reached the great room. "What in tarnation is that racket?"

"Daddy stepped on my kitten."

"Sh—sugar," Luke said. "We can't afford—"

"We're discussing it in the kitchen." Bridget nearly yelled over the kitten's yowling and over the sheer frustration of knowing what lay ahead.

For Lena, another loss, another disappointment in the adults responsible for her welfare. For the kitten, an end to undeserved suffering, and for Bridget, another reason to resent like hell the Logan Bar ranch and the men who ran it.

"Accidents happen," Shamus said, though his expression told a different tale. Half-drunk idiots stepped on hapless kittens.

"It wasn't an accident," Lena retorted. "Daddy didn't watch where he stepped, and now Tornada has to go to the vet."

Woe to the uncle who contradicted her.

"Sweetheart," Luke said, hanging his hat on a hook, "sometimes the vet can't help. Kittens are fragile."

"Tornada is not fragile," Lena said, the cat clutched against her chest. "Daddy is drunk. Again. It's his fault Tornada got hurt."

"You can choose another kitten," Shamus said before Bridget could slap her hand over his idiot mouth.

"I don't want another kitten. Tornada is the smartest and the bravest, and I want her, and she's my kitten. Uncle Luke said I could pick out one kitten for my own, and now she has to go to the vet."

Lena was crying, Bridget wasn't doing much better, and Shamus and Luke looked ready to punch something.

Patrick knelt carefully before his daughter. "I'm sorry, honey. I'm sorry I didn't watch where I was going, but Tornada can't go to the vet."

"She's my kitten, and you stepped on her, and it's not her fault she's hurt!"

Shamus got a hand under Patrick's elbow and boosted him to standing. "We're talking emergency small animal surgery, somebody coming in on a snow day. A couple grand easily, and all for nothing."

The kitten was merely wailing now, a nerve-excoriating, pathetic little distress signal, which Diana echoed just as heartrendingly from behind the mudroom's closed door.

I hate this ranch. Bridget was on the point of offering to pay for the vet bills— like she could afford that?—when Magnus reached down and gently pried the kitten from Lena's grasp.

"The injuries seem to be limited to one leg. I'll pay for the vet bills, if that's the issue. Bridget, can you drive us to the nearest small animal emergency clinic?"

"You won't put her down?" Lena's cheeks were wet with tears, her nose needed wiping, and nobody—none of the damned, idiot men to whom she was related—thought to scoop her up and hug her, so Bridget did.

Magnus regarded the child with a dead-level gaze. "I will exert myself to the utmost to ensure this kitten enjoys a long and happy life. I suspect she might lose the leg."

"Will she be able to play?"

"If there are no internal injuries, and it's simply a matter of going about on three legs, she'll be able to play of a certainty."

If Magnus used that grave, calm tone of voice to assure Bridget that unicorns were flying over the barn, she'd believe him. The guy would make a wonderful father, if he ever—

Bridget cut that thought off. Magnus wasn't looking to remarry, and Bridget wasn't looking at all.

Lena stroked her hand over Tornada's head. "T-tell the vet to take good care of my kitty."

"We will," Bridget said, kissing Lena's cheek and setting the child on her feet. "We absolutely will, and we'll call you as soon as we know something. Somebody get Lena a tissue."

Three grown men sprinted for the kitchen.

"Let's get going," Bridget went on. "If the snow stopped more than an hour ago, the plows have been out."

Magnus tucked the kitten inside his jacket.

Lena watched Bridget donning her gloves, scarf, and quilted jacket. "I wish Daddy could go to a vet. He's drunk too much."

Bridget fished around for a comforting, philosophical reply that a child could grasp. *That's for damned sure* didn't seem quite appropriate.

"You should tell him that," Magnus said. "Make sure one of your uncles is around when you do, because you're right."

For the first time that day, Lena smiled. "I'm going to tell Diana that Tornada will be fine, and then I'll talk to Daddy."

Shamus and Luke were likely *talking* to Patrick at that moment. "Do that," Bridget said, "and we'll let you know what the vet says."

The sounds emanating from Magnus's jacket had muted to more normal meowing, and outside, the sun was brutally bright on a blanket of unbroken white.

"Come on," Bridget said, leading the way through the door. "And watch your step. If you fall and squash that kitten, no power on earth will save you from Lena's wrath."

"Speaking of wrath," Magnus said as they slogged over to Bridget's truck. "You should know Shamus gave me your general ledger from last year, and the year-to-date profit and loss as well. I have questions, Bridget."

Abruptly, the moment shifted. Over the scraping of the shovels wielded by the ranch hands, the soughing of a bitter wind, and the kitten's continued lament, Bridget went from worried about her niece to furious with her brothers.

"Shamus opened my books to you without my permission?"

"He did, though given the state of your indebtedness, he might have been trying to discourage my interest in your distillery rather than secure an offer from me."

Such was the fog of Bridget's upset that she stood for a moment, hand on the truck's door handle. "My books aren't that bad."

"For the quality of your product, and the position it holds in the market, they aren't that good either. The issue now is whether you'll discuss your finances with me, or put me on the first plane back to Scotland."

No, the issue was whether to disown her brothers. "Get in. We have an injured kitten to deal with and twenty miles of hard road ahead."

At least twenty miles.

CHAPTER SEVEN

Because all defense counsel had a solemn duty to thoroughly investigate the facts of a case, even when the client stood accused of prostitution, Nate was cruising paid-escort websites when his phone buzzed.

The ringtone was *We're in the Money*, a cheerful old tune that signaled a call from Nathan's prospective father-in-law, Prescott Truman.

"Prescott, how you doin'?" Nathan asked. "Stopped snowing where you are yet?"

"Stopped snowing, started melting, and probably getting ready to snow again," Prescott replied. "Courthouse closed?"

"That it is, leaving a poor counselor at law to sit alone contemplating dreams of Cabo San Lucas. Weren't you and the missus planning a trip this month?"

"Next week. I'm off to the feed and seed to pick up my weight in dog food, or Mrs. T will leave me hog-tied in the outhouse. You got a minute, Nate?"

Nathan silently bid farewell to Luckynluvly.com and opened up a game of hearts. "For you, Prescott, I have whole hours." The rest of his life, in fact, provided Georgina Truman said *I do* in October. Georgie had wanted a year's engagement, which was fine with Nathan. He and she understood each other, and theirs would be a successful and happy, if not always faithful, marriage.

"Monday night is poker night," Prescott said.

"Sure as God rested on the Sabbath, Monday night is poker night." Nathan had been dragged along to Prescott's weekly gathering a few times, but with a guest present, the gossip had stayed mostly harmless and the drinking moderate.

"So I was playing a few hands with the usual gang of idiots, and Parker Mayhew—his boy works for the DNRC and hunts with some of the oil and gas inspectors—had some interesting news to pass along."

Prescott owned the oldest bank in town, also the largest, in part because Prescott heard all the interesting news. He played poker with the ranchers and golf with the guys who ran the colleges and universities. His missus was on the board of the ski resort's charitable foundation, and Georgie organized a charity marathon, which meant she rubbed shoulders with hospital directors and insurance company CFOs. Prescott's sons worked for mining outfits, and Georgie's younger sister was in state government over in Helena.

"I am always glad to hear interesting news, Prescott."

"There's talk of another pipeline."

Much of Montana's wealth was in the ground, and pipelines were a fact of life. "My SUV will be glad to hear that."

"So will your former law partner. Seems the route under discussion runs right across the Logan family's land."

Nathan inadvertently clicked on the king of spades and got stuck with the queen as a result. "The Logan boys are a reasonable bunch." Usually. Patrick was having a hard time of it, but grief could do that to a man.

"They lean green, or their sister does, and that could be a problem."

A problem Nathan would be expected to solve. *Well, shit.* "Green is not the smartest direction to lean if a rancher wants to make ends meet in a hard year. Don't you hold the note on their land?"

The savvy rancher rode a delicate balance, between respecting the environment and exploiting it—or developing its resources, to use the regulatory language. Each property owner tended to support certain environmental causes—preservation of the black-footed ferret or whooping crane, public access to federal land—and also had a healthy appreciation for the checks that oil and gas extraction added to the ranch's revenue.

Gotta love Montana.

"The bank owns the Logan Bar mortgage," Prescott said, "but the proposed route doesn't run across the mortgaged land. It runs across the old MacDeaver property that butts up against the Logan Bar property line."

"No mortgage at all?"

"Hasn't ever been a mortgage on that parcel. It's five thousand acres of mostly wilderness, and one finger lies along the bottom of the ridge, just begging for a pipeline to come through. Their distillery sits on that property. I can't imagine a distillery and a pipeline wouldn't be able to find a way to get along."

Nathan's hand of cards went to hell, earning him twenty-five points out of a possible twenty-six, the next-to-worst hand possible.

"The family owns the distillery, Prescott, but Bridget runs that business. She doesn't always see eye-to-eye with her brothers." Which was normal, given that Bridget was a reasonably intelligent female and only a step-sister to them.

"She might like to earn some income of her own, then, income from a commonsense business decision involving a simple pipeline easement across the back forty of what used to be her granddaddy's parcel."

Nathan dealt himself another hand of cards. This one was rife with high hearts, so he dealt again. "I can bring it up with her, but she's got odd notions where that distillery is concerned."

"Family traditions are all well and good, but nobody with any sense wants to live in a covered wagon, Nathan. Progress requires change and compromise. If she made it through law school, Bridget MacDeaver isn't stupid. Talk sense into her, and your contribution to Montana's thriving and diverse economy will be rewarded. You coming over for supper on Sunday?"

Prescott could have sold snake oil to copperheads. "Wouldn't miss it, assuming we don't get another blizzard. Any idea who's lining up for Judge Sellick's seat on the bench?"

The conversation wandered to courthouse gossip, for lawyers did love to talk, and then Prescott was off to fetch dog food for his wife, as he put it.

Nathan was losing, two points shy of ending his game of hearts, so he quit and started a new one, the better to protect his stats.

"All the man wants is for me to talk my former law partner into putting a pipeline across her family's land," Nathan said, passing three hearts to the right. "She hates me, doesn't trust me, and had to spend her life savings making sure I couldn't get her disbarred."

By the time he'd won the game, he'd figured his way through the discussion he needed to have with Bridget. Her license to practice law was still active—disbarment was still an option, in other words—her distillery had been nearly beggared by Nathan's last attempt to reason with her, and she was ripe for a reminder of how precarious her finances had grown.

"Easy-peasy," Nathan said, clicking back onto the websites that helped a guy pass the time when the courthouse was closed to all comers.

* * *

"I saw the vet's estimated bill, Magnus."

Bridget paced before the woodstove, while outside, melting snow dripped in a sun-drenched chorus. Montana's weather put Magnus in mind of the Highlands, though no obliging ocean moderated the extremes of temperature here.

"I said I'd pay that bill, and I will."

She knelt before the stove and fiddled with the dampers. "That is a lot of money for one ornery kitten."

Nearly two thousand dollars, before the white-coated vet tech had finished rattling off antibiotics, anthelmintics—whatever those were—pain meds, and post-surgical care protocols. The kitten was recovering from the loss of its front leg at the clinic.

Magnus might never recover from Lena's tears.

"The money is not being exclusively spent on the cat," he said. "I will see to it that Patrick repays me."

She rose. "What makes you think he can?"

"I'll collect in services if I can't collect in coin, but you should know, Bridget, I might have to cut my visit short."

Magnus resented the need to return to Scotland. Less than a week ago, he'd been resenting the need to travel thousands of miles to Montana. He'd sort out that contradiction when his arse was once again trapped in economy-plus seating forty thousand feet over the Atlantic.

Such a smile graced Bridget's features. "You're not going to steal my distillery?"

"Must you sound so relieved? I'd never steal your distillery, though I might purchase an interest in it, or contract with you to distribute my products along with your own."

The smile winked out. "I'm hungry. We should have stopped in town for a bite. What do you have on hand here?"

As it happened, Magnus's omelet was a dim memory, and cold weather apparently put an appetite on him.

"More salad and quiche."

"I'm not doing salad and quiche again," Bridget said, opening up the fridge. "Sit down and I'll put something together."

Magnus wanted to argue with her, but sensed that asserting control over his kitchen met some need Bridget couldn't otherwise articulate. He took a chair at the table as his phone buzzed silently in the back pocket of his jeans.

"Tell me about the distillery's finances, Bridget."

She slapped a loaf of bread down on a cutting board shaped like a pig. "Why should I hand you the keys to my kingdom?"

"Because your brothers will if you don't." They already had, in fact, which should have pleased Magnus rather than annoyed him.

"I am contemplating the pleasure of being brother-less. The only reason Shamus is still above ground and sucking air is that he might have shown you my books to wave you off, while not breaking ranks with Patrick and Luke."

She studied the loaf of bread as if deciding where to cleave a perfect gem.

"You are solvent," Magnus said. "Barely, and that can be a successful strategy if you're barely solvent for good reasons."

She went to work on the loaf, cutting off a half-dozen even slices. The knife was sharp, and she knew to let the blade do the work.

"I'm paying back my law school loans out of the distillery's revenue," Bridget said, arranging the bread on a cookie sheet. She buttered each slice, then added cheddar cheese. Crushed spices came next—minced onion, oregano, and tarragon, based on the scents.

"The law school loan repayments come from a dedicated account that's clearly documented in your general ledger. What is the loan to shareholder?"

That amount—tens of thousands of dollars—hadn't been on the previous year's spreadsheets. Bridget had raided her corporate account in a lump sum last spring, and repayments, on top of her law school loan payments, were decimating her cash flow and operating reserves.

Bridget turned the oven on and slid the cheese toast onto the middle rack. "Some of it went for Judith's final arrangements."

"Ten percent, perhaps." Uncle Fergus could wax profane about the funeral industry, but the Logans would not have been extravagant even for one for whom they all still grieved.

"Do you want coffee, tea, or hot chocolate?"

Magnus wanted answers, but he knew well the burden a business owner carried. Confide in the wrong person—even in the wrong spouse—and a dozen people lost their jobs. The damage cascaded from there, to say nothing of injured pride.

"I'll have whatever you're having."

She opened the cabinet beside the fridge, which bore a selection of teas, along with honey, agave nectar, stevia, and sugar. The honey and agave nectar went onto a tray, then Bridget put a kettle on to boil.

"I made a mistake," she said, staring at the red tea kettle. "I was the managing partner in my law office, and I made a mistake with the books. The money went to correct my error."

She wasn't lying, but she sure as hell wasn't telling the truth. "A loan between businesses isn't unusual, but you chose a different path."

A lonely path. She'd taken on rectifying her error as a personal debt, more or less.

"Nothing I did with my distillery books is illegal, Magnus. I went to an experienced business lawyer in Helena to make sure of that, got a legal memo on it, and had my CPA countersign it."

A lot of bother for a routine business transaction.

Magnus rose as the kettle began to hiss. "You followed proper protocol to a T, but say you made a mistake at the law practice. This mistake was serious enough that you left a profession you'd spent years getting qualified to work in. Your brothers apparently don't know the details, though they might suspect something, and paying off that loan to shareholder will take more than a decade at the rate you're going."

He marched up to her, lest she mistake his point. "If ever a business needed buying, it's your distillery, Bridget MacDeaver, so tell me why you'll not sell your operation to me."

"Step off, Magnus."

"Is this a bar fight?"

"No, but the toast is about to burn, and I do not forgive a man who causes me to waste good food."

Magnus backed away, but he had no intention of stepping off. He wanted to buy her distillery—that was still a sound business move, if she'd consent to it—but he also wanted to know who had backed her into a corner and how to make them pay.

* * *

Bridget felt as if the spring storm that would coat the valley in white for a few days had left a path of disruption in her life. A year ago, she'd realized that a serious error lurked in the law office's general ledger, then Judith had died, hail had wrecked much of the barley crop, and nothing had come right since.

Now Magnus was getting ready to ambush her distillery, even as he rescued gosh-bedarned kittens.

"What sort of tea are we having?" Magnus asked.

All the fixings, along with two bright red mugs, sat on the tray, but Bridget had forgotten to get out the tea.

"Irish breakfast." Good, strong black tea.

"It tastes better in Ireland," Magnus said, taking the tray to the table. "The Irish are wild for their tea, and if it's not strong enough, they threaten rebellion, at which they excel. Some tea companies blend a different brew for the Irish market than for anywhere else."

He was being polite, making small talk, though it was business small talk. "You've been to Ireland?"

"Many times. They make great whiskies, and it's a beautiful country. Shall I get the toast?"

"I'll get it. I can nuke some soup from the freezer."

"Perhaps later."

Her small-talk reprieve was to be brief. Bridget cut each piece of toast in half and arranged the triangles on a plate.

"We should have a salad."

Magnus took her by the wrist and led her to the table. "This is a friendly chat over a snack, Bridget, not the last meal of the condemned. I have more elderly relations than you have cattle, and you'll find every vice known to humankind hanging from my family tree.

"Aunt Helga is a rabid teetotaler," he went on, "because she was a raging alcoholic as a younger woman. Uncle Fergus gambled away a substantial fortune and still can't think straight in the presence of an attractive woman. Zebedee Brodie wrecks race cars when he's not funding crackbrained schemes and calling it support for emerging technologies. Cousin Elias—a mere lad in his thirties—has a penchant for breaking engagements at the last minute."

"You love these people." He spoke of them with exasperated affection, faults and all.

"They are my family." Magnus held a chair for her, something Bridget couldn't recall any of her brothers ever doing.

She sat, and fatigue settled into her bones. "We thank Thee for this food, amen. Pass the teapot, please, before I expire for lack of caffeine."

"Amen." Magnus didn't pass her the pot, but rather, poured her a mug of tea first, then filled his own cup.

"These geezers and duffers are also your board of directors, Magnus."

He stirred honey into his tea, though Bridget had the satisfaction of noting a slight hitch in his reach for the milk.

"You've been researching me. Should I be flattered?"

"Researching your distillery. Your board is composed almost entirely of family members. There's a real, live, honest-to-Pete earl in the bunch, the one you call Zebedee."

"I call him many things in addition to Uncle Zeb, when he bothers to show up at the board meetings. Will you have some toast?"

Magnus would not serve himself until Bridget had chosen a slice. That realization brought a stupid lump to her throat, and she put any old three triangles of toast on her plate.

"We thank Thee—I already said that."

Magnus took three pieces for himself. "Gratitude bears repeating, and I'm grateful for my family. If not for their stubborn distrust of my former wife, I'd have handed her my last groat and my best barrels of single malt."

He'd had family guarding his treasure, while Bridget had step-brothers trying to sell hers.

"I can't eat this." She couldn't seem to move either. Couldn't stand, grab her jacket, and flee across the slush and mud of the driveway to a ranch house that had never felt much like home.

Magnus produced a flask from the breast pocket of his vest. "For courage."

If she accepted his offer... "What sort of enemy offers me moral support when I'm running on fumes?"

He set the flask beside her mug of cooling tea. "One who isn't in a position to judge you. I might be able to help, Bridget, but you're so accustomed to thrashing through every difficulty on your own that help looks like meddling."

She picked up the flask, which was warm from his body heat. "My former law partner used to say the same thing. I was too stubborn to compromise."

Magnus sat back. "That's not what I meant, but tell me about this law partner. I suspect he's the author of some of your woes."

Bridget uncapped the flask, closed her eyes, took a whiff, and had to take another.

"That is superb," she murmured, treating herself to yet another sniff. "Vanilla pods, mint growing outside the back door, a bowl of tree-ripe mangoes sitting on the counter."

"And the palate?"

She took a cautious taste, all thoughts of Nathan and dubious solvency gone. "The mint shifts to eucalyptus, and the vanilla morphs into high church incense. There's a trace of stone dust, but that mingles so well with all the mint and a sort of peachy quality that the effect is elegant and polyphonic? Symphonic?"

The next taste confirmed all of her impressions and added yet more layers. Papayas and good old nutmeg. The stone dust drifted outdoors and hinted of pollen and the oak from which so much whisky flavor sprang.

"And the finish?" Magnus asked.

"I'm working on it." One last sample of heaven. "Quietly glorious, like profoundly intimate lovemaking recalled long afterward. That's not sensory, but I can't come at this degree of elegance any other way. This is some of the finest whisky I have ever, or will ever, taste."

"The distillery went out of business fifteen years ago," Magnus said. "That batch was thirty-four years old, and only ninety-four bottles of it were sold."

Bridget passed him back his flask. "Do you expect me to swill tea and gobble cheese toast after an experience like that?"

"No," Magnus said, "but I was hoping you might trust me enough to realize I want to help. My motives are not pure, and your trust should come with serious reservations, but I have resources you lack, Bridget."

"What sort of resources?"

He tucked the flask away. "Guile, ruthlessness, and I cut a dash in a kilt."

Now there was an image to give a lady pause. But then, Bridget had seen him wearing nothing at all. She'd also seen the guile in action up at the resort.

Nathan had been ruthless, the bastard. "Why help me, Magnus? Who or what has your balls in such a vise that you'd go thousands of miles out of your way, deal with Montana weather, my idiot brothers, and an ailing kitten just to help out another whisky operation?"

He took a sip of his tea, which had to be tepid. Stalling, then, getting his arguments lined up.

"Not my balls, but my best whisky, even better than the Highlander you just sampled. I'll share the details if you'll explain to me why you all but stole the cash reserves from your own business."

"Somebody messed with your whisky?" Even Nathan hadn't been that bold.

"With my best year, saved back in anticipation of celebrating the distillery's two hundredth birthday. I trusted the wrong people, and I will not let them win."

In a kilt, Magnus would look scrumptious, and his guile was impressive. The ruthlessness, though... Bridget liked his brand of ruthlessness best of all.

"I trusted the wrong person too," she said, "and I will never, ever make that mistake again."

CHAPTER EIGHT

Bridget likened fine whisky to remembered lovemaking. That analogy worked for Magnus, provided the memory was of intimacies he'd shared with her.

At the vet clinic, she'd been silent and tense, until the small animal surgeon had declared the kitten a low-risk candidate for a routine procedure most cats recovered from easily. Lena's three-legged pet would be the most pampered, treasured feline in Montana.

That mattered. Magnus didn't examine why.

"You said you'd make Patrick repay you for the vet bill. How?" Bridget asked.

"I'm not sure, but it occurs to me that he needs to feel useful."

"Hard for a guy to be useful when he's dead drunk."

The comment wasn't meant to carry a sexual innuendo, but Magnus manufactured one. *Down, boy.*

"I'm not sure he was drunk. Your machine shop sits directly across from the sliding glass doors in my bedroom, and somebody kept a light on all night out there." In the falling snow, that light had been pretty.

Bridget left off rearranging the cheese toast triangles on the tray. She'd eaten nothing and downed not even a sip of tea. Aunt Helga would have fussed her into taking sustenance, when all Magnus had to offer was damned whisky.

"Patrick used to draw all night," Bridget said. "His daddy kicked up one hellacious ruckus over it, until Mama stepped in. Said the boy had a gift, and who was Dan Logan to interfere with a God-given talent? I had just realized that Patrick was probably missing my mama as much as I did, and then Judith had to go and die."

Magnus let her have a moment to mull over that cheering insight while he took the uneaten food back to the counter and wrapped it in cellophane. He put away the tea things, set the kettle back on the burner, and put a teabag into a clean mug.

"You could just zap the tea in the microwave," Bridget said.

"I'm making you a cup of peppermint tea. If you're tired, you need a nap, not caffeine."

He expected her to fire off one of her prairie metaphors, but she instead got up and stuffed another log in the woodstove.

"My business partner embezzled from the law office," she said as casually as Magnus might have recited a football score. "But he was slick about it. Nathan has a whole oil spill worth of slick up his sleeve."

"Nathan?"

"Nathan Sturbridge the Third, better known as good old Nate Sturbridge, counselor at law. Good-looking Montana pioneer stock. He'll probably make judge before he's forty."

"And you hate him." Magnus certainly did.

"I can't afford to hate him. I just want him to go away."

That was the exhausted version of hate, the kind too focused on survival to bother about justice, much less revenge.

"What happened?"

Bridget rose and propped a hip against the windowsill. "I trusted him, that's what happened."

"Hard to embezzle if nobody trusts you."

The woodstove was crackling and popping, the fire finding new life.

"I don't like the courtroom," Bridget said. "I don't like all that posturing and drama. I get plenty enough of it here at the Logan Bar. Most cases settle, especially most domestics, but invariably, I got the cases that didn't settle. My clients got the crap plea bargains from the prosecutors, even the first offenders. I hated to go to work, couldn't sleep, couldn't stay away from the office."

Magnus wanted to hit somebody. "And you had law school loans."

"Not as much as many people, but some. I was smart, though. I'd found a law partner who did like to litigate. All the misery and injustice rolled right off of him. Nate is good on his feet, the judges like him, the clients trust him. I did the trial preparation, got the witnesses lined up, met with the clients, found all the cases to cite, laid cross-examination out question by question. Nate did just enough to make one hell of an impression on all concerned. Even though I still handled some cases personally, I congratulated myself on having made lemonade out of lemons."

The counters were clean, the food put away, and Magnus still wanted to hit somebody. The kettle began to whistle, so he filled the mug with hot water and handed it to Bridget.

For the sake of his own dignity, he took a seat on the couch three yards away. "You managed the books for the legal business?"

Bridget rose from the windowsill, set her tea on the coffee table, and disappeared down the hallway. Magnus at first thought she'd heeded the call of nature, but she returned carrying the quilt that had been on his bed. This one was blue and white and had a combination of circles that could also be four-petaled flowers, depending on perspective. It smelled of cedar, and despite the shop light shining in his window, he'd slept well and warmly beneath that quilt.

"I handled the books for the business," Bridget said. "How hard could that be for a two-lawyer operation? Shamus has enough number-crunching to do for the ranch, and I didn't want to impose. We had a tiny payroll—one admin, one paralegal—monthly partner draws, rent, office supplies, and client retainers. The retainers went into a trust fund until we earned our fees, and doing the bookkeeping took me less than one day a month."

She wrapped herself in the quilt and settled in the corner of the couch, not touching Magnus, her feet drawn up on the cushions.

"You kept the books as an afterthought," he said.

"We made good money, I had time for the distillery, and the clients were happy. I told Nate I wanted to cut back, take a smaller draw."

"Because you were not happy." Magnus tucked the quilt around her feet when he wanted to scoop her into his lap. That wouldn't help her get through what she needed to say, though it might help Magnus listen to her.

She took a sip of her tea. "I was content, Magnus. For most of us, life isn't a matter of spending down the trust fund."

Elias, who moved in much more glamorous circles than Magnus ever would, often said something similar.

"What about for Nathan Sturbridge?"

"Nate has expensive tastes, but his family's ranch is on the small side, and they don't have the best land. They do okay with oil and gas leases, but not all of those leases are being renewed."

"So he helped himself to the law firm's cash reserves?"

Bridget wrapped herself more tightly in the quilt. "He helped himself to a client's money. One type of law I do like is personal injury law, because again, it generally results in a commonsense outcome, once all the experts have chimed in. Our client got lucky, after a fashion, because the defendant was willing to pay up immediately and generously."

Dread formed a knot in Magnus's belly. "Mishandling client funds is dealt with severely in Scotland."

"Here too. There's a protocol observed with some of the larger settlements. The defendant pays out not to the plaintiff, but to plaintiff's counsel. Then all the necessary releases and nondisclosure agreements are signed, notarized, and disseminated while the check clears. When the paperwork has been completed, and the time for appeals has gone by, the plaintiff's lawyer cuts a check to the plaintiff and one for counsel's fees."

All of which made sense, provided the attorneys involved were conscientious and honest. "What went wrong?"

"I trusted Nathan. I got in the habit of working over the lunch hour, so I could leave early and spend a few hours at the distillery each day. Nathan would drop by the bank on his way to grab a sandwich. If we had a deposit to make or funds due from the client account, he'd handle the transaction, though I filled out all the paperwork."

Despite the roaring woodstove, Magnus's end of the couch was chilly. He rose and took the place immediately beside Bridget. "I've often done likewise, relied on my admin to make a deposit or put a check in the post."

"Well, don't hire Nathan to be your admin. I endorsed the settlement check and signed it *for deposit only*."

"He put it in his own account?"

"Nothing so obvious. He put the funds in our operating account rather than in the client security account. I always kept a few signed blank checks from the operating account under my blotter, just in case something happened while I was out of the office. Nathan used one of those signed emergency checks to move the money out of the operating account once the defendant's check had cleared. My signature was on every step of the transaction, and the money was gone before I got around to doing my monthly bookkeeping."

"How much?"

She named a figure that exceeded even the loan to shareholder on the distillery's books.

"You cleaned out your personal savings, your business reserves, everything you had rather than try to hold him accountable. Why?"

"Because I'm a coward."

Magnus put his arm around her shoulders. "You are not a coward."

For a moment, she remained in her corner, neither accepting nor rejecting him. Then she rested her head on his shoulder.

"Judith died in a riding accident. The barley crop got hit with a late storm, Patrick went to hell, Lena wasn't doing well. I might have gone to the bar association confidentially, except Nate is engaged to the bank president's daughter. The bank holds the note on the ranch, and if Nate intimated that the Logans don't keep clean books, that note might have been called. We have good and bad years—every ranch does—and our line of credit keeps us afloat in the bad years."

"But that money went someplace, Bridget. You don't have it, and Nathan does."

She closed her eyes. "How do I prove I don't have a huge wad of cash, Magnus? How do I prove Nate does? I'm not the FBI, able to get a bunch of snoopy warrants, and Nate's not dumb enough to keep the money under his mattress."

"So a man willing to commit multiple felonies continues to practice law?"

"I'm not in a position to take him down, Magnus. Nothing has really changed. We're still reeling from Judith's death, hanging on until the crops are in and the fall markets hit. I salvaged my distillery from the whole mess, and I don't intend to relinquish it to the first handsome Scotsman to come along. Now more than ever, I need the whisky to keep me going."

He knew exactly what she meant. When Celeste had left him, he'd been furious, and the only safe channel for his betrayal and humiliation had been to turn a conscientious interest in his business into an obsession.

Magnus rested his cheek against Bridget's hair. "It doesn't work, you know."

She took another taste of her tea, yawned, and cuddled against him. "What doesn't work?"

"You can't change the world by selling more whisky. I'd like to pay a call on Mr. Sturbridge in some dark, deserted alley. He betrayed your trust and took advantage of you. Worse, he profited handsomely from doing so."

Bridget was quiet, her breathing regular. Holding her warmed Magnus, though what comfort was an embrace when a woman had been dealt such a betrayal?

"I don't want to change the world, Magnus," she said after a time. "But if I can take water, barley, and yeast and make a beautiful single malt out of it, maybe I can take hard work, time, and perspective and make a life I can be proud of."

The analogy rang true, but the recipe wasn't right. Nathan Sturbridge had contaminated Bridget's dreams, and until he'd been held to account, all the beautiful, golden whisky in all the markets in the world wouldn't yield the result she craved.

"If it's any consolation, I would have given my ex-wife signature authority at my distillery but for my cousin Elias threatening to leave the board if I did. I was willing to hand her my checkbook, Bridget. She'd intimated that we could start a family when the distillery was as much hers as mine, though we'd been married less than a year."

"Conniving bitch," Bridget muttered. "We shouldn't be cuddling like this, Magnus."

"Probably not." Definitely not. But the desire to snuggle on the couch was mutual. That was something.

"Keep your friends close, keep your enemies closer."

"I'm not your enemy, Bridget, and we've been much closer than this."

She kissed him. "You're a good sort of enemy. You're a good sort of lover too."

Where was Elias when a sound arse-kicking might have stopped Magnus from turning a difficult situation into an impossible muddle?

"Bridget, this isn't wise."

"Nope," she said, shifting to straddle his lap. "It's all messy, foolish, and backward, but you just heard the worst I could have told you about me, and you're ready to pound Nathan to flinders. I like that about you."

Magnus's self-discipline was taking a beating as Bridget arranged her blanket around them both. "Anybody with an ounce of decency would want to pound him to dust. I'm after your distillery."

"You're not getting it."

He kissed her, a wee nip of a kiss redolent of peppermint. Making love again would be exactly as Bridget had said: messy and foolish. But making whisky involved a lot of bubbling wort, odd fumes, used barrels, and dark warehouses.

From messiness and foolishness might come something precious. Magnus had no idea how, and the situation with Sturbridge made the whole business more complicated.

Embezzlement, cash-flow problems, a family in disarray, and a board of crotchety elders resistant to change… all of that would have to wait, until Bridget was done kissing him.

* * *

"Where are you going?" Shamus's question came out more sharply than he'd intended, but Patrick merely shrugged off his hand.

"Out to the shop. Maybe do some sketching."

After Bridget and Magnus had left for the vet clinic, Patrick had gone up to his bedroom, shut the door, and not been seen for three hours. Now he was preparing to waltz out the front door and very likely embark on a dedicated drinking binge.

"You haven't apologized to Lena for squashing her kitten, Patrick. How can hiding in the shop be more important than that?" Though if Patrick was drawing *anything*, that was a good sign.

"For your information, baby brother, Lena is busily drawing three-legged kittens, along with a few unicorns. They look like horses to me, but she says they're unicorns who had to have their horns removed at the vet clinic. They still have their magic powers, as it turns out."

Patrick jammed his hat onto his head. Shamus knocked it off before Patrick could get a hand on the doorknob. "You didn't apologize to that kid when you nearly stomped her kitten to death."

Patrick was sober, Shamus would have bet his favorite pair of ski boots on that, but Patrick was also *different*. Shamus was terrified that difference was a bad thing, an even worse thing than Patrick's growing affection for the bottle.

Patrick looked at the cowboy hat sitting upside down on the great-room carpet. "All righty, Shamus. Let's do this. We're overdue, after all."

In the next instant, Shamus was on his ass on the carpet, six-feet-plus of older brother trying to wrestle him onto his back. The great room was the best place to roughhouse, because there was space enough and the furniture was sturdy.

A bolt of sheer, animal glee punctured Shamus's ire, because Patrick was right: They were way, way overdue for a wrestling match.

Patrick had had the advantage of surprise, but Shamus called on months of pent-up rage, bewilderment, and worry to even the match. Years ago, Bridget had demanded a rule of them—never hit your brother with a closed fist—and no brother had ever violated that rule.

Shamus was grateful for old restraint, because he wanted to pound the crap—pound the grief—out of Patrick, along with the despair and the growing indifference to everything that mattered.

Patrick apparently had a few agenda items of his own. He'd grown bony since he and Shamus had last wrestled, but he was still quicker than a summer trout going after a fly.

"You apologize to Lena," Shamus panted, gaining a momentary upper hand.

Patrick feinted, seeming to capitulate and then catching Shamus unaware as he escaped an almost-half-nelson. "I did, goshdangit. Told her I was sorry, and that only made her cry again. You're the one who didn't want to pay a few vet bills."

True, and not something Shamus was proud of. "Maybe if you put your dad-blamed backside in the saddle from time to time, did something to earn your draw, those vet bills wouldn't have been a problem."

That provoked another round of scuffling, scraping, and knocking lights over.

Patrick trapped Shamus's head against the carpet. "All you do is sit on your prissy butt in Dad's office and stare at the same numbers month after month. You know that resort better than you know your own ugly face. Why haven't you been helping Bridget sell her whisky up there?"

"She won't let me help, dadgum you."

The pressure on Shamus's body eased. "Figured as much, but you haven't offered either. When is Luke going to propose to Willy?"

"What in the blazing, stinking hell has gotten into you?"

Patrick rose and offered Shamus a hand up. "A dose of fresh mountain air. I was up drawing for most of the night because I have a few ideas that might turn into something. Saw Luke and Willy out in the mare's barn around midnight, and it's a wonder the whole place didn't burn down."

Shamus passed Patrick his hat, which wasn't exactly hat-shaped anymore. "They're getting careless."

Patrick snatched the hat and swatted Shamus with it. "Do I need to finish what we started here, Shamus Logan?"

That was the old Patrick talking, the middle brother who could walk into any confrontation and settle everybody down.

"For crap's sake, back off. I don't care who Luke falls in love with as long as he picks a consenting adult, but he and Willy think they're being discreet."

"Screw discretion. He's our brother."

"And it's his business."

"His and Willy's."

Willy was the foreman, the guy who turned decisions into action, who kept peace in the bunkhouse and knew everybody in the valley. He'd started off as a ranch hand, picked up a degree in ag economics somewhere along the way, and was gradually adding an MBA to it.

Willy and Judith had been partners in crime where the horses were concerned, and Luke probably hadn't sold the mares in part because Willy insisted that horses were profitable.

"I spend all winter wishing spring would get here," Shamus said, "then I wish to hell spring would leave us in peace. Don't suppose we can add you to the rotation when the foals start coming?"

Mares were notorious for dropping foals not only in the dead of night, but during the five minutes in the dead of night when the guy on foal watch stepped out for a quick visit to the bushes. If anything went wrong in the birthing process, though, immediate, knowledgeable intervention was the only hope of a positive outcome.

"I have taken my shifts on foal watch every year since I turned twelve," Patrick said. "Why should this year be any different?"

"Because this has been the year from hell," Shamus said, grabbing his hat from the rack by the door.

"We're still in business, and it looks to me like Bridget might have found a little bit of heaven—or Scotland. What do you make of Cromarty?"

Shamus shrugged into his sheepskin jacket. The snow was melting, but the breeze could still cut like knives.

"Cromarty isn't stupid. I don't trust him."

"Tell me something I don't know."

"I gave him Bridget's profit and loss for the past three years, and the year-to-date general ledger. He'll know exactly what he's looking at."

Patrick crossed the room to right an overturned gooseneck lamp. "He better know how to wrangle a spreadsheet, if he's buying the distillery."

"I haven't been watching Bridget's books that closely, and when I took a more careful look, I found some nasty surprises."

Patrick kicked a flipped-up corner of the carpet flat. "I purely hate nasty surprises. Is the distillery about to go belly-up?"

"Yes and no. She took a loan to shareholder last year and told me she was paying off a law school loan with it." Shamus tossed a pillow back onto a recliner, and the room looked just about put to rights.

"Nothing wrong with paying down debt," Patrick said. "It's her debt and her distillery."

"No, Patrick. It's her debt and her land. It's our distillery. She runs it and draws a small salary, but all four of us own it, and the business rents the land it sits on from her. I did some checking."

"Snooping, you mean?"

"Checking. The balances on her student loans haven't come down by nearly as much as they should."

Patrick ran a hand over scruffy cheeks. "She's stealing from us?"

"Or hedging her bets. I can't find the money anywhere. Not on her books, not on the ranch books, not anywhere."

Patrick wasn't a businessman, but his mind naturally grasped cause and effect and how parts worked together. He tossed Shamus a scarf.

"You didn't look at the law practice books, because you can't. Maybe Bridget had to buy her way out of that business. Ever think of that? Nate Sturbridge is a greedy sumbitch, and that rock Georgie

Truman is wearing on her finger didn't come from the five-and-dime."

"I hadn't noticed Georgie's ring, but I've considered a few other factors, all of which I should have seen a year ago, but didn't bother looking for."

"Come out to the shop with me," Patrick said. "Guilt will drive you straight to the liquor cabinet, and I cannot be trusted to talk you out of going there."

Shamus held the door. "What do we have to do out in the shop?"

"Keep an eye on the front door of the guesthouse, for one thing. What do you suppose Bridget and that damned Scot are getting up to?"

"No good."

"We live in hope."

* * *

Why am I about to have a relapse of foolishness with Magnus Cromarty?

The question came not from Bridget's conscience—Magnus was a consenting adult, after all—but from the part of her that had spent the last year standing back, coping, strategizing, and troubleshooting.

I'm doing this because I damned well want to. Need to.

Magnus scooted to the edge of the sofa, scooped Bridget up, quilt and all, and carried her to the back of the house. The air grew colder the farther they got from the woodstove.

"Hasn't anybody shown you how to work the heat?" Bridget asked.

"I'm conserving resources, saving them for a true necessity." Magnus laid her on the bed and closed the door. The bedroom was good-sized, with an unlit pellet stove in a corner fireplace. The four-poster bed dominated the space, and the high-beamed ceiling contributed to the lack of warmth.

He rummaged in a rucksack and tossed a pair of condoms on the night table, then pulled the curtains closed over the sliding glass doors and disappeared into the adjacent bathroom.

No time like the present. Bridget shucked out of her jeans and flannel shirt, laying them on the rocker beside the fireplace. The bed would be freezing—at first. She spread the quilt loosely over the blankets and dove under the sheets naked.

"For the love of baby bunnies, Magnus, get in here and help me warm up this bed."

He emerged from the bathroom naked from the waist up. "I'll do more than that, unless you've changed your mind."

Caution tried to rear its inconvenient head. "If you bought my business, would you keep me on as distiller?"

He paused, his jeans halfway unzipped. "You don't want to sell to me, and you're barely turning a profit because of all the debt you've taken on."

"I'm a lawyer, or I was. Indulge me in a hypothetical."

Magnus got the rest of his clothes off and turned his back to fold them on the dresser. Bridget had the uncomfortable sense he was deciding how honest to be. Again.

"I am more interested in your abilities as a distiller than in the business you run."

He wasn't flirting, wasn't flattering. "What do you mean?"

Magnus turned to face the bed. "Might we discuss that later?"

Holy prairie dogs, Batman. He was more than ready for a change of subject. "Later today."

"If you insist."

"Right now, I insist you get under these covers and wrap your big old Scottish self around me before I freeze."

He obliged, but apparently wasn't in the mood to chat. While the sheets gradually warmed, Magnus draped himself over Bridget and treated her to an excruciatingly lazy orgy of kissing—her shoulders, her neck, her brow and lips and jaw and everywhere a lady ever desired to be kissed.

Impatience joined desire. "Magnus, I don't need convincing."

"You need loving."

He would not be hurried, and after pulling his hair, wiggling, and trying to inspire him with a few other tactics, Bridget surrendered to the deliberate pleasure he offered. The cost of capitulating was to admit emotion into an exchange that she'd intended to limit to physical pleasure.

Magnus breathed her in and brushed her hair back from her brow. His fingers were warm, his caresses sweet, and his thumb tracing along her eyebrow caused an empty ache in her belly.

I'm lonely. I'm so damned lonely, and so tired of being lonely. Tired of everything— the Logan Bar ranch, grief, family feuding, responsibility.

Tired of keeping a stupid promise to a grandfather long gone.

The price of slowing down to take in Magnus's tenderness was that Bridget's emotions caught up with her.

The collision hurt like getting bucked off at a dead gallop and landing on rocky ground. Beneath the loneliness lay a fear that went back to the barely remembered time when she'd had two parents, and reached forward to the day when what family she had would be nothing but a liability. And beneath the fear, a worse ache still:

I have nobody of my own.

Magnus hitched up, cradling the back of Bridget's head in his palm and tucking her face against his shoulder. "Stay with me, Bridget."

I wish I could. "I'm here." Though *here* had become a difficult place, more intimate than Bridget had intended. She tried to re-establish some detachment, a mental perch from which to watch herself having a damned fine time with a damned fine lover.

Magnus palmed her breast and gave her an easy pressure on her nipple.

"Again," Bridget whispered. "Please."

He was relentless and inventive. When Bridget drew her knees up, the better to wrap her legs around him, Magnus caught her foot in a warm grasp. He knew exactly where to press on her sole, exactly the angle to brace her leg, exactly when to let go.

When he took an intermission to deal with protection, Bridget lay panting on her back, desire and an insistent despair bludgeoning her from within.

Lighten up, cowgirl, it's only a roll in the hay battled against a more desperate sentiment: *Why can't this be real?*

Magnus had raised the stakes—this wasn't a mere roll in the hay—and Bridget hadn't called his bet. He'd learned what nobody else knew about her, and instead of heading for the Highlands, he'd accepted Bridget's challenge to another round of intimacy.

Another level of intimacy.

He repositioned himself over her, his mouth near her ear. "Now, we let go, lass."

"I don't know if—"

Then he was inside her, all the languor and restraint, the delicate caresses and patient exploration gone in an explosion of passion.

Bridget gave up trying to mentally weigh risks and regrets and poured everything—rage, grief, determination, exhaustion, *everything*—into loving Magnus back. The bed rocked, and when the pleasure came, the satisfaction burned so bright and deep it nearly hurt.

And that felt wonderful.

Bridget lay beneath Magnus, breathing like a spent horse. Another loving like that might kill her, but even as she had that thought, she corrected herself.

Living *without* another loving like that would finish her off before the year was up. And who would have guessed—Magnus had needed loving too.

CHAPTER NINE

"You'll have bruises on your butt," Bridget said, smoothing her hand over the relevant part of Magnus's anatomy.

She had such a lovely touch. "I'll wear them with pride. You'll be sore."

He'd never made love to a woman as he just had with Bridget. Or maybe, no woman had ever made love with him like that? Certainly not his former wife, who'd liked her bedsport fairly tame and not too protracted. Magnus had told himself that married sex was supposed to be friendly like that and special in its own way.

What a load of shite. He'd wallowed in learning Bridget's every hollow and contour, in pushing her and himself past restraint to a place uniquely theirs, both uncharted and utterly safe.

So now what, laddie? Magnus rose up on knees and elbows, easing his body from Bridget's. Whatever came next, they'd go forward by negotiation and mutual consent.

Bridget shivered and gripped him by the back of the neck. "Don't be gone long."

"You all right, then?" Magnus wasn't all right, but he was righter than he'd been half an hour ago.

"I'm undone, Magnus. I'm absolutely undone. I wasn't planning on that."

"The best-laid schemes sometimes benefit from rethinking." He kissed her cheek, offered a silent apology to Mr. Burns, and got out of bed to deal with the practicalities. The bathroom was blessedly warm, and Magnus made short work of washing up.

The bed was warmer, and if Bridget was about to fall asleep, he wanted her falling asleep in his arms.

When he rejoined her under the covers, she straddled him and curled down onto his chest.

Lovely woman. Touching her soothed him as even the best whisky never had, and Magnus would not have said he was a man in need of soothing.

"Talk to me," Bridget said.

That might be the most frightening demand a woman could make of her lover. Why hadn't Magnus's ex ever wanted to prolong the intimacies with conversation?

"My whisky is in trouble."

She kissed his shoulder. "And?"

And do that again. "And if my whisky is in trouble, my family is in trouble. The elders depend on their directors' stipends. The entire crew is family even if they're not related to me. Their people worked with my people a century ago, and by virtue of my warehousing arrangements, I'm extending credit to a few other small operations. The whisky has to come right."

"It's not finishing well?"

"Five years ago, my premier batch was maturing splendidly. I'd finally brought everything together, from the water supply to the choice of barley, the malting, drying, everything. I had a legend maturing in my warehouse and made sure everybody knew about it. The culmination of two hundred years of hard work and wisdom would have my name on it at the bicentennial celebrations."

"Idiot."

"Bridget, you didn't sample what was in those casks. Compared to the wee nip you had today, my whisky was the nectar of the gods."

She kissed his forehead next. "And goddesses."

"And accountants. What's in my flask has gone for a thousand dollars a bottle at auction. My bicentennial would have opened for that much."

"Because drinking makes people drunk, but whisky can make them crazy. I'm sorry for your loss. What does this have to do with Logan Bar?"

As passionate as Magnus was about his whisky, as sexually satisfied as he'd been five minutes ago, when Bridget casually grazed his nipple with her fingernail, one thought gained Magnus's full attention:

A second condom sat three feet away on the night table.

"I need two assets from the Logan Bar distillery." *Need* was an admission, an act of trust.

"One of them had better not be cash."

"One of them will drive me daft if she kisses me even one more time."

Bridget left off using her tongue on Magnus's other nipple. "You want to hire me?"

"I want to kidnap you, *among other things.*"

She kissed him on the mouth, thoroughly, even recklessly. "You're not kidnapping me unless I get to kidnap you too. Tell me about the *other things.*"

* * *

An afternoon in the office was convincing Nate of the value of holy matrimony. He'd known Georgie Truman was a good choice—pragmatic, as gals born and bred in Montana tended to be, lively in bed, wealthy, and well-connected—but month by month she was becoming a necessity rather than a strategic move.

The phone hadn't rung the whole time Nate had been at his desk researching his latest prostitution case.

One of the ironies of the legal business was that people tended to go lawyer shopping when lawyers weren't likely to be in. Friday afternoons, holidays, during snowstorms… As if leaving a message appeased an anxiety for the client that actually hiring a lawyer would only exacerbate.

Bridget had been happy to roost in the office on the odd days—the Friday after Thanksgiving, Christmas Eve, Super Bowl Monday, New Year's Eve, most Friday afternoons. Invariably, her vigilance had resulted in new cases.

She'd had the one skill Nate couldn't pretend to claim—the ability to listen to the clients. Nate managed a close approximation of listening when picking up a casual partner for a mattress rodeo. When it came to poor schmucks crying in their beer about a seven-year itch costing them their marriage, or the inconvenience of spending a weekend in jail after their first DUI, Nate had no patience.

Nobody warned a guy that patience was a requirement for the successful practice of law.

The damned phone wasn't going to ring, and Nate's ass was tired of sitting in his damned ergonomically engineered office chair. He put his computer to sleep, rose, shut off the lights, and headed for the door. The admin hadn't come in, because it was a well-established fact that Sue Etta Grainger's four-wheel-drive worked only if she had to get to the grocery store.

"Damned women," Nate muttered, jamming his hat onto his head.

And damned weather, because as it happened, he was out of groceries himself, and Sunday supper with the Trumans was a long way off. He was still lamenting that fact when he snatched up a silly-ass red plastic shopping basket and headed for the snack aisle twenty minutes later.

"Watch where you're going, Sturbridge."

Martina Matlock had her own red plastic shopping basket, into which she'd stashed organic celery, organic baby spinach, and other horrors too healthy to contemplate.

"If it isn't one of my favorite ex-cops. There's a reason my clients call this the singles' supermarket."

"And that reason is not you, Nathan." Martina breezed past him, her down vest barely brushing the sleeve of his jacket.

She stopped a few yards farther up the aisle before a selection of soups. Why in the hell had the good Lord made such a contrary female so danged pretty that she could look sexy even handling cans of clam chowder?

"Which is your favorite?" Nate asked, surveying the offerings.

"If you're coming for dinner, I look for the brand with a little rat poison in it."

"Dang, Martina. You'll hurt my feelings. Don't suppose you've had a chance to catch up with Bridget lately?"

Martina put a can of something organic, non-GMO, ethically sourced, cruelty-free, gluten-free, and probably godawful tasting into her basket.

"You should never have forced Bridget out of the practice, Nate. Georgie has expensive tastes, and your lazy ass isn't marrying Prescott's money."

"I didn't force Bridget out, dammit. She ditched me, left me high and dry, a docket full of unhappy clients expecting me to show up in court and nobody minding the store." Nate had had enough practice telling that fairy tale that it sounded pretty convincing.

Martina went back to choosing death by sodium deprivation. "You are an idiot, Nathan Sturbridge. Bridget's sister-in-law had just died, your practice was thriving, and you wanted the whole thing for yourself. I don't know how, I'm not even sure why, but you forced Bridget out, and now you're losing more cases than you're winning."

If there was one group of people who gossiped more than lawyers, it was cops.

"That is slander, lady. Watch your pretty mouth."

She hefted a can of soup. "Truth is an absolute defense to all claims of defamation. Watch your skinny ass, little man. If you got up the balls to ask Bridget to rejoin the firm, you might just find she's entertaining other prospects."

Well, shit. Bridget entertaining prospects might make the pipeline easement more complicated.

"As if I care which bronc she's saddling. Get your mind out of the stud barn. My only interest in Bridget is that of a former partner and friend."

The look Martina gave him had probably inspired many a felon to either wet his standard-issue orange jumpsuit or confess.

"Bridget has a potential buyer for her distillery, the same good-looking Scot she was so friendly with on Friday. He's got money, connections, and class, so take your skanky little concern and shove it where the light doesn't shine."

The lawyer in Nate knew better than to react visibly, but the witness had surprised him. Surprises weren't always bad, but they were always a pain in the ass.

"Since when are you kept up-to-date on the Logan Bar business dealings?"

"Since Shamus Logan is a good friend, a concept your limited abilities won't be able to grasp, so don't try."

She sauntered off, and not until Nate got to the checkout did he realize that three cans of exorbitantly expensive and extravagantly healthy bean soup had been stashed among his guac, chips, and beer. He paid for the soup because Georgie might be over for a nooner at some point, and while she couldn't be bothered to heat anything other than water in a microwave, she'd approve on principle.

By the time Nate got out to his truck, he'd decided that for Bridget to sell her distillery was a fine thing. She'd have put up a fuss about a pipeline easement, but the Scots were a practical race.

Talking the new Scottish owner into a pipeline easement should be about as difficult as coming up with a closing argument to pitch at a jury of twelve lonely, middle-aged church ladies.

* * *

Magnus's itinerary had been shot to hell.

He'd intended to come to Montana and secure Bridget's expertise by any means necessary, including by buying her business.

Now this.

The last thing on his mind was business. Bridget lay against his side, sweet and warm. He couldn't stop touching her, whether he was drawing question marks along her arm or kissing her temple. Her hand rested over his heart, and he wanted to kiss her hand too.

"Thoughts?" she murmured.

To hell with the damned itinerary. "For the first time in my life, a woman has *made love* with me." Hochmagandy, shag, how's your father, bonk, boff... British slang abounded with casual terms for sexual congress, and any of them would have profaned what Magnus and Bridget had just shared.

Her sigh fanned across his shoulder. "Don't do that, Magnus. You're supposed to saddle up and ride into the sunset in less than a week. We have chemistry. It's not convenient, and it's not..."

Disappointment muted the glow of transcendent lovemaking. Magnus waited for Bridget to finish the job of easing him down, cooling his conviction that something precious could take root if she'd give it a chance.

"It's not like anything I've encountered before," Bridget said, "but then, I haven't done a lot of encountering."

While Magnus might have done too much. "Then I'm doubly complimented to be in this bed with you now. Can you come to Scotland with me next week?"

She withdrew her hand. "Not letting any grass grow under your boots, are you?"

"I want you to see Scotland, to meet my family, to—" To not leave his sight.

Bridget levered up on one elbow and peered down at him. "You're not trying to kidnap me so I can diagnose your ailing whisky?"

What whisk—oh, that whisky. "I can have samples sent here by Friday."

"Do that," Bridget said, kissing him. "I like a challenge, and I've never flown anywhere. Lena's mother made sure we all have passports, but the idea of flying over the ocean on less than a week's notice doesn't have much appeal."

Magnus kissed her back. "Elias hates to fly, poor lad, but how would you feel about touring a different distillery every day? Sampling three different flights every day, none of them less than twenty-eight years old? Dropping in on the Malt Whisky Society between sightseeing trips in Edinburgh?"

He expected she'd tickle him for that, or kiss him again, but instead, Bridget's expression became wistful.

"I've looked at tours online," she said, tucking close. "They have entire bus routes devoted to whisky. Did you know that?"

God, she was precious. "I've heard the occasional mention."

"I'd like to see Scotland someday, Magnus, and England and Ireland, but right now, a trip over to Billings would take some explaining and planning. Patrick's not doing well, foaling season will start any night, one of my guys at the distillery is about to become a father, and now isn't a good time to leave Lena without reinforcements."

Magnus wanted to argue, by any means necessary, but he knew exactly how she felt. "There's never a good time to get away, is there? Never the right combination of time, energy, funds, and motivation, much less the right people in place to look after your business while you're gone."

Who looked after Elias's complicated business affairs when he wanted to grab some sunshine on the Amalfi Coast? Elias was Zebedee's heir and, for all practical purposes, his errand boy too.

Bridget should have an errand boy. Magnus was tempted to apply for the position.

"I can't recall Luke ever leaving the state of Montana," she said. "Ten years ago, Patrick traveled a lot, but Shamus's idea of playing hooky is to hit the slopes in Utah or Colorado. We don't get out much."

She closed her eyes, and Magnus let her drift off. He needed time to think about the situation with Nathan Sturbridge, and Patrick, and—

His phone softly chimed on the night table. Magnus reached around a sleeping Bridget and swiped into the call.

"Elias, aren't you up past your bedtime?"

"I'm a Scotsman. We never sleep when there's fun to be had. I started to text you, but thought the matter might require some discussion."

"What matter?"

"You first. How's Montana?"

"Beautiful, cold at the moment, interesting. I'm reminded of Scotland. Plenty of room to breathe here." *And oh, by the way, I'm falling in love.*

"Met any cowgirls?"

"Shut up, Elias, and grab something to write with. I need some samples sent from the distillery."

Elias read back the list Magnus had recited. "So you'll be home for the board meeting?"

"I'm sending a proxy."

A gratifying silence lasted nearly two seconds. "I'd forgotten you could do that. Am I to know who's been taken into your confidence to that degree, or will you, like Uncle Zebedee, delight in high drama for no reason?"

"I have two candidates in mind, members of the Logan family, and you will show them every ounce of your considerable charm, Elias. Get out the kilt, quote Rabbie Burns, put plaid sheets on the guest beds, the whole bit. Remind Fergus he can vote by personal proxy as well."

"Plaid sheets give me nightmares. I don't suppose you're sending me any cowgirls?"

"More likely a cowboy, though if I can talk her into it, I'll send you one of the most talented whisky distillers on the face of the earth. If Bridget gets a bad first impression of Scotland, I will hold you accountable."

"If you want the lady to get a good first impression of Scotland, then perhaps you should make the introductions."

"Suggestion noted, but matters here are growing complicated."

"I hate complicated, and as it happens, matters here have moved in the same direction."

This was why Bridget hesitated to travel. Because the gods of mischief delighted in wrecking the plans of those fools who intentionally left their posts.

"Well, don't stop there. Let the suspense build, drop a few more hints, sigh dramatically, Elias. High drama takes effort, and so far, considering your place at Zebedee's figurative knee, you haven't impressed me."

Bridget's hand slid down Magnus's belly, then she wrapped her fingers around his cock. She wasn't even awake, and she was impressing him.

"Why has your ex asked me to join her for dinner, Magnus? She's suggested we meet right across the street from The George in Edinburgh."

Her favorite hotel. "Be careful, Elias."

"What makes you think I've accepted her invitation?"

"Because you are a randy damned idiot, and because you're not above a bit of bedroom espionage for the sake of family interests." And Celeste was beautiful and charming, no denying that.

"Are you telling me with whom I should and shouldn't *socialize*, Magnus?"

The question was careful, a balance between arrogance and curiosity. The arrogance was mostly feigned, the curiosity a mask for concern.

"She nearly destroyed me, Elias. I don't want you getting tangled up in her schemes, though tangle yourself in her sheets if you're so inclined. Her decisions in that regard have never been mine to gainsay in any case. Just be careful, and don't go getting notions about revenge or family honor."

"You're worried about *me*?"

He sounded perplexed, poor sod. "Somebody ought to be."

"And you aren't interested in getting back a bit of your own where Celeste is concerned? Have you gone English on me, Magnus? All sweet reason and diplomacy when what's wanted is a swat of the claymore to her bottom line?"

Bridget gave Magnus a luscious, little squeeze.

"You've been spending too much time around Zebedee. Just get me those whisky samples. Celeste owes me, and I'll be the one wielding that claymore. You can swing whatever puny dirk is at hand, if you're so inclined."

"I'll have you know my dirk is not—"

Magnus ended the call, and Bridget shifted so her head disappeared beneath the covers. For the next twenty minutes, Magnus strove to focus on the frigid Scottish burn that supplied the water for his whisky, and even that wasn't enough to distract him from the pleasure Bridget wrought.

* * *

"You have to tell them," Magnus said.

"I don't have to do anything." Fate had thrust three step-brothers upon Bridget. She'd quickly learned that the male animal responded well to clear, consistent boundaries.

Magnus stopped in the middle of the sidewalk. Snow was piled all around them, but in typical Montana fashion, the town had barely paused for yesterday's storm. The parking lots had been plowed, the streets were clear, and melt water formed a steady stream in the gutters and ditches.

"Let me put it to you like this," Magnus said. "Shamus knows something is wrong. Luke and Patrick will soon realize something is bothering Shamus, and then you'll have all three of them feeling hurt and ridiculous because you didn't trust them with your troubles."

They were outside the Cupcake, the noon sun finding red highlights in Magnus's hair. He'd worn a black wool kilt with hiking boots and a pair of thick wool socks that made a Highland cow look scantily clad by comparison. His fisherman's sweater was a similarly sturdy knit, and his down vest hung open.

"Howdy, Bridget. You going to introduce me to your friend?" Martina had come out of the Cupcake, a white box in her hand. She lived two blocks over and probably made this trek at least twice a day.

Magnus slapped on a smile, transforming himself from lecturing pest to Friday night fantasy.

"Magnus Cromarty." He offered Martina his hand, and she, of course, held on a little too long.

"Martina, but you can call me whatever you please, as long as it's polite and that accent is genuine."

"I saw him first," Bridget said, "and I heard him first too. Come out to the ranch for Sunday pizza, and you can listen to him while he helps Shamus with the dishes."

"Fast work," Martina said to Magnus. "You're already doing dishes with the menfolk, and you've been in town less than a week."

Her tone was friendly, though her gaze was measuring. Martina had been a cop and could send out the watch-your-step vibe without so much as lifting an eyebrow.

"Give it a rest, Martina," Bridget said. "Magnus is just passing through. I meant what I said about pizza, and to heck with Shamus's delicate nerves."

"I'll excuse myself," Magnus said, "if the topic is another man's delicate nerves. Martina, a pleasure, and I'll look forward to furthering our acquaintance over pizza." He kissed Bridget's cheek and loped off across the street in the direction of the drugstore.

"I heartily approve of a man who's not too shy to buy his own latex," Martina said. "Even if he does wear a skirt. The question is, do you approve of him?"

"Am I under arrest for something?" Bridget asked, taking a seat on the bench outside the Cupcake's display window. "Walking down the street with a guy in broad daylight?"

Which had felt wonderful, weird, and normal, all at once. Magnus held doors, he walked on the outside, he had the guy-thing down to a gentlemanly routine. He would also pick up more condoms without being reminded, and Bridget didn't know whether to be pleased, impressed, or worried.

"Walking down the street with a guy who kisses you in broad daylight and makes it look sweet."

"Are you jealous?"

Martina took the place beside Bridget. Her legs were a good six inches longer than Bridget's, but her jeans were the same shade of faded blue.

"We haven't had a quilting orgy for more than a year, Bridget MacDeaver. The company at the Bar None gets old fast."

The valley had a quilting group, and they met at least nine months out of the year, but Bridget's attendance had lapsed.

"I've been hibernating."

Across the street, Magnus held the door for a lady who had an infant in a Roo Sling and a toddler in a stroller.

"What's Magnus Cromarty doing here, Bridget? The tourist weather is months away, and he's not from around here." Quintessential Montana skepticism laced Martina's question, and maybe a little of the cop's stubborn instincts. People came to Montana to play, and Magnus was tripping Martina's alarms.

"He's after my business, sort of."

"So he has good taste in women, but what's he *doing* here? The spring skiing will turn to crap soon, the fish aren't reliably biting yet, construction won't start up for a few weeks. It's the shoulder season for every kind of fun we have to offer, and yet, here he is."

School had been canceled today, and a steady stream of teenagers banged in and out of the Cupcake. Montana schools took spring break in March as often as not, probably in defense of teacher sanity. A snow day in April qualified as another much-needed break.

"Magnus owns a distillery," Bridget said. "He's here on business. I have something he needs for his whisky, something he couldn't look for in Scotland without causing a lot of talk in a very inbred industry. He says he's interested in buying into the Logan Bar distillery, but that can't happen."

A promise was a promise, and Bridget had promised her grandpa that the legacy would be kept safe from all threats of harm, even good-looking Scottish charmers.

One of the girls coming out of the Cupcake stopped dead in her tracks when she spotted Martina, but Martina didn't seem to notice, and the kid scuttled off with her friends.

Bridget kept her voice down. "Martina, are you okay?"

"Why do you ask?"

Not a yes. "Because that kid just looked at you as if you'd arrested her uncle on multiple counts of domestic violence. You haven't quit the force, have you?"

Martina got out her phone, though it had neither buzzed nor chimed.

"Tell Shamus you're still carrying a badge," Bridget said. "If you're putting him off because you have official business to tend to, just let him know that much. He'll wait forever if you need him to, but he won't be made a fool of."

"When you were lawyering," Martina said, "you ever hear any talk about trafficking?"

Despite bright sunshine in a perfect blue sky, the day turned ominous. "Of course. It happens. Montana is the world's biggest, coldest dead end in the eyes of some girls. Whether you're stuck on a ranch or a reservation, it's easy to fall prey to the pimps and handlers when your parents don't understand you and school's an exercise in futility."

"It's the girls' answer to the gangs," Martina said. "They feel a sense of belonging, they get good at what they do, they make money at it like they'll never make money ringing up cupcakes, and whoever's handling them makes sure they're safe from other kinds of harm… until they're a little too independent, or a little too greedy."

And then the girls disappeared to a foreign market, or worse.

So… an undercover investigation, most likely. "I heard a few rumors when I was lawyering," Bridget said. "The prosecutors have that task force, and Nathan represented the occasional solicitation or prostitution client."

The penalties for prostitution weren't as severe as the penalties for pimping, and the penalties for trafficking a child under twelve included at least the possibility of a hundred-year sentence. Children over the age of twelve, though, weren't as well protected by the law.

"You ever wonder why those clients come to Nathan for representation?"

"Because Nate's good at what he does, and once you tap into a vein of work, the clients tend to give you more business by word of mouth."

Martina put her phone away and said nothing.

"I'm out of the legal business, Martina. I have no ownership interest, no stock, no seat on the board, nothing. I quitclaimed to Nathan a year ago and haven't looked back."

Careful listening had assured Bridget that the gossips concluded she'd compensated Nathan for taking on additional work, management responsibility, and business disruption. The legal effect had been a clean break—Bridget had made sure of that. She'd handed over her life savings for deposit in the operating account, though most of it went to cover the personal injury settlement.

Nate had immediately re-incorporated, meaning Bridget couldn't get the money back even if Nate came into a windfall.

"Whatever you do, Bridget, don't go back. Hang out a new shingle on your own or pass the bar in some other state, but stay clear of Nathan Sturbridge."

This went beyond advice between friends. "I intend to. You stay clear of him too."

Martina stood. "He's been asking after you, and after your Scotsman."

Bridget rose as well, though sitting in the sun had felt good. Spring would arrive, just not today.

"The last person whose concern I'd trust is Nate Sturbridge. He screwed me over, but good."

Martina put on dark sunglasses. "You ever want to tell me the details, I might be able to do something about it."

Magnus's admonition came back to Bridget: She should tell her brothers why she wasn't practicing law, why she could not practice law. Before she aired that dirty laundry with Martina, she owed her brothers a heads-up.

"Come over on Sunday for some pizza, and we'll talk."

Martina passed Bridget the white box. "For Shamus. Huckleberry scones are his favorite." She sauntered off, and a trio of young men emerging from the Cupcake stopped to goggle, their expressions reverent.

Magnus trotted across the street, his kilt flapping about his knees. "I hope I didn't abandon you at the wrong time."

"Just catching up with a friend. I invited Martina out to the ranch this weekend for pizza."

Though Martina hadn't accepted.

"So I heard. Does that mean you're refusing my invitation to travel to Scotland? I'd entrust you to no less hospitality than my own home and my own most charming cousin. You might get to meet Zebedee, the current Earl of Strathdee. What's in the box?"

"A peace offering. Martina asked me to deliver these scones to Shamus."

"And so we shall, once we've done our bit for the local economy and my own somewhat depleted reserves of energy."

"Altitude, Magnus. You have to hydrate, I'm telling you."

Nathan Sturbridge came out of the hardware store next door, a bag of rock salt in his hand. Bridget held eye contact, because backing down when Nate issued a challenge had nearly ruined her the only time she'd done it.

"Why if it isn't my long-lost, best-ever, former law partner. Bridget, how you doin'?"

He offered a bare hand. Bridget shook, glad to be wearing gloves. "Nate. I'm fine. You?"

"Just enjoying the hell out of this lovely weather. Flies will be hatching next, and won't that be the most fun ever? I'm Nate Sturbridge."

He stuck his hand out toward Magnus, and abruptly, Bridget felt uneasy—more uneasy than usual around Nate.

"Magnus Cromarty. Pleased to meet you."

Except he wasn't. Magnus's tone was cordial, his handshake friendly, but his eyes had gone as cold as a Montana sky on the nasty end of a January blizzard.

"Interesting attire, Cromarty," Nate said, eyeing Magnus's kilt. "You hail from Scotland?"

"I have that honor. You're a lawyer?"

"I'm not sure that qualifies as an honor, but it's how I earn my living. What brings you to Montana?"

"I needed a change of scene."

"Lord knows we have scenery. I'll wish you a pleasant visit. Bridget, give me a call when you have a minute. I have an interesting case I'd like to discuss with you." He touched his hat brim and headed off toward his truck.

"Right now," Magnus said, "I'd like to tackle him to the ground and pound that handsome smile right off his face."

"The longer I know you, the more I like you, Magnus Cromarty, though I generally frown on violence at first sight. Let's see what's on the Cupcake's menu before we head out to the distillery."

Magnus's gaze remained on Nate's retreating figure. "He reminds me of my ex-wife. Lovely to look at, charm oozing from every orifice, almost too good to be true. No wonder you trusted him."

"I didn't, actually, which is why I handled the books, but talking about the law practice has stirred up my curiosity about something."

Nate climbed into his truck and drove off, neglecting to either stop or signal before he turned onto the street.

"I'm curious about what he wanted to speak with you about," Magnus said. "A blackmailer seldom knows when to quit, though Sturbridge has to recall that he obliterated all of your reserves." Magnus held the door to the Cupcake for Bridget, and the warm, yeasty scent of freshly baked carbs nearly restored her mood.

Except... Nate wanted to talk to her, and that was a bad thing, like a nagging ache at the base of her skull, just waiting to blossom into a migraine.

Only worse.

"Let's get something to go," Bridget said. "I want to be heading back to the ranch before all the melting freezes and the roads turn to black ice."

Magnus ordered for her, paid the total, and carried the bags out to the truck. The afternoon was sunny, mild by post-storm standards, and pretty. Bridget was about to give a tour of the distillery to one of the few people who could appreciate her business for the gem it was.

And yet, seeing Nate had been like spotting a rat scuttling away from the feed room. Trouble was afoot, more trouble than she'd had when she'd awoken in Magnus's arms.

"You drive," Bridget said, passing Magnus the keys. "I'll do some quality assurance on the goodies."

He unlocked the doors and held hers for her. "You trust me to drive on the wrong side of the road?"

"I trust you to handle just about anything." She climbed in, and Magnus stood by the truck, his hand on the door.

"Do you mean that?"

She took the bags of food from him. One bag held ham and cheese croissants made with more butter than physics could explain. Another held a pint of broccoli cheddar soup that should have single-handedly restored the reputation of broccoli as a food source.

Bridget was more interested in the veiled question in Magnus's eyes. "I trust you, Magnus. I don't like that I trust you, and I didn't plan on it, but here we are, and the soup's getting cold."

He looked around, then leaned in and kissed her. "I trust you too."

Those weren't the traditional words signaling that a romance had found more substantial footing, and yet, to Bridget, Magnus's words meant everything. A year ago, she had failed her clients, failed her family, and failed her own expectations. Nate was circling again, like a starving coyote sniffing around a half-full dumpster.

And yet, Magnus had come to her to rescue his whisky, and she would not fail him.

He started the truck and let it idle for a moment. "You mentioned that your curiosity has been stirred up, and because there's not an inch of me you've failed to explore—God be thanked for Yankee initiative—now I'm wondering what's on your mind."

He pulled out of the parking lot at a sedate pace, while Bridget inhaled sheer, gustatory bliss.

"I'm wondering now, when I should have asked myself a year ago, *why* did Nate steal from me? Technically, he stole from the business, but the money came out of my pocket. Why? What was his motive, when he knew I'd see exactly what he'd done."

Magnus navigated the post-snowfall traffic, which was made a little trickier by occasional patches of packed snow on the road surface and the odd pile of snow narrowing the travel lanes.

"You mean, Nate essentially killed the goose who was laying golden eggs?"

"Not to be arrogant, but I ran the practice. I handled the clients, revenue was growing steadily, and we landed that big personal injury case only because I knew that aspect of the law cold. The insurance companies respected me, and more big cases were likely to come along."

"Was there anything special about that case?"

Good question. "I can't discuss details, because all parties and counsel signed a nondisclosure. It was the sort of case that puts a practice firmly on its feet, though."

"If I'm considering buying your business, and I sign a nondisclosure agreement, can you share details then?"

Bridget thought about it, while the bags of fresh food in her lap and the seat heaters under her butt and at her back cocooned her in warmth.

"If you sign a nondisclosure, I can tell you about that case, but I'm not selling to you, Magnus. I'll fix your whisky as a professional courtesy, but come locusts, auditors, or addled step-brothers, I'm keeping hold of my business."

Or the business was keeping hold of her, and her future, dang it all to perdition.

"So we'll tour your distillery," Magnus said, "and when we get back to the ranch, you can tell your brothers what happened with your law practice."

She ought to. She'd meant to. "I'll think about it."

She was stalling, though, and Magnus's smile said he knew it. The truth was, if Magnus sat in on the discussion with Luke, Shamus, and Patrick, Bridget would find a way to tell them what had happened.

How to stop them from going after Nate with malice aforethought would be a trickier challenge.

CHAPTER TEN

Distilling whisky required only three ingredients—water, barley, and yeast—but the decisions to be made between the barley and the bottle were endless.

Which barley to use? Higher sugar content was desirable but costly, and the logistics of transporting the grain affected the price and freshness of the crop.

Once the barley had begun to germinate, how long until the germination process was stopped?

How much peat—if any—to use in the fire that dried the malted barley?

What sort of yeast and how much to add?

What water source to use, and to what temperatures should the water be heated and then cooled?

Should the washbacks be Scottish larch, Oregon pinewood, or stainless steel?

The head distiller made most of those calls, and yet, for Magnus many of the decision points had been traversed generations ago. Bridget's distillery was an altogether different animal.

One entire wall was glass, bringing a panorama of Montana mountains into the plant. A fast-moving stream ran from the nearby foothills directly under the distillery, chunks of melting snow bobbing past in water so clear, Magnus could count every pebble in the streambed.

Security cameras were discreetly tucked into corners of a beamed ceiling. He'd noticed cameras at nearly every distillery he'd toured in the States. At Cromarty Distilleries no such precautions had been taken, though he'd institute them upon his return.

Bridget's office struck him as more of a bedsit than the nucleus of a business empire. Her desk was a wooden behemoth that looked to have spent time in a covered wagon. A long sofa lined one wall, three different patchwork quilts folded over the top and worn pillows tucked against the armrests. A coffee table covered with whisky periodicals sat before the sofa, and a braided rug covered the flagstone floor. A kiva occupied one corner, and the pungent scent of mesquite blended with the yeasty aroma of whisky-making.

She had a mini-fridge and microwave in another corner, but no proper table where she could take a meal. Magnus's office lacked the same feature.

"Is there a conference room or break room where we should eat?" he asked.

"The guys will be changing shifts soon, and I like to leave them their privacy." Bridget set the bags of food on the coffee table, right on top of the magazines.

Magnus organized the magazines by date and piled them on an end table. "Do you read these?" "Cover to cover, especially the ads. The whisky industry employs some of the smartest advertising minds on the planet."

She opened a set of curtains, revealing another magnificent view of the mountains and sky. From this perspective, the afternoon sun turned the rushing stream to liquid silver.

While Magnus set out the food, Bridget rummaged in a desk drawer. "You could put some honey in my tea."

He obliged—Montana organic clover honey—and waited for Bridget to join him on the sofa.

"This is a nondisclosure agreement," she said, passing him three copies of a two-page form. "It says you won't tell anybody anything about my business, except as necessary to run your business in the ordinary course. That means you can tell them where you're staying, or that you held a business negotiation with me to justify your expense report. Nothing about my whisky-making, my books, my legal arrangements, my pending liabilities, the hours I keep, who's on my payroll, or the make and model of my copying machine."

Based on the size of her copying machine, the make and model were matters of antiquity.

"I'm surprised you let me tour the facility before I signed this."

"The tours are open to the public. This time of year, we schedule them for weekends, but come summer, they'll be going six days a week."

Magnus signed the form in triplicate and folded one copy to tuck into his rucksack.

"Give that back," Bridget said, waggling her fingers. "Shamus will notarize your signature and make you sign all three forms again if he's in a finicky mood."

Magnus surrendered the release and passed Bridget a croissant.

"For what we are about to receive," she said, "we thank Thee, and if it's not asking too much, please send Nathan Sturbridge a permanent case of indigestion and boot blisters, amen."

"Amen. Remind me never to cross you."

"Remind yourself. Did you put honey in my tea?"

"Yes, ma'am." Magnus passed her a serving of chips—fries, rather. "Does hunger make you snappish, or has Sturbridge upset you?"

"Yes to both. What could he possibly want to talk to me about?"

"We'll probably find out soon enough. What are the laws here about taping conversations?"

Bridget took a bite of her croissant, closed her eyes, and chewed. "I was hungry."

Hungry. *Well.*

Magnus was dealing with an interesting case of chronic arousal. Watching the Montana breeze whip a strand of hair across Bridget's mouth, he got *ideas*. Seeing her utter concentration around the equipment and employees making her whisky, those ideas became imaginings.

Watching her sit, knees splayed, while she devoured her food, the imaginings became fantasies.

That he could be sexually preoccupied while in a whisky-making facility was a profound relief, and a little amusing.

"I was hungry too," Magnus said. "And you have a lovely distillery. Is that stream your water supply?"

"You betcha," Bridget replied, considering a big wedge of fried potato. "I own—and I do mean I, and I do mean own—about five thousand acres of those foothills, and that stream originates in a spring-fed pond at the lip of a hanging valley. I own the valley, the pond, and the water, thanks to my sainted grandpap's will. I lease the water rights to the distillery on a nonexclusive basis year to year."

In Scotland, drought was a foreign concept, an inconvenience suffered by English farmers, poor blighters. In the American West, water was serious business, and Bridget's ownership of water rights was enviable.

"And you grow your own barley?"

"Try to. Last year, that didn't go so well. Damned hailstorm. Are you going to eat that croissant?"

Magnus bit off a mouthful of takeout heaven. "Tell me about the distribution arrangements for your product."

While finishing off her croissant, Bridget described a convoluted set of liquor licensing and distribution laws, the likes of which Magnus had never encountered. Breaking into this market from outside the United States, even from outside of Montana, would be a complicated undertaking, and here again, Bridget's position was ideal.

She was an attorney admitted to the Montana bar who understood both the liquor laws and the whisky market. She was within easy delivery distance of resorts that catered to those with spare time and spare money.

Scottish distillers would hire her to consult and pay handsomely for her expertise, irrespective of her ability to age whisky to its maximum potential.

"Do we spare Shamus a scone or destroy all the evidence?" Bridget asked, taking a considering sip of her tea.

"The issue is not the scones, Bridget. It's Martina's thoughtfulness."

"Right," Bridget said, opening a small white box. "And two scones can be as thoughtful as four."

She'd learned that reasoning from her brothers. "Or three. I'll pass for now."

She shrugged, broke a scone in half, and tore off a corner. "Nathan Sturbridge is up to something."

And Bridget's mind never rested, except in those lovely, drowsy moments after a thorough loving. Magnus brushed her hair back over her shoulder.

"Tell me about the case he used to blackmail you. I've signed the nondisclosure, and we have privacy."

Also a nice long couch, three quilts, some pillows, and a door that locked.

"The case was easy. One of the smaller ski resorts didn't correctly count the chairs on its longest lift at the end of the day. A seventeen-year-old boy ended up spending the whole night sitting thirty feet above the hillside. At seven thousand feet in mid-March, that could have been a death sentence."

"He survived?"

"He was fine. The night was unusually mild, no wind to speak of. He was a local boy and had dressed for the slopes, right down to a water bottle and a few protein bars in his fanny pack. By morning he was cold and pissed off, but he had no medical issues."

"So why the lawsuit?"

"Because American tort law, dude. Pain and suffering, mental trauma, slap any label you want on it. The resort's lawyers were desperate to ensure the kid kept his mouth shut about the whole thing. A lawsuit was a way to back up that desperation with a fat check and a signed court order. I knew his mom from my quilting group, so I got the case, and a fine case it was too."

"Until Sturbridge turned to thievery."

Bridget put the unfinished half of her scone back in the box. "Him again. I don't even begrudge Nate the money. If he'd come to me and said he needed it to get his mom into a decent assisted-living facility, I would have passed over the funds without question and worked out some long-term repayment. But Nate cheated me out of something valuable that I worked hard to earn. That, I cannot forgive."

Magnus kissed her cheek, because she'd put his own sentiments regarding his ex into words. "Nor should you." He was considering turning the kiss into something more, when Bridget's phone vibrated against his side.

"If this is one of my brothers…" She scowled at the screen. "It's Nathan Sturbridge."

"Will he keep calling?"

"Yes." She swiped into the call and gestured for Magnus to lean close enough to hear both sides of the conversation. "Nathan, what the hell do you want now?"

Magnus heard an indrawn breath on the other end.

"Now, Bridget," Sturbridge crooned, "is that any way to talk to the man who could still cost you your license to practice law and see you sent to prison for embezzling?"

* * *

Dealing with Nate always upset Bridget. Most of the upset was fear.

Fear that he'd want more money, and she wouldn't have it.

Fear that he'd go after the ranch somehow, fear that he'd find another way to put her fingerprints on shady business.

Fear that she'd lose her distillery, the last link she had to her father and to the grandfather who'd made a distiller out of her. The distillery and the land it sat on were the last resources she controlled that might be some protection for her brothers and any family they might have.

She took a slow breath, a tactic she'd learned in the courtroom. Make the bastard wait until she was good and ready to reply.

"That, Nathan Sturbridge, is how I talk to lying, cheating weasels who are a disgrace to the Montana bar association. What do you want?"

"The statute of limitations in Montana for most felonies is twenty-one years, sugar pie."

"It's five years except for murder and a few other forms of homicide, which have no statute of limitation." For theft involving breach of a fiduciary obligation, the fuse was a lot shorter: one year after discovery of the offense. Sexual misconduct against minors had some other specific provisions, which Bridget wasn't about to recite for Nate's edification.

"Whatever, darlin'. Your dainty signature is on a check for a huge sum of cash that should never have gone anywhere but straight to the client. Nobody but thee and me know that I was the one to cash that check. Do I have your attention now, or should I file a complaint with the nice folks at the Office of Disciplinary Counsel?"

Never accept a forced choice. That was Bridget's advice for a witness being asked leading questions on cross-examination.

"What do you want?"

"To talk a little business. Seems your property is under consideration for an easement request. Nothing major, but it could result in some revenue for all concerned."

All concerned being Nate, of course. "What sort of easement?"

"Just a little bitty pipeline. No big deal. I'm in a position to negotiate sweet terms for you, if you're willing to see reason."

His proposition was so outrageous, so audacious, that Bridget nearly dropped the phone.

Magnus covered her hand with his own, as if he sensed the depth of her upset.

Her rage. That was what lay beneath the dorsal fin of fear circling her life. A growing ire that wouldn't count the cost when it came to taking back from Nate Sturbridge what he'd stolen from her.

So this is revenge? This savage, empowering delusion that an eye for an eye was the solution to all problems? A year ago, Bridget would have recoiled in horror from her own reaction.

Today, she struggled to balance her anger with self-preservation and her family's safety.

"The Logan Bar doesn't exploit mineral resources."

"The Logan Bar is a ranch teetering on the brink of extinction, and all that wealth sitting in the ground doesn't do anybody any good unless you go after it. I'm only talking about an easement, Bridget—nobody says the pipeline will ever be built—and you don't own that distillery all by your lonesome. I'm sure Patrick would be willing to talk to me if you're determined to be mule-headed."

Patrick, the most environmentally aware of the Logan brothers, might kill Nate for mentioning a pipeline easement. Thank God that Bridget had never discussed the particulars of her family business with Nate.

Magnus scrawled something on a sticky note. *Keep your enemies closer.*

Bridget grabbed for the sticky note, ready to crumple it up and toss it in the trash. She snatched it off the notepad, her anger swiveling to include all the men—*because it was always men*—who presumed to tell her how to run her business and her life.

Magnus scrawled another word: *Please.* Then, *I want a future with you.*

Well… Dayum.

"I've stunned you with the generosity of my offer," Nate said. "I'm willing to turn over a new leaf and put the past behind us. You were going to have to buy your way out of the practice anyway, and you know it. All you have to do is agree to some reasonable terms on an easement and allow me to handle the money end of it as your lawyer. It's a simple transaction, unless you force my hand."

He was such scum, such lying, manipulative, evil, vile, walking, smiling, flirting scum. Starving buzzards would have given Nate Sturbridge's rotting carcass a fail on the sniff test, he was such a disgrace to the food chain.

His reasonable tone dripped with the victimhood of the abuser: *You drive me to violence. It's not my fault you deserve a whuppin'.*

"Send an email to my business addy," Bridget said, because Nate was her enemy and always would be.

And maybe because Magnus wanted a future with her, or thought he did.

"No can do, sweet cheeks. Emails live forever and are discoverable, as we both know all too well. This little easement project hasn't hit the public-notice phase yet. Meet me at the Bar None tonight."

Magnus shook his head, though Bridget had no intention of letting Nate order her around.

"No can do, buttwipe. I have a Scottish whisky baron strutting around the Logan Bar expecting five-star hand-holding. If you and I talk, it's at the time and place of my choosing."

"He's a lucky baron. We'll talk, just make sure it's soon."

Bridget ended the call and passed Magnus her phone, lest she pitch it through the window.

"I truly do hate him," she said. "I hate him with a burning, thousand-sun, relentless, soul-deep conviction that Montana would be a better place without that pusillanimous polecat above ground and sucking air. That I even think such thoughts ought to scare me. I'm still an officer of the court and a decent human being, I hope, and Nate isn't half so clever as he thinks he is."

Magnus wrapped his arms around her. "You were magnificent."

Bridget leaned against him, her heart beating erratically. "I'm terrified. Terrified he'll wreck my life, terrified I'll do something I regret to wreck his. I'm tired of being terrified, and furious, because Nate depends on fear to work his stupid schemes."

Magnus produced a handkerchief. The sight of it—white cotton, a purple thistle with greenery embroidered in one corner—coincided with a trickle of warmth against Bridget's cheek.

"Crap. I hate to cry."

Magnus settled her in his lap on the sofa until she'd cried herself past all dignity. Her eyes smarted, and her nose stung, and she probably looked about as appealing as roadkill. The sheer relief of giving in to emotions grown too heavy to carry alone, though, left a lightness behind and sense of gratitude for Magnus's company.

"Sturbridge made you cry," he said. "For that alone, I agree with your estimation of him. I hope you realize he admitted his wrongdoing in my hearing."

Snowmelt was warmer than Magnus's tone, but his hands tracing Bridget's features were tenderness itself.

"Hearsay," Bridget said, rubbing her cheek against Magnus's chest. "I can't get him convicted on the basis of hearsay, but I'm still glad he admitted before a witness what a weasel he's been."

Magnus produced his flask and passed it to Bridget. She sat up enough to take a fortifying sip, then another.

"If he admitted it once, he can admit it again," Magnus said, taking a nip and capping the flask. "We'll make sure that when he does, we're there to hold him accountable."

Bridget indulged in a few more minutes of snuggling in Magnus's arms. The distillery was a peaceful, happy place, where she was queen of all she surveyed and damned good at it. Showing Magnus around had felt a little awkward, a little foolish.

And a lot wonderful. She had promised her grandpap to defend this citadel at any cost, but Grandpap had never envisioned a future with Magnus Cromarty.

Bridget got off Magnus's lap, collected the nondisclosure agreements, closed the blinds, and tucked his sticky note into her pocket.

"Time to go," she said. "The roads will freeze as soon as the sun sets, and that's worse news by the mile."

Magnus collected the leftovers, kissed her, and held the door. "Time to talk to your brothers?"

A suggestion, a question, a mere observation. The guy had good instincts.

"Time to talk to my brothers. Are you hydrating, Magnus? The croissants were salty." She didn't tell him he looked tired to her. Neither of them had gotten much sleep the night before.

"I'll refill my water bottle from your stream, if that's allowed. I'm curious as to the taste. My uncle Fergus insists the water we use is half the reason our single malts are such good quality."

"You can take the distiller out of Scotland…"

Bridget warmed up the truck while Magnus knelt by the stream, the late afternoon sun slanting over his shoulder. Prospectors had settled this part of Montana more one hundred and fifty years ago, and one of them might have crouched in that very spot, though he wouldn't have looked half so handsome.

While Magnus chugged from his water bottle and then refilled it, Bridget adjusted the heat.

He'd written *I want a future with you* plain as day, and Bridget had the evidence tucked into the pocket of her jeans. No sense denying the obvious just because it was stupid, inconvenient, irrational, and doomed.

She wanted a future with him too.

* * *

Celeste MacKinnon, formerly Celeste Cromarty, was a striking woman. She moved with the benevolent confidence of a lady who knew herself to be attractive, powerful, and smarter than most of the people goggling at her.

Elias thus refused to goggle, though every time he saw Celeste, he understood a little better why Magnus had been smitten.

Fascinated was a better word.

Elias rose and kissed Celeste's cheek, and all around him, he could feel the other diners, the men especially, envying him that privilege. One of Celeste's greatest assets was her sense of timing. She lingered near for only a moment, but in that moment, women speculated, men shifted in their seats, and the wait staff preened to see such an elegant lady among their patrons.

Elias resisted the urge to wave away a cloud of Joy, though he generally liked that scent on other women. On Celeste, the fragrance lacked its usual appeal.

"Elias Brodie, if you grow any more handsome, somebody will have to marry you for your own safety. How are you?"

He wasn't *that* handsome—tall, auburn-haired, as most Cromartys tended to be, with a good-sized beak, the better to sniff whisky—but when Celeste smiled at Elias, offering to admit him to the friendly conspiracy of the very beautiful, he felt handsome.

She was a strawberry-blond cross between Grace Kelly and Julia Roberts, leggy and lush, with eyes the color of wood hyacinths. She wore a wrapped V-neck silk blouse of the same blue and a taupe pencil skirt that showed off her hips and legs without being too tight or too short.

A slim gold bracelet draped about her wrist, and a scarf knotted into a loose choker echoed the blue and the taupe along with soft greens and a shade of pink that likely flattered both her nipples and her lips.

Magnus had once missed a board meeting to take Celeste scarf shopping in Budapest. At the time, Elias had envied his cousin the courage to indulge in such romance. Soon after, he'd felt sorry for the poor bastard.

"I am well," he said, "and you look to be thriving. I trust Daryl is in good health?" Daryl MacKinnon was the present Mr. Celeste. He prided himself on knowing everything worth knowing about making whisky. The rumor among distillers was that MacKinnon was a competent distiller, but nobody had taught him much about making money.

"Daryl has abandoned me for the last of the polo matches." Celeste affected a pout. "I suspect he's fonder of his ponies than of his wife, but one bears up under these tribulations. Are you hungry?"

She reached for the menu and shot a little smile at Elias that suggested he might be hungry for her.

"Famished, and envious of Daryl's adventures on horseback. I haven't been on the polo field in far too long."

She lowered her lashes. "Do you miss time in the saddle?"

Oh, for feck's sake. Abruptly, Elias wished he'd stayed home in his sweats watching reruns of European football championships and sending nosy texts to his cousins.

"I don't miss being sore for days at a time, or getting pitched on my arse at forty miles an hour so my horse can play leapfrog with my battered carcass."

She smirked at her menu, as if Elias had said something adorably masculine.

"I have to ask how Magnus is," she said, slowly turning a page. She'd doubtless have the grilled salmon and pick at it, chicken being too pedestrian and prawns too untidy. For dessert, chocolate truffle cake with Grand Marnier ganache, though she wouldn't finish that either.

Elias had been engaged when Magnus and Celeste had married, and he was still great friends with his former fiancée. She'd not liked Celeste, and at the time, Elias had thought his fiancée a wee bit jealous. Celeste was beautiful, charming, gracious, and poised, after all.

Elias's fiancée had claimed that everything was a prop for Celeste—clothes, food, cutlery, cars, pets, men, *everything* was a potential performance-enhancing convenience. Elias had eventually agreed that even a husband could fall into the same category.

Thank God that Magnus had slipped from Celeste's grasp with his soul and his business intact.

"Magnus is off in Montana on a holiday," Elias said. "Spring skiing, trout fishing, casinos, I'm not sure what all is involved."

Celeste pretended to peruse the menu, but she'd paged past the dinner selections and was well into the wines and whiskies.

"Montana? Isn't it still winter there?"

"I can't say. Does anything on the menu tempt you?"

She frankly inspected him. "I'll have the salmon. What about you?"

"Steak." A man had to keep up his strength when behind enemy lines.

Celeste patted his hand, except her gesture was more of a caress, and well she knew it. "We can be honest with each other, can't we, Elias?"

"I'd rather you didn't attempt to deceive me."

Another pat. "Magnus doesn't take holidays, so you've already told one fib. Is he soliciting funds from American investors? I've told Daryl there's opportunity in that direction. What Americans lack in respect for tradition, they make up for in extravagant investment schemes."

Elias consulted to numerous not-for-profit organizations throughout the European market. Celeste might credibly have turned the topic to business, but she instead chatted interminably about mutual acquaintances and asked about Cromarty and Brodie family members to whom she'd never sent so much as a greeting card.

She nibbled her sesame-glazed salmon. She pronounced a fine Gewürztraminer too arrogant for such a subtle and complex main dish, though pleasant enough as a complement to certain cheeses. She named several of those cheeses—the notably stinky Maroilles among them—and patted Elias's hand a half-dozen times.

Good God, the woman was tiresome.

"Will you share a dessert with me, Elias?"

"I'm as fond of a sticky toffee pudding as the next man."

"That was always Magnus's favorite." She glanced around, as if half of Edinburgh was hanging on her next words. "I worry about Magnus, you know."

Ach, finally. "Any particular reason?"

"It's been years since the divorce, though we remain quite fond of each other. I've noticed a change in him lately. He's preoccupied, perhaps even a bit... anxious?"

Elias considered and discarded several honest rejoinders, among them: *If I'd been married to you, I'd need medication for my anxiety.*

"Perhaps Magnus needed a holiday."

"He's not on holiday, Elias. Magnus doesn't know how to relax. They make whisky nearly everywhere in the States. He's looking for a buyer, a white knight."

And dear, dear Celeste was just eaten up with concern for poor Magnus? "I'm on his board of directors, Celeste. Without violating confidentiality, I can assure you the business is sound and Magnus has never mentioned looking for a buyer."

"Elias, I love you dearly, but a gold-plated academic degree and a few quarterly meetings don't give you the feel for the industry or for Magnus Cromarty that I have. I'm the tenth generation of my family to deal in top-quality single malt, and I tell you in strictest confidence that Magnus is about to step on a land mine. His books won't show the problems he has in his warehouses."

"His inventories are all regularly audited, and his products sell well."

Celeste fell silent while the kilted waiter whisked plates from the table.

"We'll take the rest of that fish in a box, please," Elias said, "and the last of the steak."

"Of course, sir. Are we having dessert this evening?"

"Celeste?"

She lifted her wineglass, holding it so that it caught the candlelight. "Perhaps a small serving of the chocolate truffle. Elias, I trust you'll share a few bites?"

Would this meal never end? "Of course, and the sticky toffee pudding for me."

The waiter left, and Elias waited for Celeste to drop the other stiletto. Magnus was so well rid of this woman, Elias would congratulate him on his good sense the very next time they spoke.

"Magnus has a ticking bomb in his warehouse, Elias. His bicentennial year is a disaster in the making. Some of his own employees have said as much. It's getting grimmer by the year, and everything he's tried has made the situation worse."

Like all good liars, Celeste wove a plaid of truth and falsehood. Magnus did have a problem in the warehouse, but his employees wouldn't say a word about it to anybody—if they even knew. The distiller alone was responsible for sampling casks as they matured and making adjustments as necessary. The warehousemen, distilling staff, and other employees would no more sample the inventory uninvited than a banker would help himself to a handful of cash from the till.

Celeste had also misrepresented Magnus's efforts to deal with his ailing batch of whisky. He'd only recently become aware of the problem, and Magnus was the sort to gather information before taking action.

"What are you asking of me, Celeste? The distillery is all Magnus has, and he manages it without interference from me or the board." A slight exaggeration.

She set down her wineglass and leaned forward. "Let me help, Elias. If Magnus will give me a controlling interest in his distillery—all I need is fifty-one percent—I can trade him comparable shares in the MacKinnon operation. I'll quietly substitute some of MacKinnon's best batches for the dreadful mistake Magnus would serve as his bicentennial batch. Somebody needs to do something about this now, before Magnus draws attention to the situation."

The quiet substitution was easy. No distiller kept an entire year's inventory in one warehouse. If a warehouse burned to the ground, flooded, or collapsed under tons of snow, the risk was shared by many businesses rather than wiping out one or two. Casks of whisky moved from place to place all the time, and Celeste has likely exploited that fact to get the whisky into the wrong casks in the first place.

But that other detail—*give me a controlling interest in his distillery*—was asking Elias to commit a sin worse than treason.

And asking so prettily too.

"Assuming the problem you allude to is real," Elias said, "and not an overreaction to gossip or misinformation, your offer to help is appreciated. I can neither negotiate for nor obligate a business I do not own, however."

The desserts arrived, Elias's redolent of warm whisky sauce, Celeste's glistening with rich, dark ganache.

When the waiter had withdrawn, Celeste lifted a forkful of truffle cake. "You can both negotiate for and contractually bind Cromarty Distilleries, Elias. If Magnus is out of town, then you have his delegation, don't you? You're authorized to act in his stead until he returns, and that means you more or less own the business until Magnus is back. I'm trying to save that business and offering you an excellent opportunity to both diversify and avoid a very public disaster. Magnus will thank you for it, once he accepts that he's ruined a substantial portion of his most anticipated year."

She made a quasi-erotic production out of nibbling her cake.

Elias toyed with his whisky sauce.

Other than Magnus, only the person who'd mishandled the whisky in the first place would know there was a batch going sour in the Cromarty warehouse. Celeste had incriminated herself with that admission alone, though Elias wouldn't be able to prove her guilt.

"You have a memorandum of agreement drafted?" he asked.

"I do. Agreement in principle, good faith, due diligence, the usual safeguards. Cromarty's will get an interest in MacKinnon's equal in value to my controlling interest in Cromarty's, and nobody needs to know that Magnus has a disaster literally brewing."

Elias started on his sticky toffee pudding, which was some consolation for the whole bother of meeting with Celeste.

Her proposal presented several problems.

First, her memorandum doubtless held all manner of hidden traps and potholes. The Cromarty family attorneys would delight in finding those and neutralizing them.

Second, Magnus would be left with his ex-wife for a boss.

Which raised the third problem: Magnus would kill Elias, slowly and painfully, many times over, if Elias gave Celeste's scheme even an appearance of approval.

"I'm expected elsewhere later tonight," Elias said. "Send me your memorandum, though I make no promises or representations, Celeste. Liquidation of any significant asset requires board approval, as you well know."

"And you have a board meeting next week." She took another bite of her dessert, sliding the fork slowly from her mouth.

The waiter returned with the boxed leftovers and a bill, which Elias paid on the distillery's credit card. This was business, after all.

Nasty business.

"What a marvelous meal," Celeste pronounced when Elias had done justice to his sticky toffee pudding. "Will you walk me over to my hotel?"

"Of course. I'm parked on that side of the street."

He tended to all the gentlemanly inanities his aunties had pounded into him from boyhood: held the lady's lovely, utterly impractical silk jacket, held the door, offered his arm when they crossed the street. Celeste accepted each gesture as if indulging a favored vassal.

When they stepped back up onto the sidewalk, she kept her arm laced with Elias's. His car sat like a trusty steed not twenty yards ahead, just beyond the hotel entrance.

"You know, Elias, I believe in mixing business with pleasure. Will you join me for a nightcap?"

Elias recalled his last discussion with Magnus, and two impressions came to mind. Magnus had warned Elias to be cautious where Celeste was concerned, though even a cautious man occasionally slept with the enemy.

And Elias liked sex rather a lot. Always had, something of a family tradition, said to date from the first earl of Strathdee and his countess, who'd been separated for nearly ten years early in their marriage.

Accepting Celeste's invitation—the nightcap would be served in her suite, if not in her very bed—also created a tactical advantage: Adultery was considered proof that a Scottish marriage had suffered an "irretrievable breakdown." Elias could cheerfully testify for Daryl MacKinnon, if that poor soul ever sought to divest himself of Celeste's company.

The idea appealed—some.

Though Magnus had also said he did not want Celeste destroyed, an admission that had both pleased and surprised Elias. A year ago, Magnus would have delighted in Celeste's downfall.

"Will you come upstairs with me, Elias?"

The aunties mentally booted Elias in the arse for even considering it. "I honestly haven't got time, alas for me. Thank you for an enjoyable meal, and I'll look for an email from you by Monday."

"I've already sent it," Celeste said, leaning up to kiss his cheek.

She prowled away, the street lights providing Elias an excellent view of her retreat. She had pressed close—provocatively close—but all that had earned her was a grease spot on her jacket where she'd mashed against the bag of leftover sesame salmon.

CHAPTER ELEVEN

What sort of man—what sort of idiot—informed a woman he wanted a future with her by scratching his sentiments on a pink sticky note while that woman did battle with her enemy?

A man in love, that's what sort.

Magnus shoved a log into the guesthouse woodstove and resumed his place on the couch. He gravitated toward the corner where he'd cuddled with Bridget—more idiocy—and indulged in the further lunacy of wrapping himself in one of her quilts.

She was at the ranch house, having dinner with her brothers. Magnus was to join the family afterward for what amounted to a counsel of war.

His phone buzzed, and his heart leaped in hopes Bridget was summoning him.

Life was just full of disappointments. "Elias, greetings."

"You owe me," Elias growled. "You owe me until our progeny are squabbling over whose turn it is to visit us at Hogmanay."

"We'll be dropping in on them," Magnus replied, "because I'll be bringing the whisky as first footer, and you'll be tagging along with me. What has you up past your bedtime now?"

"I had dinner with Celeste. She's after your distillery."

Magnus tucked the red and brown quilt closer. "Bold, even for her." And he hadn't seen that maneuver coming. "What's her strategy?"

"She's being gracious in victory. She gets a controlling interest in your distillery, you get a comparably valuable chunk of stock in MacKinnon's, and she'll keep her mouth shut about how you've wrecked an entire year's worth of fine single malt. She'll even give you a few barrels of decent MacKinnon to take its place."

Magnus leaned his head back and studied the knotty pine ceiling paneling. "A controlling interest in Cromarty Distilleries? Let me guess, my stock is to be signed over to her personally, not to MacKinnon's, so that when she leaves Daryl sitting on his arse in the dust, there's no question the Cromarty stock is hers. My reciprocal interest in MacKinnon's, however, will be held by Cromarty Distilleries, which means Celeste is essentially getting half my business plus fifty-one percent of whatever MacKinnon stock she transfers to me."

"Took me an hour of puzzling out the fine print, but that's essentially her scheme. There's more."

"With Celeste, there's always more."

"She knows you're out of town and knows I have your delegation. She pressured me to sign a memorandum of understanding in your absence, agreeing to the deal in principle."

The logs in the woodstove fell, sending sparks dancing up the flue. "Or she'll start the talk about my bicentennial year being the most pathetic excuse for single malt ever to come out of an oak barrel. By the time I bottle it, I won't be able to sell it as anything other than industrial disinfectant."

Despair wound around Magnus's mood, like the cold drafts that blew along the guesthouse floors. Who knew where they leaked into the dwelling, but even with the woodstove roaring, they were a reminder of snow on the ground.

Melting snow.

"Elias, I'm sending you a water sample. Please get it to the lab straightaway for analysis." Delicious water, if such a thing were possible. Full of minerals, would be Magnus's guess.

"I'm so touched. You said please. The aunties would be proud of you. What the fuckity-fuck-fuck-fuck am I supposed to do about your ex-wife?"

Dinner with Celeste had unnerved Elias, which was hard to do. "Nothing, at the moment, though I'll get back to you in the next day or two."

"You'll *get back* to me? I'm supposed to facilitate a hostile takeover of your business, cast my ethics to the wind, betray half the elders on our notably spindly family tree, and risk Zebedee's rare but substantial wrath, while you fish for *trout*—"

"I need to discuss the situation with Bridget. She has instincts I lack and whisky I love."

"Bridget? She's the cowgirl with the distill—"

Magnus disconnected from Elias to accept a text from Bridget: *Get your handsome Scottish behonkus over here. Brothers are about to come to blows over the pumpkin pie.*

Magnus was off the couch in the next instant. He paused only to close the dampers on the woodstove before grabbing his jacket and heading out the door.

* * *

Bridget had been parted from Magnus for a little over two hours, and the sight of him still did her heart good. He was in jeans and a flannel shirt rather than his kilt, which made it a little easier to resist hugging him in front of her brothers.

"I have never had pumpkin pie before," Magnus said, sliding into the seat next to Lena. "Will I like it?"

Lena's gaze was half worried, half bemused. "It's mushy, like pudding, but good, like gingerbread and cinnamon toast. You should try it to be polite, but I can finish your piece if you don't like it."

"No fair," Shamus groused. "Little girls get little pieces of pie. Big guys get—"

Magnus speared a bite of Shamus's pie. "Big guys get a lesson in manners. The person who makes the pie deserves the biggest piece."

"I helped roll out the dough," Lena said.

Bridget set a good-sized slice of pie before Magnus, topped with whipped cream, ginger, nutmeg, and cinnamon.

"My thanks," Magnus said, saluting with a forkful of spiced whipped cream. No time like the present. "I got a call from Nathan Sturbridge today."

Patrick shut off the water at the sink and turned, resting his hips against the counter and crossing his arms. "What the hell did he want?"

"Swear jar, Daddy," Lena mumbled around her last mouthful of pie.

"He wanted to discuss a business proposition involving my grandpap's land."

Luke paused, his spoon poised above the bowl of whipped cream. "I don't like the sound of that."

"Princess, why don't you take a dollop of whipped cream to the patient?" Shamus suggested. "Never met an ailment that didn't respond to a judicious dose of whipped cream."

"Tornada can have whipped cream?" Lena asked.

"One kitten-sized serving," Patrick said. "If your uncle Luke is willing to spare a poor, three-legged feline even that much. Don't let Tornada lick off the spoon."

Luke passed Lena a spoonful of whipped cream. "I'll expect Tornada to share a nice, juicy dead mouse with me some fine day. You be sure and tell her that."

Lena grabbed the spoon and scampered from the kitchen. She'd been smiling, and watching her go, her uncles were smiling too.

"I love you guys," Bridget said.

The words surprised her, but years ago, these three men—teenagers, then—had watched a younger version of Bridget with the same affection they showed Lena. They were good guys, and they were her family.

"I will kill Nate Sturbridge," Shamus said. "If he's rattled you so badly you're getting all mushy on us."

"What's he done?" Patrick asked, taking Lena's plate to the sink.

"Love you too," Luke said, passing Patrick the empty whipped cream bowl.

"Always have, so don't think we'll get stupid on you just when you need us most—except for Shamus. He's always stupid."

Shamus tossed a balled-up napkin across the table, Magnus winked at her, and Bridget nearly started bawling.

"Nate wants to put me in jail unless I give him a pipeline easement across my land. He doesn't know the property is titled exclusively in my name and thinks you three will convince me to agree."

"As if," Luke snorted.

"Like you were going to convince her to sell her distillery to me," Magnus said. "This pie is delicious. The whipped cream needs a wee dram of an unpeated single malt."

"Water's different from business assets," Luke said. "Water is where the whisky comes from and without water, there's no good grass if you want to raise livestock."

That Luke grasped how essential water was to making whisky surprised Bridget.

"Tell us about going to jail." Patrick resumed his place at the table. "I want to hear all about that."

Bridget didn't want to tell them. Now that the moment was upon her, she couldn't quite find the spin that would excuse her decisions, or make her look anything other than weak, stupid, and gullible.

Magnus regarded her over a half-eaten slab of pie. He wrote outrageously brave words on sticky notes, maybe he could...

"Sturbridge embezzled from the law office," he said. "He did it in such a way that Bridget's signature was on the relevant documents—a check for cash, a deposit slip that put client funds into the wrong account. Sturbridge used a signed blank check to move the money to where he wanted it, and he withdrew the actual cash, but he did so over Bridget's signature."

"Is that legal?" Luke asked.

"No," Shamus replied. "No more legal than forging Bridget's signature would have been."

"I never have liked Nate Sturbridge," Patrick said. "He was a year behind me in school and couldn't keep his hands to himself. Judith didn't like him, but the guy is always inviting me for a drink when I run into him in town."

"Now we have to hate him," Luke said.

"While you're hating him," Magnus interjected, "he's threatening to have Bridget investigated for mishandling the funds. If she doesn't let him negotiate this pipeline easement, that investigation will go forward, and Bridget will have to explain where the money went."

"The money I don't have, because I handed over all of my money to replace what Nate stole."

"That is screwed up," Shamus said. "You never had the law firm's money, and your books will show that."

"My books won't show a damned thing," Bridget retorted. "It looks like I stole the money from the law office, then replaced it with distillery funds as soon as Nate noticed the client account was short. Nate will doubtless swear a huge wad of ill-gotten cash is still stuffed under my mattress or in some whisky barrel."

That earned her a squabble between Shamus and Luke about what Bridget's books would reveal, with Patrick observing that a walk with Nate into some dark alley would reveal a lot more.

"Can't do that," Luke said. "Nate's engaged to Georgie Truman, and if Prescott Truman got wind we'd had a two-fisted talk with Nate, our line of credit would dry up faster than a mud puddle in a prairie fire."

"Well, Bridget can't have a damned pipeline running through her land," Patrick shot back. "That's one of our best water supplies, and Bridget needs that water for her distillery. I'm not rabidly opposed to developing mineral resources, but one teeny, tiny leak in Nate's pipeline, and she's out of business and we have a whole lot of thirsty livestock."

"Thirsty people too," Shamus added. "The reservoir for the ranch house draws from the same springs as that stream. We have others, but we'd have to lay a lot of pipe."

"And we'd have to borrow from the bank to lay the pipe," Luke said, "so that's not happening either."

Bridget was encouraged that her brothers hadn't castigated her for trusting Nate in the first place, though the practice of always having some signed checks on hand was one her own mother had instituted at the ranch.

"Speaking of the bank," Magnus said. "Does Nathan make transactions at the bank window, or use the drive-through?"

"He stops by to flirt with the tellers," Bridget said, "or shoot the breeze with old man Truman. That's what he said he was doing. Bank errands were usually added to Nate's lunch outings."

"What difference does it make?" Patrick asked. "Almost all the ranchers use Prescott's bank. The merchants tend to use First Finance and Trust, and the resorts pick and choose, though Prescott has the largest of them."

"I ask," Magnus said, "because here in the land of the free, you use a bloody lot of security cameras. I thought it had something to do with all the guns. At the petrol stations, grocery stores, drugstore, everywhere, you have security cameras. If Nate got all that cash from a bank teller, the transaction was recorded on a security camera. The film quality might be poor, but it would be good enough to implicate him in any investigation."

Bridget sat back and simply stared at Magnus as he finished his pie. *I should have thought of that* warred with a compulsion to call the bank.

"A year is a long time to keep security footage," Shamus said. "Casinos keep security data just about forever, but a bank…"

"I know somebody we can ask," Luke said. "Somebody who used to be in law enforcement and has been a good friend to this family."

"Somebody who does a mighty fine two-step," Patrick added.

Thank God for friends and family. "I've invited Martina over for pizza this weekend. I'll make sure she's coming."

Magnus rose and took his empty plate and fork to the sink. Bridget liked watching him strut around in his kilt, but he did lovely things for a pair of jeans too.

"Now that we have that settled," he said, "which one of you fine gentlemen is traveling to Scotland in my place?"

* * *

The whisky samples arrived on Saturday, much to Magnus's relief, along with a text from Elias confirming that the sample of Logan Bar water was at the lab.

"This reads like a book of the Old Testament," Bridget said, setting Celeste's memorandum of mayhem on the coffee table. "You can't keep all the heretofores and wherefores straight long enough to get the gist of the story."

"And the Old Testament is crammed full of violence and betrayal," Magnus replied.

While Bridget got up to feed the woodstove, he poured a flight of three tasting portions. He detected the scent of his ailing batch without even bringing the glass to his nose.

"You can't be considering this deal," Bridget said. "You're being used as a back door to give Celeste a greater share of her spouse's business, while you give up control of your own."

Straight to the heart of the problem. "Celeste's scheme comes to fruition only if I accept MacKinnon stock on behalf of Cromarty Distilleries, and transfer the Cromarty assets to Celeste personally, which even in an alternate universe, I would not do."

He set the tray before Bridget and took the place beside her.

"This is your problem child?" she asked.

"One of them is. Taste cautiously."

She kissed him. "I always do. Relax, Magnus. I've signed a nondisclosure too."

Bridget had insisted on that courtesy and made her brothers do likewise regarding Cromarty Distilleries. Lena had been included in the family pact by virtue of a pinky swear with Magnus, which she'd promptly dashed off to explain to her three-legged kitten.

His first pinky swear, as it happened.

Bridget lifted the glass of ruined whisky. "That is the smell of trouble." Her expression became meditative as she held the glass under her nose, then moved it away, then held it under her nose.

"Do you dare taste it?" Magnus asked.

"Shush. Of course, I'll taste it." She did, taking several small sips. "I need to think about this."

"Don't think too long. I have a bicentennial year coming up."

"How long has this been in the barrel?"

"A little more than five years."

Magnus fell silent, because nattering wouldn't change what was in the glass or ease the tension gripping him.

"Do you have access to competent coopers?" Bridget asked, setting the glass down.

"For a price, and with enough notice, I can gain access." Kentucky had a thriving community of barrel makers, and their livelihood was ensured in part by a law prohibiting the use of their products in the bourbon industry more than once. The used barrels were purchased by whisky distilleries for reuse, sometimes for more than one batch of whisky.

"I'll need to make some phone calls on Monday," Bridget said. "And I'll want to taste this again before then."

"I'm surprised you're willing to."

Bridget patted his knee. "Some whiskies are like infants. They keep you up all night, don't smell very nice, and cost a lot simply to warehouse. A few years with the right kind of nurturing in the right environment, and you get an adorable toddler, a computer genius, or a concert violinist."

"Or a disaster."

She kissed him again. "Or a disaster."

Magnus rested his forehead against hers. "You'd tell me if it was hopeless?"

"I would, and it might be, but I don't know that yet. What's in the other two glasses?"

"Consolation." Magnus passed her a drink. "This one's the same age as I am, and I got the last bottle."

They sipped in silence, the fire in the woodstove snapping and popping, while outside the eaves dripped even as the sun set.

Bridget sampled her whisky. "Oh, that is… grassy, minty, a hint of bleached sheets drying on the clothesline. Everything sunny and mild, maybe a touch of the sea… Lovely. What will you do if I can't fix your whisky, Magnus?"

Cry. And Bridget alone might understand his tears. "I have some other years that could finish very nicely."

"You'll let me have a taste of them?"

"I was hoping you'd ask."

They finished their drinks in silence, but Magnus's burden had eased. Bridget would try to rescue his whisky as a professional courtesy, and she'd assist with finding a substitute if necessary. The problem wasn't solved, but it was shared.

For a Scotsman far from home, that was nearly the same thing.

So why wasn't Magnus feeling more pleased with life and with the prospect of returning to Scotland with his mission accomplished?

* * *

Once upon a time, Nate had loved to ski. Montana was the sort of place where you either learned to enjoy the fun to be had, no matter how cold, hot, dusty, or drenched that fun, or you went somewhere less challenging.

Having passed the Montana bar, and only the Montana bar, going elsewhere wasn't an option. Nate no longer went up into the mountains either.

And now, he'd have to start avoiding the Bar None.

"Nate," Mandy Glascock said, sliding onto the stool next to his. "Been a while. How's business?"

Mandy's family owned a spread that straddled the valley and the slopes, and they'd made bank selling off chunks of road-front acreage for trust-fund palaces. On the western boundary, their land abutted the Logans' property, then ran along state land for miles.

"Mandy, nice to see you. Business is fine, and you look fine too." He made no move to touch her, not so much as a handshake, though she was a well-built brunette with a friendly smile.

On the dance floor, the weekend fishing trip was in full swing with locals, tourists, ranch hands, and a smattering of student types scootin' into pairs. Nate would have been out there—a cute little mojito-drunk blonde had been eyeing him up for the past half hour—except Georgie sometimes dropped in at the Bar None and her tolerance had limits.

"Haven't seen you on the slopes much this year." Mandy caught Preacher's eye and tipped the bottom of her longneck in his direction.

Preacher uncapped a cold one, poured it to a perfect head, and set the mug and bottle before Mandy. Nate said a prayer the bartender would hang out and make small talk, and Preacher moved right back to the drink station to take the next order.

"Been busy," Nate said. "Solo practice is like that. Never rains but what it pours." Trouble was like that too, and trouble sat right beside him.

"I understand you might be handling a little land transaction for the Logans."

How in the hell...? "Now where would you hear something confidential like that?"

She took out her phone, tapped a glossy red nail on the wallpaper of a cowboy on a bronc, and an image of Nate appeared, grinning with all the stupidity of a man who thinks he has privacy.

"Look at the time." Mandy stared at her phone for an excruciating progression of instants, during which Nate's lovely, comfortable life flashed before his eyes.

"Here's the thing, Nathan. That land transaction for the Logans will make possible another land transaction for my dear daddy, and I like to keep my daddy happy."

The words were meant to carry a creepy undertone, and they did. "I've already approached Bridget, and we're setting up a time to discuss the details. These things require discussion, as you well know, and nothing has been officially said about the pipeline by anybody who matters."

She shoved the phone into the pocket of her denim jacket. "I'm pleased to hear that you've made a priority out of this, Nathan. Very pleased. You'll keep me posted?"

He wouldn't have to. He'd be watched everywhere, and just when he thought he'd sidled off the radar, Mandy and the very nasty people she called friends would yank him back where they wanted him. He'd considered turning state's evidence, but the resulting mess would doubtless cost him his license to practice law.

And—when had this begun to matter so much?—his engagement to Georgie.

All over a roll in the hay he'd been too drunk to properly enjoy.

"When the deal goes down, you'll be the first to know," Nate said. "And it will go down."

"Good," Mandy said, patting his shoulder. "I knew I could count on you."

She prowled off, swingin' it, though Nate wasn't in any mood to appreciate the taunt.

"You paying for her beer?" Preacher asked.

"I'm paying," Nate said, slapping a twenty on the counter. "From now until hell freezes over, I'll be paying."

Preacher took the money and headed off to the register, but first, he gave Nate the same sort of look he'd give a college boy overdoing the shots. *Stupid, stupid, stupid.*

And the look was deserved, because sure as shit, in that picture Mandy had of Nate, he'd been wearing nothing but a bit of latex and a smile, the girl— because she was a *girl*—in the photo had been wearing even less than that.

"You want another one?" Preacher asked, coming back with the change.

"Why not?" Nate replied. "Monday is a long way off, and I've got a powerful thirst."

Oddly enough, his thirst was not for the mojito-swilling blonde, or even for more rye whisky. His thirst was for a life with Georgie and a couple kids on a nice little spread not too far from town. He'd eventually have his judgeship, Georgie would stay busy with her charities and the children, and life would be sweet.

Until the next time Mandy came around, demanding another piece of Nate's soul.

* * *

The whole time Bridget drove into town for pizza, the whole time she stood with Lena carefully deciding to have the same thing they had every week, the whole way back to the ranch, she mulled over the problem with Magnus's whisky.

"Are you sad?" Lena asked as Bridget turned off the highway at the Logan Bar sign.

"Not particularly. I'm thinking. What about you? Are you sad?"

Lena stared out the window at a landscape that included wet, bare ground, patches of snow on the shady side of swales and ditches, and bright winter runoff rills crisscrossing the fields.

"Sometimes, I'm sad. I miss Mom. Do you like Magnus?"

The truck hit a mud puddle, splashing dirty water even onto the windshield. "I do. I like him, and I respect him."

"He talks funny, but he has honest eyes."

Slow hands too. "He makes whisky in Scotland, which is far, far away. We might visit him sometime."

Lena shot a glance at Bridget, then resumed studying land she'd seen nearly every day of her life. "I could go with you?"

"That would be up to your daddy, but Shamus is going to visit there this week."

"Will Uncle Shamus come back?"

"Yes."

But would Magnus come back? What did it mean when a man scrawled *I want a future with you* on a sticky note, trusted you with his worst whisky, and made no plans beyond the end of next week?

"Why does pizza have to smell so good?" Lena asked. "The uncles wouldn't notice if I had just one pepperoni."

Why does Magnus have to be such a good man? "Split a cheese stick with me."

Lena's version of splitting was a division into exactly equal portions. She ate as daintily as a child could, while Bridget wolfed her half down in two bites.

"Whose truck is that?" Lena asked as Bridget pulled into the ranch house driveway.

"Martina Matlock's. She's sharing our pizza and maybe staying to do some quilting. Would you like to join us?"

"Can Tornada quilt too?"

The three-legged kitten was allowed to sleep in Lena's room, breaking years of cat-less precedent in the ranch house.

"Yes, unless Martina's allergic to cats. Please carry the cheese sticks for me."

Bridget hadn't taken two steps into the great room before Shamus relieved her of the pizza, and Luke took the cheese sticks from Lena. Martina, looking delectable and tidy, was giving Shamus's suitcases a silent inspection.

"Uncle Shamus is going to Scotland," Lena said. "It's far, far away, but he's coming back."

"First, I'm having half this pizza," Shamus said. "Bridget, hadn't we better round up your Scotsman?"

"I'll get him," Lena said, darting back out the door.

Patrick watched his daughter leave. "I don't know who she's taken a bigger shine to, Magnus Cromarty or Montana's most expensive kitten."

"Are you complaining?" Bridget asked.

"Nope. I'm not standing around here when there's warm pizza on the premises either."

Lena dragged Magnus into the kitchen by the hand and insisted he sit beside her. Martina took the place beside Shamus, and Bridget was just reaching for her first hot, cheesy slice of perfection when Luke started grace.

Magnus smiled at Bridget across the table, and perfection abruptly became something other than a thick slice of pepperoni with black olives.

This—this family meal, with noise, banter, sincere gratitude, humor, and a side of cheese sticks—was perfection. If the looks Martina gave Shamus were any indication, he'd soon be straying in her direction permanently. Patrick seemed to be doing better, and Lucas and Will might one day get around to tying the knot.

Life went on, and Bridget's whisky would age in its barrels, while she…

"Ladies first," Magnus said, holding out the box of plain cheese pizza to Lena.

"Tornada's a lady," Lena said. "So's Aunt Bridget and Miss Martina."

"I'm a hungry lady," Martina replied, and for a time, nobody said much besides, "Pass the chili verde," or "Who stole my last jalapeño?"

When Lena had been sent off to watch a video of barrel-racing championships, and coffee was brewing, Shamus put on the kettle.

"I have a plane to catch, so we'd best get this confab underway."

"I'm all ears," Martina said.

"I'm in trouble," Bridget announced. "But if you're still an officer of the law, what I can tell you about that trouble is limited."

Martina peeled the paper from a chocolate cupcake. "I was a friend to this family before I got my first pony, and I will be friends with the Logans until the day I die. Unless you're selling heroin to schoolchildren, what my friends tell me in confidence goes no further."

Not quite an answer to the question of Martina's present occupation, but answer enough.

"Nate Sturbridge framed me to take the blame for embezzlement from the law office client fund," Bridget said. When she'd tried to explain the situation to her brothers, that admission had been difficult. Now, it made her purely furious. "He has the money, or he had it, and I have no proof."

Bridget ran through the sequence of events while Martina licked the frosting from her cupcake, Magnus poured coffee, and Shamus fixed tea for the ladies.

"So you want to know what the bank's security tapes might show," Martina said, "but you don't want to tip off Prescott Truman about why you're curious."

"We don't know if the bank even has tapes that go back a year," Shamus said. "Storing that much data would cost a pretty penny."

Martina took a bite of chocolate cupcake and got a dash of frosting on her nose. Shamus stared hard at the clock, and Patrick and Luke exchanged smiles.

She used a red-checked napkin to wipe away the frosting. "As it happens, Prescott does some business with the casinos, and they require very, extremely, endlessly fancy security measures. They have to keep a lot of cash up at the resort—enough to cover every chip in play, plus a margin—and that means significant reserves are sometimes kept off-site. Eat your cupcake, Shamus."

"I'll eat his cupcake," Patrick muttered.

"No, you will not." Shamus set his dessert beyond Patrick's reach. "Be nice to me, or I might not come back from Scotland."

"You'll come back," Luke retorted. "Lena would miss you."

"So would Tornada," Bridget added, straight-faced.

Magnus helped himself to a cupcake. "About the tapes. We don't need to see any footage, but we need to know if they exist and if they could be brought into evidence."

"Easy enough to find out," Martina replied.

"How?" Bridget asked. "Patrick, you touch my cupcake, you die."

The moment turned awkward—Judith had died. A silence hovered, until Patrick swiped Bridget's cupcake, took a bite, and put it back on her plate.

"They taste better when they're stolen," he said. "Tell us how you'll get access to Prescott's security information without letting him know what's up."

"I'll ask Georgie," Martina said. "She's on my bowling team, and there's nothing about that bank she doesn't know, but that doesn't solve Bridget's problem."

"If those tapes exist," Luke said, "they give Bridget the leverage she needs to tell Sturbridge to step off. That's enough for now."

Martina considered the last of her cupcake, then considered Shamus. "You promise you're coming back from Scotland, Shamus Logan?"

"I promise."

"Nathan Sturbridge is under investigation by authorities who've been trying to bring down a trafficking ring for more than a year. I can't tell you which agencies are involved, can't tell you specifics, but Nate made some classic stupid moves. I suspect that's why he needed Bridget's money, and why he won't have it stuffed inside his mattress even if I were able to get you a search warrant."

"I'll kill him," Luke said.

"I'll help you," Patrick added.

Shamus set down his cupcake. "I'll bury the damned evidence."

"Swear jar," Magnus said. "This investigation has been going on for more than a year?"

"Nearly two years," Martina replied. "It's… complicated. One part of it is a setup: The john has a good time, and when he's ready to saunter on his merry way, he's told that he was with an underage female, and the encounter was recorded for posterity. The john pays for silence, even though as near as we can tell, the women involved are of age. They just look underage."

"So the crime committed isn't trafficking underage women," Bridget murmured, "it's merely prostitution, or possibly pimping, and the money is great, because the johns are chosen for their ability to pay."

"The money is great if you don't mind committing extortion," Martina said. "Sticks in my craw to ignore felonies."

"But the extortion is probably reserved for the select few who have the ability to pay well," Magnus pointed out, "meaning at least some of the people managing this dirty business are local."

"My, my, my," Luke murmured. "Trouble in River City."

"I don't want to put Nate behind bars," Bridget said. "I just want to run my distillery without him threatening me over a pipeline."

"You don't want your money back?" Martina asked. "You don't want him kicked out of the profession of law?"

"Of course I want my money back, and of course Nate's a disgrace to the legal profession, but you say the money's gone, and I believe you. My distillery could be in business for the next hundred years, but if the water supply gets messed up, I got nothin'."

"The ranch doesn't have much either," Shamus said.

Patrick rose and gathered up cupcake wrappers. "So where do we go from here? We don't know if the bank has tapes that would incriminate Nate, we can't get to those tapes if they exist, and Bridget's supposed to meet with the guy tomorrow."

"Don't cheer us up or anything," Luke muttered.

"Patrick's right," Bridget said. "In a sense, I'm worse off because of what Martina has told us."

"I told you jack squat," Martina said. "I'm here to work on a new pillowcase for my hope chest."

"Worse off, how?" Shamus asked. "Nate had a motive to steal from you, and now we know what that motive is."

"Bridget is worse off," Magnus said, "because if Nate had a motive to steal once, that same motive will probably inspire him to steal again. Extortionists don't leave a signed receipt and ride off into the sunset. Even if Bridget signed an easement for the pipeline, Nate could well come after her next time to sell her land or sell her business."

"And I'm not selling," Bridget said. "I'm not selling an easement. I'm not selling my business."

If Magnus thought she'd changed her mind on that score, then he'd better take Shamus's place on that flight bound for Scotland.

"You're not selling," Magnus said, "but Nathan doesn't know that."

Martina downed the last of her tea. "If this is about to get illegal, I'm about to get scarce."

"Not illegal," Magnus replied. "Devious, perhaps."

"Well, get devious in a damned hurry," Shamus said, "or I won't be on my plane, and then we'll have two distilleries in trouble."

CHAPTER TWELVE

Another storm—ice and freezing rain, for variety—gave Bridget an excuse to push the scheduled meeting with Nathan Sturbridge back until Wednesday, and Magnus used the extra two days to get better acquainted with Bridget's distillery.

Getting better acquainted with Bridget had stalled, for which Magnus blamed Sturbridge and his meddling.

"You are full of ideas," he said as Bridget parked a skid loader in her warehouse. The building was of recent construction, as whisky warehouses went, sectioned off into separate temperature-controlled areas, with modern lighting and ventilation throughout.

"I have to be full of ideas," she said, climbing out of the vehicle. "Where you come from, it's malt whisky, period. Might be single cask, might be blended, but all the other variations—rye, corn, blended spirits—aren't competing in your bailiwick. We have to be not only the best whisky option, we also have to be the best spirits, period."

She was lecturing, nearly ranting. "Bridget, what's wrong?"

She pulled off a pair of work gloves and tossed them onto the seat of the loader. "You mean, besides my law-partner-turned-pandering-blackmailer threatening to put my water supply at risk?"

Magnus had a nagging sense Bridget was keeping something from him. He'd had the same feeling when Celeste had been plotting her exit from the marriage, spreading rumors among the employees, quietly stashing money into her personal checking account, and liquidating nearly every piece of jewelry Magnus had given her.

When he'd finally noticed she was wearing the same earrings and slim gold bracelet to every occasion, she'd told him they were her favorites.

He let Bridget lead him to her office, which necessitated a dash across the frigid parking lot. Montana weather raised fickle to a high art, which was doubtless part of the reason the warehouse had to be climate controlled.

"You interested in some hot tea?" Bridget asked, pouring water into a chipped blue mug.

"I have water." Magnus had filled his bottle at the stream when they'd arrived, and he took a sip while Bridget put her mug in the microwave. The water was wonderfully cold and had a sparkly feeling going down. "Have you analyzed your water? I like it."

"Of course I've analyzed it, and lo and behold, it's wet and makes great whisky. I don't like what you have planned for Sturbridge."

So much for the whisky-maker's version of small talk. Magnus capped his water bottle and took Bridget in his arms.

"The plan is not mine, but ours, and it's the best we can come up with when time is of the essence." The statute of limitations on raiding the till was only one year, and that year would soon be up. Then too, Bridget should not have to endure one day more than necessary of Sturbridge's perfidy.

"Nate is lazy, he's not stupid," she said.

"While you and I are neither." Magnus kissed her, not to make a point, but because he longed for the taste of her. Bridget had been increasingly distracted since the family war council on Sunday, and any hopes Magnus had entertained about sharing a bed again had gone nowhere.

He'd endured a trail ride with Patrick and Lena yesterday before the weather had turned up nasty again. He'd admired a new foal that had arrived on Sunday night, and watched Bridget stitching away on a quilt for Lena. He'd played damned chase-the-string with the kittens and generally exhausted his stores of gentlemanly deportment.

Now, he needed to kiss Bridget.

She apparently needed to kiss him back, because the next thing Magnus knew, he was being pushed up against her behemoth desk, and she was yanking his shirttail out of his jeans.

"I want this," she muttered against his mouth. "I want you. Now."

Magnus's body leaped at the invitation, and as Bridget locked the door, he shucked out of his boots and shirt and got his belt buckle undone.

"Don't stop there," she said, pulling her sweater over her head. "We're burning daylight."

"I didn't bring—"

"I did," she said, tossing a condom on the end table beside the sofa. "And that's not all I'm bringing, Magnus Cromarty."

Her T-shirt—Distillers do it with spirit!—joined the heap of clothing on her desk, followed by a lacy lilac bra and her jeans.

"The curtains are open," Magnus said, an inane observation when Bridget MacDeaver was nearly naked less than two yards away.

"I like wild scenery." She prowled close enough to ruffle the hair on his chest. "I like you."

This wasn't a happy admission, which Magnus would worry about later. "I more than like you and hope what we start here can continue in my bed tonight." And for many nights to come.

"You," she said, pushing him down to sit on the couch. "On your back please, now."

Magnus obliged, and Bridget straddled him, took care of the protection, and pretty much took care of his every fantasy and coherent thought over the next thirty minutes. By the time she was panting and spent on his chest, Magnus couldn't recall the day of the week, month of the year, or which continent he found himself on.

But he'd never forget the feel of Bridget's lovemaking.

"You're worried," he said, drifting his hands over her back. "That was worried passion, Mary Bridget MacDeaver."

"It was a lot of things, and anybody would be worried in my position. Go to sleep."

Their bodies had slipped apart, and Bridget's breathing became even. A few years ago, maybe even a few days ago, Magnus would have nodded off, content with intense physical satisfaction and good memories.

With Bridget, he wanted more. Her desire for him had been real, but she'd also used sex to distract him. From what, he didn't know, and questioning her was pointless. When Bridget MacDeaver made up her mind, there was no unmaking it.

He liked that about her—no deception, no underhanded scheming—but hoped she'd made up her mind to trust him.

Because he certainly trusted her.

He'd barely closed his eyes when a phone vibrated against the scarred wood of the end table.

"That's yours," Bridget muttered, pushing away from him. She stretched to get his phone, which put her breasts within nuzzling distance.

Magnus resisted, because the chime had signaled a text from Elias. "The board meeting should be starting about now," he said, accepting the phone.

Fergus gave Celeste his proxy and your man from Montana hasn't arrived yet. Celeste is spreading mutiny one smile at a time, and we're supposed to convene in fifteen minutes.

"Bad news?" Bridget asked, passing him his shirt.

"Disaster for Scotland," Magnus replied, quoting the old sportscaster's lament. "Or for Cromarty Distilleries."

* * *

"I miss Uncle Shamus," Lena said.

Oddly enough, Patrick missed him too. "He'll be back this time next week, or that's the plan."

"Do you have any sevens?"

Patrick passed over the seven of clubs. "You're cleaning me out, Lena Lilly Logan."

She was very serious about her go-fish and put the pair of sevens face-up on the table. "Do you have any twos?"

"Go fish."

She picked up a card, wrinkled her nose, and gave Patrick an expectant look.

"Do you have any elevens?" he asked.

"Daddy, I'm not a little girl."

Yes, you are, and to me you always will be. "Sorry. Do you have any threes?"

Even the number was painful. Mother, father, and child were a threesome, but Patrick and Lena were down to deuces. That purely stank.

Lena passed over the three of hearts. "How far away is Scotland?"

"Across the ocean, thousands of miles. Way, way, way far away."

"Aunt Bridget said we might visit there." Lena was asking a question— several questions, in fact.

Patrick pretended to rearrange the cards in his hand. "You like Mister Magnus, don't you?"

"He's not loud, but he's nice. He can't ride a horse as well as you used to. If you have a pair, you're supposed to put them down."

Patrick put his lousy threes on the table, and good riddance. "Aunt Bridget likes Mister Magnus too. He lives in Scotland, and she might like to visit him there. He has a distillery, just like she does."

"But his distillery is in Scotland, and ours is here."

"That does appear to be the case. Would you like to visit Scotland, Lena?"

She put her cards down. "Jason Prescott goes to Mexico with his grandparents. He says it's always warm there, and everybody is nice."

"What else does Jason say?"

"That I'm too poor to go anywhere, and only poor people never take vacations. Tara Huxtable said Jason is stupid, and some people have to work for a living."

Patrick assessed Jason's snide remarks for racial prejudice and found only a small boy's small-mindedness.

"Some people have to wander all over the place because they don't know home when it's staring them in the face. Your mama told me that. I love it here at the Logan Bar, Lena, but if you want to go with your Aunt Bridget to see Scotland, we'll make that happen when school's out." How they'd make it happen wasn't immediately clear.

She tidied up her pairs of cards. "Would you come with us?"

"You worried about your old man?"

"You used to be fun to beat at cards, Daddy."

I used to be a lot of things, including happily married. "It might surprise you to know that I am interested in visiting Scotland. They are way, way ahead of us when it comes to renewable energy. They're good at things like windmills, solar power, and tidal power. I have an idea for a solar tree, and Mister Magnus said his uncle might be willing to fund it."

"What's a solar tree?"

"It looks like a real tree, but it's collecting sunlight like a solar panel. In Scotland, they have cell towers that look like trees, and—why are you collecting my cards?"

"Because you weren't even trying to win. I think it's time I taught you how to play crazy eights."

As best Patrick recalled, crazy eights could last for hours. "How about if you come out to the shop with me and do your homework while I do a little sketching?"

Her smile was surprised and eager. "Can Tornada come?"

"If you set her up a litter box and bowl of water, she can come next time."

"I'll get my drawing paper and my library book." Lena was off like a shot, the kitchen door swinging in her wake.

"What has gotten into my niece?" Luke asked, coming through the doorway.

"I'm not sure, but how would you feel about setting up some prototype solar windmills over the summer?"

"What'll it cost us?"

"Spare parts, time, my labor. Maybe a round-trip ticket to Scotland to meet with Magnus's rich, eccentric uncle."

Luke opened the fridge and drank straight out of a quart container of half-and-half. "Magnus this, and Magnus that. The guy has been in town less than two weeks, and it feels like he's taken over my family."

"Our family. Cromarty knows about you and Willy."

Luke slammed the door to the fridge. "What in the hell business is it of Cromarty's what I get up to with whom?"

"The milk mustache kinda ruins that glower, Lukey-poo. You and Willy were amorous under the moonlight last week, and Cromarty saw you. I don't reckon it matters a hill of beans to Magnus who you want to tango with as long as everybody's a consenting adult."

Luke wiped his lip with a tea towel. "A fine thing when a man can't even have privacy in the middle of the night on his own property."

"Like you weren't peering in the guesthouse window when you stacked all that firewood?"

"I didn't peer in the windows, exactly. Or listen at the keyhole much."

Patrick tidied up the cards, cut the deck, and shuffled. "Of course you didn't. Word of advice, though: Stop wasting time, Lucas. You and Willy want to tie the knot, then be about it. His horse steps in a gopher hole, a drunk driver gets in the wrong lane, or a bar fight goes south, and you'll be out of time. If he makes you happy, and you make him happy, then go for it. Lena could use some cousins, and we know Shamus will take forever to lasso Martina."

Judith's horse had stumbled, she'd gone flying, and broken her neck. She died before Patrick had been able to get her helmet unbuckled, much less dial 911. Full of life one minute, gone the next.

Luke opened the fridge and stood with his back to Patrick. "Cousins."

"Never had any, but Cromarty speaks highly of the concept. Something to think about."

The door swung open. "Daddy, I'm ready!"

Luke remained at the fridge, his shoulders suspiciously tight.

"C'mon, princess," Patrick said. "I'll show you how to draw a tree that can do magic."

They were at the door when Luke called out, "You'd be my best man?"

"Hell, yeah, and I'm sure Shamus would stand up for Willy, if Bridget didn't wrestle him for the privilege."

"Swear jar, Daddy."

Patrick took Lena's hand. "It's time we got rid of that damned jar, because you're a big girl, and from time to time, in the right company, under appropriate circumstances, your speech might get a little colorful. You're a Logan, after all."

Lena dragged him to the door, her brows knit. She was working up to something, something her mother might have been able to anticipate but Patrick had to wait for, one hand on the doorknob.

"What?" he asked.

"Damned right, Daddy. No more swear jar. That's for little kids."

* * *

Bridget helped Magnus dive into his clothes, while her mind spun frantically over what she knew about articles of incorporation, bylaws, and directors' meetings.

Precious damned little.

"Elias," Magnus muttered, "answer the damned—Elias. You haven't heard from Shamus Logan?"

"Not a text, not a phone call, not a damned fart in the wind." Elias spoke softly, nearly growling.

"Language, dear," murmured an elderly female voice.

"Give Aunt Hildy my love," Magnus said, "and explain to her that Fergus's head has been turned by a pretty traitor."

"Explain that to her yourself," Elias said. "You have ten minutes, Magnus, and Celeste is carrying a briefcase that I'm sure is just full of plans to take over your company."

Bridget wrapped herself in a blanket and sat close enough to overhear this exchange. "Give me the phone, Magnus."

He passed over the phone without so much as blinking.

"Elias, I'm Bridget MacDeaver, outside counsel for Magnus Cromarty. Your first action as chairman of the meeting is to exclude Celeste because her proxy is invalid."

"Magnus, are you there?" Elias asked.

"Right here, and you are to trust Bridget with your life, also with my distillery."

Bridget wished he hadn't said that, even though his words also warmed her from the inside as good whisky did.

"Elias, listen fast," Bridget said. "According to the boilerplate bylaws of any organization worth its salt, a proxy must be free of conflicts of interest, personal or professional, and free from the unresolved appearance of conflict. Celeste owns stock in a competing venture and is married to its primary shareholder. Boot her from the meeting."

Magnus kissed her, then whispered in her ear, "Does Shamus have a conflict?"

Well... Bridget held the phone away. "We're not rivals, Magnus. I will never, ever sell to you or to anybody else. I'll close my business before I'll do that."

He drew back as if she'd slapped him. "Then we're not rivals, and Shamus has no conflict."

"Hello?" Elias barked. "Is there intelligent life in Montana? You want me to just announce that Celeste isn't welcome and get on with business as usual?"

"No," Bridget said. "If Shamus isn't there, you don't have a quorum. You thank everybody for their time, apologize for their trouble, and reschedule the meeting for a time and date to be announced."

"If you think I'll survive telling half a dozen elderly, cantankerous, Scottish curmudg—I'm getting a text. Hold on."

"Are you sure about the conflict-of-interest business?" Magnus asked.

"Sure enough that Elias should be able to bluff it. The potential for the exact scenario Celeste has set up is too great—a disgruntled director, whose loyalty ought to be to the company, summons the devil in a weak moment, and all hell breaks loose."

"Is that Magnus on the phone?" the same elderly lady asked. "Fine thing, when a young man has time to frolic but not to attend his own board meetings. I could be home quilting instead of—who is this?"

Shamus? Magnus mouthed.

"He's here," Elias said. "Looks like he slept in the gutter, or possibly at Heathrow, but if Logan wears a cowboy hat and the boots to match, he's here. I've a meeting to run and a rat to evict from your warehouse."

The call ended, and Magnus remained sitting beside Bridget, staring at a screen that used the blue and white Scottish saltire flag for wallpaper.

"That was too close for comfort," Magnus said. "Much too close. Celeste will follow up with emails or chatty little notes to every one of my directors, a copy of her takeover plan attached."

Bridget rose and reached from beneath her blanket to pluck her shirt from the pile on the desk. "At least in the United States, she'd be guilty of tortious interference with an advantageous business relationship."

"English, please, love."

Without dropping the blanket, Bridget sat back down and pulled her shirt over her head. "Where are my...?"

Magnus swiped her panties from the arm of the couch, ran his fingers over them, and passed them to her.

"When somebody has a business arrangement with you," Bridget said, "such as a vendor agreement, contracted work for hire, or a fiduciary relationship, the whole marketplace benefits from the expectation that those situations will honk along on the terms negotiated. When the agreement has run its course, everybody is free to go on their merry way, forming other associations."

"Like a handfasting."

"Whatever that is. In any case, if you have such an agreement—and your directors absolutely had to sign agreements to serve on your board—then somebody who acts with intent to harm you by wrecking your done deal is liable for damages, at least here in the States. It's a tort, meaning you have to prove damages, but I have to wonder about Celeste's business acumen if she'd pull a stunt like this."

Magnus rose from the couch and passed Bridget her jeans—she was still wearing her wool socks.

He tucked in his shirt tails and fastened the snap on his own jeans. "You're suggesting Celeste is desperate?"

"Desperate or not too keen on business in a businesslike manner. You would have sent meeting minutes to your lawyers, they would have taken a look at what Celeste got up to and told you after the fact that all of her motions, seconds, and submitted documents were invalid due to her lack of proper proxy status."

Even rumpled—especially rumpled—Magnus was an imposing figure. He propped his butt against the desk and did up his Celtic knot belt buckle.

"My Uncle Zebedee has a bit of advice in situations like this: When your opponent is acting like a fool, apparently playing straight into your hands, assume you're the fool and your opponent is brilliant. Rethink the situation from every possible angle before you make a move."

Putting jeans on under a blanket was an awkward undertaking, but Bridget wanted the layer of modesty.

"Is Celeste brilliant?"

"I don't think so. Shrewd, driven, manipulative, but not brilliant."

"She dumped you. In my book, that takes brilliant off the table."

Magnus's phone chimed again. He stared at the screen, then passed it to Bridget.

Celeste evicted, round one to Cromartys. Hilda and Heidi promising to have a talk with Fergus he'll not soon forget. You owe me forever.

"Will there be a round two?" Bridget asked. "If there is, you should be in Scotland when that round goes down."

"Trying to get rid of me, Mary Bridget?"

Well, yes, in a sense. "Let's get through this week, then ask me again."

Magnus got his boots on, Bridget did likewise, and then it was time to leave. Before Bridget had fired up the truck and turned for the ranch, more freezing rain was falling.

* * *

Magnus let Bridget focus on the messy roads during the short drive to the ranch house, while he thought through next steps. He wasn't sure there was a next step for him and Bridget, at least not until Nathan Sturbridge had been dealt with.

Magnus was also waiting for Bridget to come to a decision regarding the bicentennial whisky, and the passivity of waiting bothered him sorely.

"Will you stay with me tonight?" he asked as Bridget backed the truck into a slot between two other vehicles in the ranch house driveway.

She regarded him as if, rather than his whisky, he was the product that puzzled her. "I want to."

Then what in the hell is stopping you? Because something was, something other than Nathan Sturbridge.

"Is there a but, Bridget?"

"No." She climbed out of the truck and walked beside Magnus to the guesthouse. "Do you still have a return flight for next week?"

"I do. I can change it." *Ask me to. Smile, hint that you'd like to be in the seat beside me when I fly home.*

"Let's see what happens tomorrow. I still don't like this plan."

Martina didn't like it, and she was law enforcement. Shamus, Luke, and Patrick loathed Magnus's suggestion, but saw its usefulness. More significantly, they didn't have anything to suggest in its place.

"You still think I'm after your distillery." Magnus spoke aloud, though he shouldn't have. He pushed open the guesthouse door and waited for Bridget to precede him through.

She remained on the porch, the wind whipping strands of her hair across her cheek. "If you think you can beg, borrow, steal, or otherwise convey to yourself any interest in my whisky operation, then you'll be sleeping alone tonight, Magnus. Don't lie to me about this."

A good dozen windows on the ranch house faced the guesthouse porch, and a brother or two might be watching from any one of them. Magnus gestured for Bridget to lead him inside, and she complied.

He was hungry, tired, thirsty—now that some helpful soul had made him more aware of his own bodily needs—and he wanted to have a long talk with Elias about the day's board meeting. More than that, he wanted Bridget to smile at him as she had the first night they'd met.

He closed and locked the door. "Listen to me, Mary Bridget MacDeaver: You hold the fate of my distillery in your hands. You hold the security of much of my family, by blood and otherwise, in those same hands. If you think I'll jeopardize my legacy and livelihood to take over your operation, then you don't know me at all."

Magnus was ready for a rousing argument, provided that argument settled things between him and Bridget.

She pulled off her gloves and stuffed them into her jacket pockets. "My own brothers brought you here with the intent to sell you my business. I'm still not over that."

"And Fergus gave his proxy to my enemy," Magnus said. "What has that to do with us?"

She draped her quilted jacket over the back of a chair at the kitchen table. "Maybe nothing, but I'm snakebit, Magnus. My law partner set me up for felony charges, my brothers tried to wheedle my business from me. Two weeks ago, I'd never laid eyes on you. Now one of those same brothers is in Scotland doing your bidding."

"Shamus is having a wee holiday, and Elias is probably getting him drunk right this minute, if my aunts Hilda and Heidi haven't already. An hour ago, you were making passionate love with me."

That earned him a haunted smile, and frustrated desire gave way to a sinking pessimism.

"My office will never be the same," Bridget said. "What should we do about dinner?"

The change of subject was a proper kick to Magnus's balls—or to his heart. "I'm hungry for protein, and I want to hear your thoughts on my ruined whisky."

They threw together a salad, Bridget fired up the grill on the porch, and a half-dozen beef shish kebabs later, Magnus was feeling less pessimistic.

"You asked about your whisky," Bridget said when the dishes had been done. "I've been pondering possibilities, and I'd like another taste."

"You're daft if you think it will improve with further acquaintance. I have nightmares about that whisky."

"There's a way to fix it, Magnus. I just can't see it yet." She went off on a flight about phenols and esters, tannins and fat-soluble odor compounds. Magnus, as her professional peer, should have been able to follow the discussion, but she left him in the dust.

"You're dead on your feet," Bridget said, snuggling closer. At some point between a diatribe on the effect of temperature on absorption rates and speculation regarding vertical versus horizontal barrel storage, she'd draped herself along Magnus's side.

He tucked the quilt over her shoulders. "I thought I was passionate about whisky, but I'm merely conscientious and enthusiastic compared to you. I should have heard from Elias by now."

"Not if he's trying to get Shamus drunk. That could take all night. Did I overhear that one of your aunts is a quilter?"

"Both Heidi and Hilda are quilters. They go to quilt shows, quilt festivals, quilt everythings. You'd get on well with them."

If you ever came to Scotland to meet them.

"Ask your aunts why Celeste would be desperate enough to crash your board meeting. Quilters talk almost as much as they sew. If there's anything to be learned on the extended family grapevine, those two will know it."

"Celeste hasn't a domestic, much less a quilted, bone in her…"

"What?"

"Celeste has an aunt who knits. She's chummy with Hilda."

"Bush telegraph, works every time. Call your cousin, and let me think about your whisky."

Bridget scooted down, laying her head in Magnus's lap. His phone sat two feet way, but he made no move to reach for it. The hour in Scotland would be fiendishly late, while the moments with Bridget were too precious to waste.

Magnus stroked her hair while she dozed and mulled over his whisky. His nightmares were entirely survivable—a bad batch of whisky was a serious, expensive problem and a mortifying embarrassment, but not a tragedy.

Nathan Sturbridge had threatened Bridget with jail, disbarment, disgrace, and penury. For that, Magnus was determined that Sturbridge suffer a lifetime of nightmares, at least.

CHAPTER THIRTEEN

The Bar None was a friendly place to do business. Nate had met clients over a drink, joined other lawyers for the occasional meal, and in years past, done his share of boot-scootin' on the dance floor and in the parking lot. This was his turf, and if Bridget wanted to conduct their negotiation here, that was fine with him. Plenty of witnesses to keep her from getting all het up, and plenty of good rye whisky too.

Bridget was the punctual sort, so Nate was early, the better to wet his whistle. Martina was trying to ignore him from a corner table—no Shamus Logan to dance attendance on a weeknight—and Preacher was at his usual post behind the bar.

God was in his heaven, and all was about to come right in Nate's world.

At two minutes past the hour, Magnus Cromarty strutted into the Bar None, a kilt swinging around his knees.

"You know how to make an entrance, Cromarty," Nate said, standing to offer his hand. "Bet it gets a little breezy in that getup come December. Don't suppose you caught a ride to town with Bridget?"

Cromarty wasn't bad-looking, though the guy had a twitchy quality Nate associated with prosecuting attorneys.

"Bridget won't be coming. Seems her brothers know how to get into her email, and she thinks you had to reschedule this meeting again."

Cromarty looked like he wanted to smile, and Nate did smile. The Logan brothers had no interest in brewing whisky, that was common knowledge. Plain as day, Cromarty had come to talk a little business.

"Have a seat, Mr. Cromarty. Drinks are on me."

"Generous of you."

Nate's guest ordered twelve-year-old Logan Bar single malt, which wasn't cheap. Preacher left the bottle on the table with the chips and salsa, the bastard, but Cromarty didn't so much as sip his drink.

"I'm here to discuss a commercial transaction with you, Mr. Sturbridge." Cromarty took out a fancy phone and set it on the table. "I typically record business negotiations, because taking notes calls attention to the discussion when we both benefit from discretion, and relying strictly on recall introduces avoidable errors."

Somebody sure was anxious to cut a deal. Nate considered the agenda and considered his rye—the third of the evening, negotiations being a thirsty undertaking.

"If you're that forgetful, record any damned thing you please. We'll be discussing hypotheticals for the most part, won't we?"

Nate would be. Lawyers excelled at discussing hypotheticals, though a cut of the revenue from a pipeline easement would be wonderfully real.

Cromarty smiled at his drink. "I'm not a lawyer, Mr. Sturbridge, I'm a businessman. I prefer to discuss possibilities and facts. Bridget claims you approached her about a running a pipeline across her land."

Very likely, Cromarty had charmed that admission from Bridget between the sheets. "And if I did?"

Cromarty held his drink up to the light. "I am in Montana as a result of extensive correspondence with the Logan brothers, who have no expertise with making whisky, poor lads. My family has been making whisky for more than two hundred years, and I *am* interested in the Logan Bar distillery. Very interested."

If Bridget was smart, she'd lead Cromarty on a dance and then make him pay through the nose for the damned distillery. Bridget was smart, but alas for her, she wasn't devious.

"What has this to do with me?" Though Nate could connect the dots easily. Cromarty was buying the Logan Bar distillery and wanted to control the terms of the pipeline easement. Nate drank to that good news, because Cromarty would save him the trouble of convincing Bridget to see reason.

Preacher was drying glasses with a red towel, Martina waggled her fingers at Cromarty, and Joey Deardorff was sulking at the end of the bar, probably trying to find the nerve to buy Martina a drink. Several other couples had taken up tables at the edge of the dance floor, but the place was mostly empty, it being midweek and early for the singles crowd.

Nate should do business here more often. The informal atmosphere was good for loosening tongues, and the service was good.

Cromarty brought his drink to his nose, then set it aside. "You ask what my business aspirations have to do with you." He hit a few keys on his phone, and tucked it into his breast pocket, suggesting the negotiating was about to get productive. "Bridget MacDeaver hates you, and that bothers me. I've seen the books for her distillery, thanks to her brothers, and on those books is a substantial loan that she made essentially to your law practice."

Bookkeeping was not Nate's strong suit, which was why the Almighty had created legions of gray-haired women in sensible shoes who delighted in spreadsheets and stray pennies.

"I can assure you, Mr. Cromarty, that my law practice is under no obligation to Bridget MacDeaver or her distillery. Just the opposite. When her sister-in-law died, Bridget bailed on me with no notice, left me holding about eight different bags, and had the decency to pass along token compensation for my inconvenience. No loan to me or the law practice was made, and no payments on that loan will be forthcoming, regardless of what her brothers might have intimated."

Half of lawyering was storytelling, creating a tale from facts and evidence. Bridget had doubtless nearly bankrupted her distillery to cover the law office's shortfall, but Nate's embellishments had sounded convincing to his own ears. She *had* left the practice, and he *was* doing the work of two lawyers as a result.

More or less.

Sorta.

"Would you like another drink, Mr. Sturbridge?" Cromarty gestured with his chin at Nate, and the nice waitress—who had nice legs too—brought over the bottle of rye.

"Much obliged," Nate said. "Any other questions, Cromarty?"

Cromarty poured Nate a generous shot. "I'm what you might call snakebit—did I use the term correctly? My ex was in the whisky business, still is, and she left a path of destruction from my bank account to my distillery to my board of directors. Five years on, and I'm still looking over my shoulder for some female to wreck what I've rebuilt."

That made sense, women being women regardless of nationality. "Sorry for your troubles, Cromarty. I didn't appreciate it when Bridget left me a mountain of work to do, and no time to prepare the cases. The bar association frowns mightily on lawyers who drop the ball, but I felt sorry for her because her family was going through a hard time."

Cromarty capped the bottle of rye. "Good of you. I appreciate the warning too, because a woman who will welsh on a partner bears watching. What do you know about making whisky and about selling whisky in Montana?"

Guys were supposed to look out for each other. If that wasn't part of the code of the west, it was certainly part of the code of the locker room.

This question about whisky was probably Cromarty's real agenda—free legal advice, same as half the valley wanted at some point. Nate rambled on convincingly about nothing much in particular—he preferred criminal defense to corporate law—while Cromarty appeared to be swilling down every word.

Thinking himself quite the clever corporate raider, no doubt, a regular whisky tycoon in a skirt. Over the course of couple more shots of rye, Cromarty waxed eloquent about tradition, pot stills, the challenges of breaking into international markets, and God alone knew what. The accent—or a bit too much drink, maybe—made some of his bull tiresome to decipher.

"Timing is everything," Nate observed. "So when will you buy that distillery out from under Bridget?"

"An acquisition always requires due diligence, Sturbridge. I'd sign a memorandum of understanding first, take a very close look at the books and the facility next, and execute a contract of purchase thereafter, assuming Bridget and I came to terms. This business of Bridget leaving a law partner with no notice doesn't sit well with me at all. Though you've been very helpful, I still have significant questions about the Logan Bar's finances."

Well, crap. Significant questions meant significant delays. "What questions, Cromarty? I've known the Logans all my life, and they run a good outfit. Distilling is your bailiwick, but Bridget's a hard worker and doesn't half-ass anything. I was in business with her, and I oughta know. There was a death in the family, the hailstorm from hell came through... I cut Bridget some slack."

Cromarty leaned nearer, glancing around first, as if his piddly little whisky deal would be of interest to couples intent on getting horizontal with each other before midnight.

"Then answer me this, Sturbridge: Why would a woman planning to run out on her law partner be entering her appearance in court cases right up until the day she left?"

The Bar None had begun to fill up, and the noise level made Cromarty's words harder to grasp. "Beg pardon?"

"Bridget MacDeaver was taking on cases and meeting with clients right up until the week she made that loan to the law practice. Why would she jeopardize the distillery she loves to cut out on a business that showed every evidence of earning a healthy, steady income?"

Damn, Cromarty was like a dog on a bone, but the guy was right to be cautious where Bridget was concerned.

Nate took another sip of patience. "I'm tellin' you, there wasn't any damned loan." Preacher shot them a mildly curious look. Nate leaned closer to Cromarty. "There wasn't any loan from the distillery to the law practice."

Cromarty looked unconvinced. "So if I were to examine the books from the law practice, they wouldn't show an influx of cash equal to what Bridget took from the distillery?"

Not a question Cromarty could ask Bridget directly, so Nate didn't take offense. "I already told you, Bridget compensated me for the trouble of taking over the whole law office, and what does any of this have to do with agreeing to a pipeline easement?" The question, for reasons Nate would recall any minute, seemed pressing.

So did a trip to the john.

"I can't acquire a business with dirty books, Sturbridge," Cromarty said, keeping his voice down. "The whisky industry is heavily regulated, particularly when the product is shipped internationally, and dirty books are soon obvious. If you can't tell me what really happened with that money, I'll be on a plane back to Scotland in less than week. Just between us, you should also know that Bridget will never permit an easement to cross her property—and it is her property, not her brothers'."

Well, hell. Nate dipped a chip into the salsa, but the chip busted before he could scoop up a decent serving.

"How do you know the land is hers?"

"Because land records are public, and the distillery I might buy sits on that land, for now."

Cromarty must really want that distillery, if he was personally checking land records this soon after hitting town. If Bridget knew she had the poor bastard by the balls, she'd grip and twist with a vengeance.

"How badly do you need to close this deal?" Nate asked.

"Bridget MacDeaver is sitting on a gold mine," Cromarty said, sending another nervous glance around the room. "Her products are undervalued and underdistributed, and she doesn't know what to do about it. If she won't expand with my help, somebody else will come along and make her an offer she can't refuse, probably one of my competitors. Does that answer your question?"

"You want it bad." Which was good, for Nate.

"I am *exceedingly* interested, but if Bridget isn't managing her business on the up and up, I can't afford to make an international investment in a dodgy venture. The distillery's books aren't adding up, which means Bridget could finish the job my ex started. I can't take another hit like that."

So… to get the pipeline easement through, Nate had to do Bridget a genuine favor, and talk Cromarty into buying her distillery. Why did life have to be so complicated?

As skittish as Cromarty was, he'd ride off into the sunset, unless Nate explained about the money.

A niggling sense of caution warned him not to do that—Nate had been played for a fool and didn't like admitting that to a stranger—but self-preservation voted in favor of securing the easement sooner rather than later.

"I took a little unscheduled loan from the law office," Nate said. "Got painted into a corner, the kind of corner only a wad of cash could get me out of. Bridget handled all the money, but she always had a few signed checks where I could get to them in an emergency. She made it too easy to help myself, so I did. She got all worked up about it and replaced the money, then left the practice. It wasn't any big deal."

Cromarty drew a finger around the rim of his untouched drink. "A cash-flow problem? I despise cash flow problems."

"Exactly. I had a personal cash-flow problem, got tangled up with some mighty impatient folks you'd never want to meet in a dark alley. I might have eventually paid it back, but Bridget left in a huff, so why bother?"

A comforting bit of logic, come to think of it.

"I'm not sure I understand. You took a business check Bridget had signed, used it to solve this personal cash flow problem, and haven't reimbursed Bridget or the business for the funds you appropriated?"

Lord abide, Cromarty was slow. Maybe all the whisky fumes had addled his business brain. "You make it sound like I stole that money, when it was Bridget's signature on the check."

"Her signature?" Cromarty's expression was befuddled, as if simple monetary transactions weren't something covered in Whisky-Making 101.

How had this guy stayed in business at all, much less come from two-hundred years of whisky-making stock?

"You bet it was Bridget's signature on that check, which is why Bridget replaced the money in a big-ass hurry. As far as anybody knows, she wrote the check, therefore she got the funds."

Nate was still pleased with himself for being clever enough to put the whole thing together. Not like Bridget was using that money anyway.

Cromarty used a thumbnail to peel the label on the bottle of rye. "Correct me if I'm wrong, Sturbridge, but doesn't your federal government keep an eye on transactions in excess of ten thousand dollars?"

Nate scooped another chip through the salsa and got most of it to his mouth, except for a bit that dropped on the table.

"We occasionally handled sums over ten thousand—as retainers, settlements, and the like—and nobody ever asked us about it. Do I look like some whoop-de-do securities and finance lawyer to you, Cromarty?"

Damn, it was time to see a man about a horse.

Cromarty tore a strip off the label on the bottle of rye, then sat back, his gaze flat. "You look like a criminal. The worst kind of criminal, who has no remorse for his wrongdoing and takes advantage of anybody to avoid being held responsible for his crimes. If the cash was disbursed to you, then the security cameras at the bank very likely recorded the whole transaction."

Cromarty's expression was serious enough to make any sane person uneasy. He wasn't angry, he was in the grip of an ice-cold rage that could have dropped Harley Gummo with a single punch.

And yet, Nate couldn't quite make sense of what Cromarty had said. "What *transaction?*"

"Somebody counted out a lot of money at a teller window, probably counted it several times, while you stood waiting. Then you—not Bridget, you—walked out of the bank with the money. That's all on tape somewhere, Sturbridge, and I'm guessing the bank will not appreciate you using them to embezzle from your business partner."

Embezzle was a word Nate had avoided even in his imagination. Embezzling was… stupid, dishonorable, not something a bank president's son-in-law could get caught doing.

"So I helped myself to the money," Nate said. "What of it? Bridget could spare it, and nobody's the wiser. You going to agree to that pipeline, or has this little tête-à-tête been a waste of time?"

"You admit to stealing from Bridget MacDeaver?"

"For crap's sake, yes, I stole from Bridget. I also admit she made taking that money too easy. Wasn't all that much, she could spare it, and the alternative for me was something you wouldn't wish on your worst enemy."

Cromarty finally took a sip of his drink. "As it happens, you're wrong. You are my worst enemy, Sturbridge, and while everybody makes mistakes, not everybody breaks the law, fails to take responsibility for those mistakes, and exploits the trust of business associates to ensure the burden falls on the innocent instead of the guilty."

Cromarty raised his hand in the direction of the bar, though Nate was not about to get stuck with the bill for this farce.

"Judge me all you please," Nate said, pushing to his feet. "I got the money when I needed it, and a friendly word to the wise: If you want that distillery, then I'm the only guy who can get Bridget to sell it to you. All I have to do is remind her whose signature was on that check and what the bar association would do to a woman who steals from her own law practice. She'll turn up sweeter than wild clover honey."

Cromarty remained seated, which meant he'd be paying the tab. A fitting retribution for having wasted Nate's evening.

"You threatened Bridget with disbarment to get her to leave the practice?"

"I didn't threaten her, Cromarty, I promised her. If she made any trouble for a guy who was down on his luck and a little short of cash, then I'd make trouble for her right back. I did her a favor, if you want the truth. She isn't much of a lawyer and was never going to love the law the way she loves that distillery. Let me know when you're ready to deal, but don't wait too long. I'm a busy man."

Nate's stroll away from the table was meant to take him in the direction of the facilities, except he caught his toe on the leg of a chair and stumbled. Martina Matlock caught him, and lordy, the gal had a serious grip.

"Thank you, darlin'," Nate said. "I'm off to drain the dragon, though if you're interested in a dance, I could oblige you when I've tended to my business."

Martina kept hold of Nate's arm. "I appreciate the offer, Nate, but you and I will be taking a little ride."

"Not until I take a piss, 'scuse my French. I've been negotiating over a drink or two, and nature calls."

Martina snapped something cold around Nate's wrist, tucked his arm behind him, and secured his second wrist. "I am arresting you, Nathan Sturbridge. You can either come quietly and we'll finish this discussion in private, or you can resist arrest."

Her tone delivered a frigid slap to Nate's buzz. At Cromarty's table, a guy in a dark suit collected the phone Cromarty had tucked away most of a bottle of rye ago. The phone Nate had assumed had been turned off.

Shit.

The words *arresting you* sank in, and the handcuffs—Martina Matlock had *put him in handcuffs*—drove reality home.

"Martina, I really, truly have to take a leak."

"Nice try, but you really truly are under arrest."

She urged him toward the door, and Nate went because, as a lawyer, he knew all too well what could follow when some fool resisted arrest. A few feet away, Magnus Cromarty sat studying his whisky as if it held the secret to eternal life, while Preacher refused to spare Nate so much as a glance.

* * *

Magnus left a few bills sitting amid the crumbs, napkins, and empty glasses on the table and headed to the lounge. He wanted to get away from the noise, the gathering crowd, and the scent of rye.

He needed to see Bridget.

When he got to the lounge, she sprang out of her chair and wrapped him in a bear hug. "Martina escorted Nate in handcuffs across the parking lot. A big guy in a suit climbed out of a Dodge Charger and helped her get Nate into the backseat. I'm babbling."

Magnus held her close enough to feel that her heart was pounding like a fiddle player's at the end of a medley of reels.

"Sturbridge incriminated himself in half a dozen directions, and I made very, very certain to start the evening by getting his permission to record our conversation."

"You're sure?"

"I'm sure. If your lectures about wiretapping laws were any more detailed, I'd be teaching the subject to federal agents myself."

He smoothed a hand over her hair, which was loose this evening, no tidy bun, no fancy braid. "Sturbridge truly betrayed you, Bridget. His remorse was microscopic at best. If I hadn't intimated that he was caught on tape walking out of the bank with all the cash, I doubt he'd have admitted to stealing from you."

Bridget sank back into her chair. "But there are no tapes."

Martina had discreetly established that the bank kept no more than ninety days of security data. "I gambled on Nate being too lazy to have ascertained that fact himself, because laziness is consistent with everything you've told me about him. He never checked the land records before broaching the easement with you, for example. He didn't even prepare his own cases in the courtroom."

Soon, relief would begin to seep through Magnus's rage, but for now, he was still furious. Sturbridge had bragged about taking advantage of his own business partner, bragged about threatening her.

Bridget touched Magnus's hand. "You okay?"

Patrick and Luke came strutting through the door.

"Martina called," Patrick said. "Nate barely let her get out the Miranda warnings before he started singing the state's evidence school anthem. Cromarty's recording probably won't even come into evidence."

"I'm guessing Nate's arrest will leave a bunch of legal clients sorely in need of representation," Luke added, taking a chair. "Bet you Sue Etta would help you get that situation sorted out, Bridget. You could take up where you left off, step right into—"

"Lucas,"—Patrick appropriated the fourth chair—"now I know you were dropped on your head once too often. The last thing Bridget needs to worry about is hanging out a shingle to clean up after Nate Sturbridge."

Magnus watched emotions flit through Bridget's eyes: bewilderment, impatience, and then a grudging willingness to consider Lucas's idiot suggestion.

"Don't do it," Magnus said. "You have more distilling talent in your left little finger than I could find in all of Speyside, which isn't particularly relevant, but you didn't enjoy being a lawyer, and that's relevant as hell."

"Swear jar," Lucas muttered as Patrick smacked him on the arm.

"Bridget is that good with the whisky?" Patrick asked.

"She is so far beyond good that I could line up consulting clients for her from one end of Britain to the other. Her whiskies finish spectacularly and she grasps both the art and science of the distilling craft with instinctive genius." So why hadn't Bridget told Magnus how to fix his ailing batch?

Maybe because Nate Sturbridge had been threatening her freedom and her livelihood, and maybe because Magnus's problem could not be solved.

"I don't want to talk about whisky right now," Bridget said. "I don't want to talk about Nate Sturbridge, or law offices, or anything. I want Magnus to take me back to the ranch, and tomorrow—probably after noon—I'll call Martina and get a bead on where things stand. Magnus?"

He rose and, without so much as nodding at Patrick or Lucas, took Bridget by the hand and led her out to the truck.

"You want me to drive?" He could—the wrong side of the road felt normal now.

"If you're okay to drive."

"I've had three sips of whisky over the past hour and a half. I'm fine."

He wasn't fine. He was relieved for Bridget's sake, angry at Sturbridge, and worried, not so much for his whisky as he was for his future. For *their* future.

"Thank you," Bridget said as Magnus navigated mostly empty streets on the way out of town. "You've solved enormous problems for me that could have wrecked years of my life, if not my whole life."

"Sturbridge was already on the law enforcement radar. We merely chased him into the net." Bridget had explained cross-examination techniques to Magnus, taught him applicable laws, and in every way armed him for battle. "You were a first-rate lawyer, by the way. I'd know that even if Martina hadn't told me. If you want to resume practicing law, then you should."

"I was an unhappy lawyer. I love my distillery, Magnus."

While he loved her. Magnus kept that sentiment to himself, hoping it was among the items Bridget would make time to discuss tomorrow. She came right into the guesthouse with him and, as soon as the door swung shut, kissed him within an inch of his life.

They left a trail of clothing from the front door to the master bedroom, and Magnus considered indulging in a bout of wall sex, but the pressing need to get a condom out of his wallet—and Bridget out of her jeans—dissuaded him from that delight.

And get her out of her jeans and into bed, he did.

CHAPTER FOURTEEN

Bridget's desire warred with profound resentment, because the legacy Magnus had safeguarded for her was about to become her prison. Maybe Mama had sensed that about the whisky business and had chosen to fall in love with Daniel Logan instead.

Bridget would worry about family history tomorrow, after she'd spent the night—the whole night—making love with Magnus. A lady needed memories to store up against a lonely future.

"Don't be so careful with me, Magnus," she panted between kisses. "Don't hold back."

His clothing had borne the scent of the Bar None—beer, spicy cooking, perfume, and leather—but naked on the bed, he was simply Magnus. Soap, fresh air, and man.

He smoothed Bridget's hair from her brow. "Holding back can add to the pleasure."

"Add to the pleasure next time. Cowboy up this time."

She was desperate to have him inside her, and just plain desperate. Rather than let him start a conversation, Bridget groped for the condom and passed it to him.

"Are we in a hurry?" he asked, fingering the edge of the foil.

"Yes."

His smile as he braced himself over her was sweet and wicked. "Fools rush in, Mary Bridget."

He tormented her with a slow, easy joining, then drove her mad with soft kisses, and just when Bridget was about to break all swear-jar records expressing her frustration, Magnus drove into her with a measured determination that sent her soaring.

"Better?" he murmured when Bridget was a limp heap of satisfied female beneath him.

"A little."

He moved again, and the aftershocks were nearly as intense as the main event. "Magnus, I need a minute."

He eased to a halt, hilted inside of her. "I need you, Bridget MacDeaver."

Arousal shifted to encompass impending loss. Magnus would get on some damned plane and fly off to Scotland, and for years Bridget would read all the whisky journals hoping to catch a mention of him. She'd Google him once a week—no need to be extravagantly pathetic—and she'd eventually hear of his marriage to some leggy British whisky princess.

His whisky would win prizes, he'd find a boutique distillery in Colorado to purchase, and—

"Have I loved you to sleep?" he asked.

"Not even close, Magnus Cromarty. I'm just catching my breath between rounds."

"You're awfully quiet about it."

"Plotting my revenge."

He moved lazily, but Bridget knew by now that wouldn't last. Magnus was like the best whiskies, growing more complex as the flavor blossomed, until a solo became a symphony, and words failed.

She ran her hands over the warm contours of his back and buried her nose against his throat. Why did he have to be such a good man, such a decent, smart, honorable, brave, wily, kind, sexy, wish-come-true of a guy?

Then she was coming, and crying, and silently cursing her distillery and all whisky everywhere, and through it all, Magnus held her and loved her, and loved her some more.

When she lay along his side a few minutes later, gathering what composure she could, Magnus wrapped an arm around her and kissed her temple.

"Care to tell me what that was all about?"

Of course, he wouldn't just roll over and go to sleep. Not Magnus. "I know how to fix your whisky. It won't be cheap, and you'll have to be quiet about how you did it, but the result will be worth the effort."

Magnus rolled to his side so he faced her and drew a single finger down her forehead, her nose, her lips, chin, and midline.

"I came here determined to rescue that batch of whisky, but at the moment, I don't much care what becomes of it. I care far more about what will become of us, Bridget."

So did she, not that it would matter. "Let's have that discussion in the morning, after I've explained what to do with the whisky."

She felt him weighing her words, deciding whether to force a confrontation or allow her a few hours of grace.

He gathered her in his arms. "In the morning, we'll talk. Now, we make love."

* * *

Magnus would never have come up with the solution on his own. Probably no Scottish distiller could have figured it out.

"You make little barrels," Bridget said, tapping the drawing she'd sketched on a paper towel. "They are still technically barrels, still oak, but because they are so much smaller, more of the whisky comes in contact with the wood, and the flavor develops more quickly."

"Wee barrels?" Magnus muttered, staring at his bright red mug of tea. "Are you sure?"

Sitting at his kitchen table, Bridget went off on a discourse about the ratio of volume to surface area, then waxed enthusiastic about temperature fluctuations ensuring the whisky interacted with the wood on an accelerated schedule, all of which made sense.

But none of which mattered. "So you can rescue my whisky."

"I can restore that whisky to the promise it held before it was sabotaged, at least. I'm guessing the result will be spectacular, if you can make the barrels as I've suggested."

She'd steered him toward a very expensive French red wine for the barrels. Procuring enough barrels to rebuild into smaller casks would take every connection Magnus laid claim to, much of his cash reserves, and all of his guile.

"What if I instead shipped that whisky here?" Magnus said. "Could you develop other options for it?"

They'd wolfed down buttered toast with huckleberry jam and chased it with strong black tea. Bridget wore one of Magnus's plaid flannel shirts, while he'd pulled on jeans and a turtleneck. The morning was dreary with gusts of rain slapping against the windows, and for Magnus, the aftermath of a night of thorough loving blended with growing unease.

If Bridget had meant to stay for the morning, she'd have started the woodstove.

"Why would you go to all the expense of shipping the whisky here?" Bridget asked, putting the lid back on the jam jar.

"Because I want to do business with you, among other things."

She stared out at gray skies that obscured the nearby mountains. "I'd better get dressed."

Well, shite. "I'll clean up."

Before Magnus was done wiping down the table, Bridget reappeared in the kitchen fully clothed. Her hair was still in disarray, from which he took minor comfort, but she'd put on her boots and draped her jacket and purse over the back of a chair.

"I'm not looking for a partner, Magnus. I've been honest with you about that. I appreciate what you've done for me, and for my distillery, but I'm not selling you any interest whatsoever in my operation."

She was selling something, and Magnus wasn't buying it. "We don't need to merge assets to do business with each other or to have a relationship. I can distribute your products internationally, you can sell mine here in the States. All that takes is a pair of straightforward agreements."

Bridget shrugged into her jacket, the pretty quilted one that was soft to touch. "And reaching those agreements will take time, and wrangling, and mixing business with pleasure, and I'm not interested."

"You were fascinated for most of last night, and so was I."

"That was then, and this is now, and I'm saying no thank you."

A gentleman never argued with a lady, but Magnus wasn't feeling very gentlemanly. "Why no thank you? Why not even a maybe, Bridget? Why not at least listen, consider options, hear me out?"

"Because I like being in charge of my own show, Magnus. The distillery is all I have, and as soon as I can, I'll buy my brothers out. The last thing I need is you complicating that situation with your bright ideas and bad whisky."

Bridget's insult reassured Magnus that she was upset, because for the most part he made very good whisky. She knew that, which meant she was trying to provoke him into arguing.

Into leaving without a backward glance.

Fortunately, Magnus still had his pride and still had a fine measure of good old Scottish cunning.

"I'm in your debt for saving my whisky," he said. "Your talents as a distiller are rare and worth a pretty penny. Send me a bill for consulting services, and if you'd ever like to take on similar projects, I'm sure many a Scottish—"

She kissed his cheek and fled, not even bothering to close the door. Magnus stood for a moment in the kitchen, letting the hurt and confusion wash through him as cold air gusted into the room.

He'd get on that plane for Scotland and put in motion the steps Bridget had laid out for saving his whisky, but then he'd be back, and he'd get to the bottom of whatever was coming between him and Bridget, if it was the last thing he did.

Which, given her stubbornness, it very well might be.

* * *

"We're here to apologize," Luke said. "Shamus would be with us, if he wasn't skiing in France."

Happily skiing in France, because Magnus had found a way to pry Shamus away from his spreadsheets. Bridget kicked a stone into the creek that ran beneath her distillery a hundred yards to the east.

"Apology accepted. Don't you two have work to do?"

Patrick slung an arm around her shoulders. "You don't even know what we're apologizing for."

Bridget sidled away when she wanted to throw them both in the creek.

"You're apologizing for betraying me by inviting Magnus here, for not realizing Nathan had me in a corner, and for failing to see anything but the ranch and your own concerns."

Her brothers exchanged a look that Bridget couldn't translate.

"We're sorry for all that and more," Luke said. "Now it's your turn to apologize to us."

I'm sorry to see Magnus go. "You're pushing your luck, guys."

"Not like you to dodge a challenge," Patrick said. "C'mon, Bridget. We're your family."

The water babbled by, a happy counterpoint to soft breezes and the fresh scent of the valley welcoming spring. Bridget loved this spot, within sight of her distillery, in the shadow of the mountains she called home.

She loved Magnus too, though, so very much. "Now is not a good time," she said, turning her back to her brothers. "If one of you would take Magnus to the airport tomorrow, I'd appreciate it."

"I can't oblige," Luke said. "Willy and I are going ring shopping over in Bozeman."

"About time, Luke, but then, you always were on the slow side. Patrick?"

"Nope. I promised Lena a trail ride and a picnic if the weather's nice."

Well, hell. "I'm sorry I didn't trust you with my problems," Bridget said, the understatement of the millennium. "I'm sorry Magnus and I aren't going to work out, not personally, not professionally. He's a great guy, and he's saved my bacon, and—I damned hate to cry."

Patrick—the dad of the two—wrapped her in a hug. "You stink at apologizing. He's not gone yet."

"But h-he'll go tomorrow," Bridget wailed, "and he got you straightened out and talked to his uncle about funding your windmill trees, and he shook Shamus free of the damned office, and kicked Nate to the curb, and he loves my wh-whisky."

"And you love him," Luke said, patting her arm. "If you want to move to Scotland, then go. Hire somebody to mind the still, come back every few months, teach one of us what we need to know. Three ingredients, right? How hard can whisky-making be?"

"Really hard," Bridget said. "Really, really hard, and lonely, and…"

Patrick and Luke watched her as if she had something profound to add to that sentiment, when all she had was a broken heart.

"If Magnus Cromarty is who and what you want," Patrick said, "then don't let anything stand in your way. Not us, not the still, not your grandpap's sainted memory, or the ghost of Nathan Sturbridge. More than anything else, Bridget, we want you to be happy."

"And what we do not want," Luke added, "Is to put up with you moping around for the next thirty years because you let Magnus Cromarty get away.

There is nothing on this ranch, in the distillery, or in all of Montana that's worth turning your back on a guy who'd lay the world at your feet if you'd let him."

"Be a pioneer." Patrick punched her arm gently. "In the grand family tradition, bet all your worldly goods on a hunch and a hope."

Magnus had done this too. Turned overworked, grouchy, unhappy step-brothers into the family Bridget very much needed. He'd saved the ranch, which was nice, but he'd also saved Bridget's heart.

Nothing on earth was worth passing up a guy like that. Sunlight struck the stream, turning the water to a flowing cascade of silver and gold.

"I love you both very much," Bridget said, "but I'm scared and I have something to tell you."

"Don't you dare name the kid after Shamus," Patrick said. "He's ornery enough without having a namesake."

"I'd like another niece," Luke mused. "Lena would probably vote for a girl too."

"Cripes sake, I wouldn't even know if the rabbit had died yet, and that's not what I have to tell you."

"So what does that leave?" Patrick asked.

Luke folded his arms. "If the quilting club is meeting at the ranch again, you have to warn us in time to evacuate."

Oh, they were the worst, best brothers. Bridget started talking and hoped they'd still consider her family by the time she was done.

* * *

Magnus had emailed Shamus and arranged to book the guesthouse for most of June. By then, he'd have set up the great whisky rescue, replaced a certain aging board member or three, turned his lawyers loose on drafting distribution agreements, and endured as much separation from Bridget as he could tolerate.

"I don't understand why you can't do all that from Montana," Elias said. "I've done a fine job of minding the tiller in your absence and learned a lot about making whisky."

Magnus switched the phone to his other ear and tossed the last of his flannel shirts onto the open suitcase. Shamus had driven the rental car to the airport, which meant Bridget would at least have to provide chauffeur service.

"You've doubtless drunk my best stock, taught my cats to sleep on the kitchen counter, and let Uncle Zeb have a peek at my books, while neglecting half your clients and any number of supermodels."

"Uncle Zeb's quite enthusiastic about your windmill-tree project, and I swore off supermodels two fiancées ago. There's really no need to hurry home, Magnus, and I suspect you aren't hurrying so much as you're running away."

The damned suitcase would never close. "I am coming home, Elias, and when I get there, I'll deliver you a proper thrashing for that bit of disrespect."

"Tell me about your cowgirl, Magnus. Tell me why you aren't setting up a home on the range with her."

"I'll thrash Shamus too, next time I see him, for telling tales out of school."

"You took enormous risks for that woman, when you're the last man who ought to be exerting himself on behalf of the ladies."

"What are you babbling about?" And where had Magnus's belt…? He spied it looped around the back of the chair at the master bedroom's desk.

"Celeste. Seems Husband Number Two has served her with divorce papers, and she's being told to either slink away quietly, or face uncomfortable inquiries into her business dealings behind his back."

"Tell him to take away her keys to the warehouse before he does anything else, even before he changes his passwords and terminates the credit cards." Putting on a belt while holding a phone was impossible.

"I'll pass that along, or you can tell him yourself when you get home. Did you get the water analysis results I sent last night?"

Last night, Magnus had indulged in a wee dram too many, such as a man might when frustrated with the love of his life.

"Water is water, Elias. I have the distillery's supply monitored for purity and mineral content, but it hasn't changed in twenty years."

Thank God. Ruin a distillery's water supply, and you ruined its future.

"Not your distillery, *hers*. I sent you the results, and you haven't even bothered to look at them. Some micromanager you are. I'm off to feed your cats their salmon pâté."

"That's not cat food, you daft excuse for a deranged—"

"They like to eat it right off your marble counters. Take a look at Bridget MacDeaver's water, Magnus. It's not like yours at all."

Elias ended the call.

Magnus stared at his phone, resisting Elias's taunt for about two seconds before scrolling back through his messages. The complete lab report on Bridget's water was only a few pages, but it took some skimming to get down to the interesting parts.

At first, Magnus couldn't believe what the screen was telling him, because her water was, indeed, very, very different from his. Then bits and pieces of conversation, stray glances, and odd silences came together, and he whooped out loud, tossed the phone in the air, and fished out his kilt.

He and the lady were about to have a long, honest talk. If she told him after that to leave Montana and never come back, he'd abide by her wishes, but he'd bet everything—his distillery, hers, his heart, their future—he could persuade her to come see Scotland instead.

* * *

"Luke and Patrick elected me to take you to the airport." Bridget had argued, she'd pleaded, she'd even tried stonewalling, but given what else she'd had to tell them, they'd guilted her into this penance.

Magnus was traveling in his kilt apparently, the plain black work kilt that swung around his knees and made her think wicked, hopeless thoughts.

"We have time for a wee chat before I catch my plane, Mary Bridget. Let's take a walk to the foaling barn."

As good a place to say good-bye as any. In the past week, two more foals had been born, an elegant chestnut filly and a friendly black colt who looked like he'd take after his plow-horse mama in size and temperament.

"Will you be glad to get home?" Bridget asked.

"Overjoyed."

He didn't sound overjoyed. "Magnus?"

"I'll come home to two dyspeptic cats who now think I owe them salmon pâté served on the family silver. Aunt Helga will stop speaking to me when I retire Fergus from my board of directors, though he's apologized profusely for allowing his head to be turned by Celeste's pretty face. At his age, that he can see a pretty face is amazing."

"I'm sorry," Bridget said, because Magnus was very likely reciting facts. "But you can salvage your whisky, right?"

"I can. Uncle Zebedee is hunting up the requisite wine casks for me, because his connections on the Continent are vast and complicated, and Daryl MacKinnon is lending me a team of coopers as a gesture of goodwill or commiseration, I'm not sure which."

The doors at both ends of the foaling barn were open because the day was mild. A pregnant mare who looked ready to drop her foal any minute stuck her head over her Dutch door and whuffled.

I want to have children with Magnus, and we leave for the airport in ten minutes.

"Hello, Katydid," Bridget said, giving the mare a scratch under the chin. "Not long now." The mare lipped at Bridget's jacket pocket, looking for treats that weren't there. "I love the smell of this place. The horses, alfalfa, sweet feed, spring on the breeze… It's a good combination, home and hope."

"Then make a whisky that brings those scents to mind."

Bridget wanted to make a life that brought those scents to mind. "You don't want to miss your plane, Magnus."

"Yes, as a matter of fact, I do. I've analyzed the water supplying your distillery, Bridget. You're sitting on a gold mine."

He wasn't making a marketing claim. He was accusing her of something. Something serious.

"My business has potential," Bridget replied carefully. "Someday—"

"Someday, you will tell your brothers that upstream from your distillery, very likely on the property you inherited from your grandfather, there's actual gold. The kind people hoard. The kind entire economies have been built on."

Bridget's middle went cattywampus on her, and the solid dirt floor felt wavy beneath her boots. "You can't… That's not…"

"The lab report fairly sparkles with traces of gold in the water, not merely the occasional part per billion, but enough to get the attention of any respectable geologist. Whose secret are you guarding, Bridget?"

By some miracle, a pair of straw bales were stacked right where Bridget needed to sit.

Magnus *knew*. He'd analyzed her water, connected the dots, and leaped to a conclusion that generations of MacDeavers had sworn to keep secret.

"You can't tell anybody, Magnus. Not a soul, not your cousin, not your drinking buddies, not your uncle Fergus. My land would be swarming with trespassers in nothing flat, and then the politicians would get involved."

He took the place beside her, sharing her straw bales. "And you'd lose your distillery forever."

"I'd lose my self-respect forever. The first MacDeaver to settle in Montana made a choice. We could make great whisky with the water running down from those hills, or we could tear up the countryside looking for a great fortune. The whisky has kept us housed and fed, while gold is a recipe for misery."

Magnus took Bridget's hand. "But a lack of coin is a recipe for misery too, and the Logan Bar ranch was testing your promise not to go for the gold."

"Not the ranch, but the need to look out for my family. They are my family, I know that now." How right it felt to lace her fingers with his.

"Do you also know they can look out for themselves, and for you too, Bridget?"

"I'm willing to entertain the theory. Will you keep my secret, Magnus?"

He wrapped an arm around her shoulders. The mares in their stalls munched alfalfa, a barn cat leaped from the rafters to a feed rack to the floor.

"I come from at least ten generations of whisky-makers, Bridget. Do you think I, of all people, would jeopardize a successful distillery, with all its tradition, wisdom, and business potential, for something as transitory and bothersome as gold?"

His question was a riddle that only the heart could answer. He was washed in the water of life, had traveled halfway around the world to rescue a batch of whisky, and wanted nothing more than to see his children and grandchildren thriving in the same industry Bridget had made her passion.

"You'll keep my secret."

They sat side by side, the peace of the moment settling Bridget so thoroughly, she was a different person, a happier, better person, for having this discussion.

"I have a question for you, Mary Bridget."

Please don't ruin this. "I should have told my brothers years ago, I know, but I didn't, and then it got awkward, and then the ranch hit some tough years, and I couldn't trust them to respect my wishes."

Magnus kissed her knuckles. "Can you trust them now?"

Clearly not the question he was determined to ask.

"I hope so, because I told Luke and Patrick yesterday. They made me promise I'd teach Lena the trade, and if she wants to go into the business, to at least consider that. If Shamus will take over my bookkeeping, I'll have more time to focus on the whisky."

"Better and better. May I ask you my question now?"

He rose, and Bridget braced herself to be offered a job, a distribution agreement, a scolding. "Ask."

Magnus stood before her, his arms looped around her shoulders. "I'll keep your secret to my dying day and guard it with my last breath. Will you keep my heart, Bridget? To have and to hold? Until we're old and crotchety and driving our offspring daft with our opinions and arguments? Will you raise a family with me, God willing, and cobble together a life that might involve a lot of travel and no little frustration?"

Bridget leaned forward, bracing her forehead against Magnus's chest. "Is that a proposal?"

"Afraid so."

He embraced her gently, and Bridget wrapped her arms around his waist. She wanted to honor his offer with something profound, meaningful, and memorable.

"Hell, yeah, Magnus Cromarty. Hell, yeah, I'll marry you."

Then they were laughing and kissing, and Bridget was crying, while Magnus cursed the cat trying to strop itself against their boots. Luke showed up on a skid loader and called Patrick, who texted Shamus, who must have texted Elias, and pretty soon, all the ranch hands and Lena were gathered around, until some considerate soul took Magnus's luggage back to the guesthouse, and Bridget was again alone with... her fiancé.

"This will be complicated, Magnus. We'll rack up frequent-flier miles and miss the hell out of each other and probably need two houses, and the lawyers will get involved."

"Stop," Magnus said as they reached the porch of the guesthouse. "Just stop. In the first place, I'm marrying the only lawyer whose opinion matters, and in the second, I hope this door is unlocked."

"Sure it is. Why—Magnus!"

He'd scooped her up in his arms. "I believe the important matters are deserving of practice. If you'd get the latch?"

Bridget pushed the door open, and Magnus carried her over the threshold. The symbolism felt appropriate—trusting him, making a fresh start, and shutting the rest of the world out for the intimate parts.

"Thank you," Bridget said, kissing him. "For the chivalry, for the proposal, for everything, Magnus, but this is still going to be complicated."

"Not it isn't. Three ingredients, Bridget: you, me, and love. If we can make whisky, we can make a lifetime of magic with just those three ingredients."

As it happened, the fourth ingredient, a yowling red-haired terror named Sean Fergus Cromarty, added himself to the recipe before his parents had been married two years. Several more ingredients came along, and with each addition, the recipe yielded more magic, more happiness, and more love.

For Bridget, Magnus, and their offspring.

For dear cousin Elias... well, that's another story.

Nov 2019

Manufactured by Amazon.ca
Bolton, ON